Somewhere South Of Here

Somewhere South Of Here

William Kowalski

W F HOWES LTD

This large print edition published in 2002 by
W F Howes Ltd
Units 6/7, Victoria Mills, Fowke Street
Rothley, Leicester LE7 7PJ

1 3 5 7 9 10 8 6 4 2

First published in 2001 by Doubleday
a division of Transworld Publishers

A CIP catalogue record for this book is available
from the British Library

ISBN 1 84197 525 7

Typeset by Palimpsest Book Production Limited,
Polmont, Stirlingshire
Printed and bound in Great Britain
by Antony Rowe Ltd, Chippenham, Wilts.

For Alexandra
and also young Theo Hansen

ACKNOWLEDGEMENTS

The author wishes to thank those many friends and family members who provided their encouragement and support throughout the writing of this novel. Also, thanks to Donald P. 'Tex' Dorsey, Steve Stickley, Barb Piatt, Bill McBride, Sgt. Bjorn Dahlin, USMC (ret.), Mel Ewing, Paul Owen, and Maj. Bruce Wincentsen, USMC (ret.), for their background information on the role of United States Marine Corps snipers in Vietnam. Thanks to the Beltrandel-Rio family for their assistance with Spanish phrases and vocabulary; to Candra Day for information on the Sausalito water-front; and to Lhasa de Sela, chanteuse extraordinaire, are also in order. Also thanks to my agent, Anne Hawkins, who is 'bad' in the good sense of the word, and my very fine editor, Marjorie Braman, whose patience is bodacious.

– W. K.

Somewhere South Of Here

RUNNING OUT OF SUERTE

Consuelo Gonzalez, the former acrobatic child prodigy and tightrope princess of the Strawberry Family Circus, is such a heavy sleeper that not even the Great San Francisco Earthquake of 1989 was able to wake her, or so she claims. At the time of the earthquake, Consuelo, then twenty-one years old, was napping on the couch in the house she shared with her five sisters – all of whom were also circus performers – and her three parents – her father, her biological mother, and her other mother, Claudia, who'd married Consuelo's father when the original Señora Gonzalez was still alive and in perfect health, and when Consuelo herself was only six years old.

The quake struck just before the third game of the World Series, which was going on at that very moment in Candlestick Park. It was the worst earthquake San Francisco had seen since the fiery devastation of 1906. Television cameras at the game captured the field rippling like a blanket, the crowded stands waving back and forth as gracefully as a forest of kelp. Miraculously, they held, and

1

none of the fans was hurt. But outside the stadium, San Francisco was collapsing like a house of cards for the second time in less than a century. Miles upon miles of bridges and highways that were thought to be quakeproof were shaken to pieces in moments. Several massive buildings, also supposedly quakeproof, fell in on themselves and burst like water balloons, spewing human beings and furniture into the street. Thousands were injured; sixty-three people died.

Consuelo, however, slumbered on peacefully, unaware that her family had fled the house in terror – the Gonzalezes, being only a poor circus family, had no illusions about *their* house being quakeproof. The outraged earth rumbled and heaved, pictures and books succumbed gracelessly to gravity. A section of roof fell not a foot from her head. When she awoke, it was to find that her home had been almost leveled, and that one of her parents – Claudia, her other mother – had been knocked out cold by falling debris.

But thanks to the grace of the Virgin, and the vigilance of Consuelo's angels, none of the Gonzalez family was dead. Even more astonishing was the perfect circle of calm in the devastation, a magic zone that by some miracle was free of collapsed beams and broken glass and even of the tiny particles of plaster that had been shaken loose and fallen everywhere, like snow – a circle at the center of which was Consuelo herself, as fresh as a daisy and completely unharmed.

The Quake of '89 was, for her, the final proof that she was blessed, that she was protected by guardian angels – not just one angel, like most people have, or two, as very lucky people have, but eleven. I don't see how she could be so sure she even had guardian angels in the first place, or that there were eleven of them. It seems like an outrageous number of angels to have. But Consuelo, who knows her angels well, knows each of them by name, in fact, said: 'Don't you see? I *needed* eleven. My work was very dangerous.'

Consuelo's work *was* dangerous. According to her, it was these ethereal guardians who kept her aloft all the years she walked the tightrope for the circus – without a safety net, in the tradition of the great Flying Wallendas, whom she idolized. To use a net would have been to doubt the power of the angels. They would have resented it, and might even have gone permanently off duty, figuring their work was done and they weren't needed anymore. But as long as Consuelo performed netless – a feat which consistently drew record crowds to the Strawberry Family Circus, larger crowds than even the Fire-Eating Wolf Boys of Guadalajara or El Stretcho the Human Rubber Band could command – they hovered about her in an invisible swarm, supporting her like a flock of solicitous Tinkerbelles. And it's these eleven angels who will carry Consuelo on to fame and fortune in

3

her new career as a singer. They used to appear in her dreams and tell her so when she was just a little girl.

It's an outrageous story, I know, but I've never doubted any of it for a moment – by which I mean, *I* believe that *she* believes in them. For myself, I'm not so sure. But if I needed hard evidence of every little thing I believed in, I wouldn't have much left. So I listen to her stories. But I always pretend not to believe them, just to keep her on her toes.

'Ask my sisters! They saw them too!' Consuelo pouts. But her accent toys with her words: she really says *axe my seesters*!

'How could your sisters see them if it was your dream?' I ask.

'Ha! Phooey!' she says. *Phooey* is her favorite English word, though when she says it it rarely makes sense. 'You don't know the rules of magic. They saw them, all of them, flying around my head. Every night.'

'Yeah. Whatever.'

'Whatever, whatever. I hate this word You use it too much. You are loving me, Beelee, yes?'

'Yes. I am loving you.'

'Then you must believe me.'

'No.'

'*Caramba!* You tease me! I can see it in your eyes!'

She's got me there. Part of me does believe her. Consuelo says all children see these lights, but most grow up and forget about them. If I think back to

4

when I was a kid, I do have faint memories of tiny luminescent spots dancing around by the ceiling, but they never talked to me. Besides, I can't tell now whether I really remember them or whether she's just got me thinking I do, which is why I pretend to think she's lying.

But Consuelo hasn't got it in her to lie; in fact, she's probably one of the most honest people I've ever met. And as if the story of the earthquake isn't proof enough of the existence of watchful spirits, there was the time she really did slip and fall from the wire in the middle of a performance, made a rapid descent of nearly forty feet, and landed – once again, completely unharmed – on the floor of the main ring below. This I know from a yellowed newspaper article that she'd cut out and saved. Those who saw Consuelo fall – the reporter who wrote the article happened to be in the audience that day – said that instead of plummeting to the ground like a rock, as she should have, she *fluttered* down, like a piece of paper. She lit on her feet as neatly as a cat, made a deep bow, and walked off into the wings to thunderous applause from the audience, who thought her fall was part of the act. It wasn't, however, and backstage Consuelo had a nervous breakdown that spelled the end of her career as a circus performer. She was then seventeen years old.

'That was when I decided to become a singer,' she tells me now. 'It wasn't that I didn't trust the angels any more. I just didn't want to use up all my luck on something as stupid as walking the wire. I could feel their *hands* on me, Beelee. Eleven pairs of tiny little *manos*. It was scary.'

'You were glad they were there, though, I bet,' I say. 'Right?'

'Yes. But it was *spooky*, I'm telling you.' *Spooky* is another of her favorite English words; she likes any words with an 'oo' sound in them and uses them every chance she gets, because they don't have quite the same sound in Spanish – close, but not quite. Of the two languages, she says, Spanish is the more beautiful, and English the sillier.

'Well, I don't think walking the wire is stupid,' I say. I'm a former daredevil myself: a veteran of countless leaps from ten-foot roofs and hare-brained stunts on a souped-up lawnmower, small-town tricks performed for an audience consisting of myself, and sometimes my grandfather. I feel deep admiration for Consuelo's acrobatic abilities, almost a professional respect, if you will, even though back then I never knew there were such things as circuses and wouldn't have been allowed to go to one if I had. Even now, although she's given up the circus life for good, she still keeps herself in practice. Sometimes, as I sit typing in the bathroom, I can hear the squeaks and crashes that mean she's on her unicycle again, juggling empty wine bottles – another part of her old high-wire act. For a while I begged her to allow me to string a length of cable across the street from our roof to El Perrero's roof, just so she could put on

6

the occasional neighborhood show. But Consuelo refuses to tempt fate again.

'I don't want to use up all my luck,' she repeats. 'You only get so much *suerte* in your life, Beelee, and it's stupid to waste it.'

That's one way of looking at it: you're born with only so much *suerte*, and if you use it up you're . . . well, you're shit out of *suerte*. It makes sense. Lots of people run out of *suerte* at the worst possible time. Look at Amelia Earhart, who I once believed was my mother, back in the days when I was still free to imagine who my mother was. She ran through her supply of *suerte* right in midair.

Lately I've been wondering to myself if perhaps we haven't both already used up all the *suerte* that was allotted to us from our very earliest days. I don't mean to complain, but this is the plain truth: these are lean times for Consuelo and me. We don't eat much, and if she didn't have a job at the Cowgirl we wouldn't ever go out, either. She's twenty-two now, still waiting for the angels to deliver on their promise of fame and fortune in the singing world. In the meantime, she's cleaning toilets at the Cowgirl Hall of Fame – which is not a museum, as the name implies, but a bar – in the mornings, and singing on the tiny stage there two nights a week.

As for me, I'm almost twenty, a college dropout, a trust-fund baby whose trust in the world – both financial and otherwise – has nearly expired. And although as a child I was not without guardian angels of my own, our protectors seem to have abandoned us both for the time being. That is, they've kept us alive, but not much else. These are the days of Ramen noodles and one-dollar beers, of cigarettes bought with handfuls of change and hoarded jealously throughout the week. I will continue to get a five-hundred-dollar check from my grandfather's estate every month, which will allow me to spend that much more time on my novel – if you can call what I'm writing a novel yet, considering all it has is a beginning – and it will also allow Consuelo to get by working only a few hours a day, leaving enough time to practice her voice lessons in the afternoons. But after the money runs out, which will be in eleven months and ten days, I don't know where any other money is going to come from. I've run through all the money I saved from my old job back in Mannville, which wasn't much to begin with, only several hundred dollars; it was gone in no time, an *astonishingly* short time, spent on nothing more luxurious than rent and food and firewood. Maybe by next year Consuelo's angels will have come back to life, and she'll feel the touch of their invisible hands again. Maybe they'll carry us up and away into something better, out of Santa Fe and into some wild blue yonder where everything is as it's supposed to be, where we can afford to eat decently as often as we want and where I won't have to account to myself for every damn quarter I spend. That wouldn't surprise me too much. Consuelo is magic; she's just the sort of person to whom things like this could happen.

But to be honest, neither of us minds being poor all that much – or maybe I should say we've been poor so long it's never occurred to us to complain. I was raised on a diet of oral history and fried-baloney sandwiches, and for me hunger was a country always just barely visible over the horizon. For Consuelo, however, hunger wasn't a distant place. It was the land in which she lived, the place where she'd put down roots and called home. She grew up – or claims to have grown up – in a school bus in Mexico, traveling around with her family and eating at most once a day. That part of her story is one I never pretend to disbelieve; it would hurt her too much. I can see the lingering effects of childhood malnutrition in her jutting, countable ribs – of which she seems to have more than the average person – and in her pale, translucent skin, beneath which pulses a network of fine blue veins. I see it also in her teacup eyes, eyes accustomed to looking at nice things she knows she'll never have. I must have had the same look in my eyes when I was a boy. I never felt the same kind of arm-biting hunger she did, but my world contained mostly stories and ghosts – nothing more than hot air, intangible things, memories of a time when our family had once been glorious and strong, a time that had long since faded away into dust, and I knew with utter despairing certainty that there was a whole world of things I was never going to have.

'But,' I tell her, 'at least you got to go to the circus!' – to which she will only roll her eyes.

Consuelo is also an artist. Our bedroom in the little house on South Blossom Street, in downtown Santa Fe, is papered floor to ceiling with Consuelo's angel portraits. Sometimes they're depicted individually, each with their own name, with distinctive facial features. There is Señor José, Guardian of the Right Foot; Mr Patrick Murphy, Guardian of the Left; Elena the Beautiful, Angel in Charge of Balance; Tom, the Angel of Enlightenment; Maria Tomasita Evangelina – I forget the rest. I've come to think of them as distant relatives of hers, as though her paintings were really family photographs. In other paintings, the angels appear as indistinguishable points of light, circumnavigating her sleeping head like a cloud of fireflies. Consuelo puts herself in her paintings, too. In each one she's a little girl snoozing blissfully, no more than a lump under the covers with a smile on her face – which is exactly how she looks in real life each morning, when the alarm clock goes off like some kind of shrieking electric insect, and I'm jolted out of dreamlessness into another day.

I always set the clock for 5:00 A.M. That's the prime writing hour.

'I don't know why you can't be a little easier on yourself,' she says sometimes. 'You could write

10

just as well at seven as you could at five, no?' *Leetle, sebben, fife*. I love her accent. It makes me want to bite her.

'No, I couldn't,' I say, because there's something about five o'clock. The sun isn't up yet. The birds are barely stirring. Coffee smells more heavenly, the first cigarette tastes a little better. I like the smells of sleep, of last night's love. My dream mind is awake, but my thinking mind still sleeps – my imagination is laid bare and I plunder it like treasure, getting as much as I can on paper before I have time to think about it. The way most writers *write* about writing, you'd think every moment of it is some kind of blessed event, with sunlight streaming in the window just so and a sleeping cat perched nearby on top of a bookcase, and the writer closes his eyes and is filled instantly with grand ideas. That's just so much bullshit. There's a sort of panic involved, if you want to know the truth. At least, that's how it is for me. Once I wake up too much, the words stop coming, and since that's the whole reason I get out of bed in the first place, the rest of the day is just me waiting to go back to sleep so I can get up and do it all over again.

But even sleep holds its own kind of terror for me lately, some bizarre mystery, the very existence of which is an unassailable plague. The thing is, I don't dream any more. At all.

'You don't dream because you write,' Consuelo says. 'Your whole life is a dream. You're *always* dreaming. If you stopped writing—'

11

'Shh,' I say, clapping one hand over her mouth. 'Don't talk about not writing.'

'It doesn't matter.' She pulls my hand away. 'I was just saying. Just a joke.'

'Not even in a joke.'

'Phooey,' she says. 'You are too super . . . super . . . what is the word?'

The word she's looking for is *superstitious*, but I'll be damned if I'm going to give it to her. 'Handsome,' I say instead.

'This is not the word I want to say!'

'Say it anyway.'

'Phooey to you!'

'Phooey to you, my enchilada.' I can't help it any longer – I bite the delicate seashell of her ear, but gently.

Consuelo was first a plug in the hole of my heart, then grew to become my heart itself. I've never told her about Annie, but I think she knows anyhow. I can't say Annie was the one who put the hole there in the first place. That would imply she did it on purpose. But I love Consuelo in a way Annie would never let me love her. And so I nip her ear with my lips and wrestle her down, gently, always gently, and even when she wrestles back it's the most delicious kind of fighting, the kind that makes us one.

After Consuelo moved in with me, I started keeping my typewriter in the bathroom. This is not for her sake – if an earthquake of magnitude 7.1 can't wake her, the clacking of my keys

12

certainly won't. I just happen to prefer writing in the bathroom because it's the warmest room in the house. The other rooms are theoretically heated by our wood-burning stove, but the house is old and drafty and the insulation around the windows imperfect, and after only a few months in the mountains of the high desert my blood has grown thin – I get cold more easily than I used to, like an eighty-year-old man.

Around eight o'clock every morning Consuelo stumbles into the bathroom, pees, showers, gets dressed, and as always tries to sneak a peek over my shoulder at what I'm writing. Also as always, I block her view with my body.

'You *cabron*,' she says, swatting the back of my head. 'You *cabroncito*. How you ever going to manage to publish a book if you can't even let *me* read it?'

'You can read it when it's done.'

'When will that be?'

'I don't know.'

'What are you writing about?'

'Nothing.'

'A lot of time you spend on nothing.'

'Yeah. Whatever.'

'Whatever, whatever, *ay, Dios mio!*' she chants, flouncing out of the bathroom. She clacks around the house for a while in her high heels, which she wears everywhere. She's the best-dressed toilet cleaner in Santa Fe, New Mexico. As she clacks – and clicks and stomps – she sings. Her voice is

13

lovely, as light as air and as clear as glass. Consuelo sings constantly to herself, as though she can't help it. I've learned enough Spanish to know that she's making up the words as she goes along, that she's telling herself a tale without beginning or ending. She sings the story of her life, not as it happened but as it's happening. Occasionally I hear my name in there, and I know she's singing about me. Most of the time, however, her song is a mystery, and when I ask her what she sings about she merely smiles.

'You tell me what you write,' she says, 'I tell you what I sing.'

So I've learned not to ask, but merely to listen, which makes me content. Her voice is light, clear, strong. It makes me want to sing myself, and it illuminates even the darkest corners of my mind.

Consuelo clacks in her heels out of the house and up to the Cowgirl, where she will clean the bathrooms, mop the kitchen floor, and practice her scales on the rickety old piano until the bar opens. I'll sit in the bathroom all morning and into the afternoon, until she comes home and cooks dinner. I would cook dinner myself, but I'm not allowed. Consuelo has tasted my cooking before, once. Once, she says, was enough.

'Very few men belong in the kitchen,' she says, with a conviction a thousand years old, 'and you are not one of them. You make the living, and I make the food. That's the way it is.'

It never pays to argue with Consuelo. She considers my monthly check from Grandpa's estate as proof that my writing is generating some sort of income, and no amount of explaining will convince her otherwise. I've told her repeatedly that in less than a year, these checks will run out. It doesn't seem to worry her. She has faith – whether in me or something higher I don't know, but I certainly hope it's something higher.

Someday, maybe, I'll take her back to Mannville and introduce her to Mildred, and Mildred in turn will introduce her to her newly discovered principles of feminism. Until then, things will keep on as they are – the planets will continue on their groaning paths around the sun, early snow will fall in the mountains, and I'll keep typing away in the bathroom, pondering the deeper mysteries of life and trying to ignore the growling in my stomach.

CHAPTER 1

THE EAGLE DREAM

My name, for what it's worth, is William Amos Mann the Fourth, and I arrived in Santa Fe on the back of my steelgray 1977 Kawasaki KZ1000, bringing with me only what I could carry on the back of it: an antique typewriter, some books, and a few articles of clothing. It was then late in the summer of 1990. I'd just turned twenty years old, or so I assumed – my exact date of birth, like my origins, was unknown, so my grandfather had had to invent one on my behalf.

Grandpa'd had to do a lot of things on my behalf over the course of my life; I'm referring to those tasks that normally fall to parents, of which I had none, due to the mysterious absence of my mother and the untimely death of my father in the skies over the South China Sea just before my birth. Grandpa was my sole care-giver, and a tough old shoe; I know from casual observation that it's not easy for two people to raise a child, let alone one, let alone an aging, lonely man who is too fond of the bottle, but somehow he pulled it off. He might have begrudged my very existence, interfering as it did with his plan of alcohol-induced suicide, but

16

Grandpa was at heart a generous man, though I was one of only two people alive who knew it. *He* knew a considerable amount, although by his own admission none of it was very important; he'd concerned himself all his life with things that were mostly trivial and never applied himself to learning anything with any weight to it. That was why, in his own words, Grandpa was a failure at everything he did: he failed in business, he failed in marriage, and he even failed at fatherhood – though that was not his fault. It was the fault of Vietnam. The only thing he'd succeeded at, in sixty-six years of living, was raising me.

Nevertheless, over the course of the eighteen years we were together as grandfather and grandson, he tried to teach me everything he knew, and not all of it was worthless. For example, he taught me how to read and write, before my existence was discovered by the county and I was forced to go to school. He taught me how to work on engines of both the motorcycle and car varieties. But most significantly, and probably because he thought he was doing me a favor, he taught me the entire history of my once-glorious family – the Manns of Mannville, New York, who to hear him tell it were nothing less than a race of superpeople. Some of this was boring and some wasn't; I liked his war stories the best, but I could have done without hearing about how great we Manns were. All I had to do was look at him to know this wasn't true.

While not exactly up on the finer points of child

rearing, Grandpa managed to see me through my childhood in one piece and, despite my disbelief in our greatness, to instill in me a deep pride in who I was. The only problem was that I didn't actually *know* who I was. That is, I didn't know who *half* of me was, the half of me that came from my mother; neither, for that matter, did Grandpa. I was delivered to him in a picnic basket – a fact of which I was always slightly ashamed, until he reminded me that Moses had arrived in a basket, and so had numerous other notable persons throughout history. There was nothing to be embarrassed about; there was a fine tradition associated with baskets. This happened when I was only a few weeks old: my arrival, I mean. Presumably I was put in that basket by my mother, on that strange morning in 1970. I must have known her for a short time, but of course I don't remember anything from those days; and Grandpa never even got a glimpse of her as she dropped me off on the back steps and promptly fled the scene.

I'd wondered about my mother all my life – what she looked like, how she smelled and sounded and acted. Lately this wondering had grown to encompass a curiosity about the kind of people she herself came from, because they were my family, too, after all, even though I knew nothing about them. I'd no idea whether they were loud or soft-spoken, funny or boring, preferred chocolate to vanilla, if they liked movies over books or the other way around. I wondered whether any of them had ever done anything magnificent in their lives, or if they were the kind of folks who were satisfied with just getting by. These things were important – knowing them would help me to know myself, and the only way that would happen was if I went and looked for her. Not to make accusations, but simply to find out, as I have said, what she was like.

And if, for some reason, she was no longer among the living, well, at least I'd have tried. That was why I finally decided to leave town, more than two years after my graduation from high school. I wouldn't regret having looked for her and failed, but I would regret it infinitely if I'd never looked at all.

I'd spent the previous two years saving money from my job as a delivery boy for Gruber's Grocery and General Merchandise, and also writing in my bedroom – mostly short stories, but also a number of letters. I didn't show the stories to anyone, but the letters I mailed to an address in Santa Fe, New Mexico, where I knew my mother had lived once upon a time, before I was even born. This address wasn't much to go on, but it was the only clue I had. But none of my letters was answered. Most of them were returned, stamped 'Addressee unknown,' and a few of them simply disappeared into the ether.

The letters themselves said nothing important – they were all identical, in fact. In each I wrote the following:

Dear Resident,

If Eliza McMeel is still living at this address, please ask her to write back to me. I have something important which belongs to her and would like to return it.

Sincerely,
W. A. Mann

The 'something important' was me, of course. But I hesitated to come right out and *say* that; I didn't know who would be reading these letters, and I wanted them to be as noncommittal as possible, while still intriguing enough to make her respond. I didn't think my mother would know exactly who W. A. Mann was, although she would certainly recognize the last name as belonging to my father. But my caution was all for naught. I spent many a sleepless night staring at the ceiling, wondering if she would ever respond, but two years passed without any reply.

I lost patience. If I wasn't going to find my mother through the mail, then my only course of action was to go and have a look for myself. That was why I decided to leave Mannville, pure and simple. I had no interest in going to college, which would have been my only other reason for leaving home. Though I'm ashamed now to admit this, I might have been content to live the rest of my life in the old farmhouse that my great-great-grandfather had built, delivering groceries on my motorcycle for Harold and Emily Gruber and writing short stories in my bedroom during my spare time. I was already regarded in town as a bit of a lackluster young man, just like many other young men in small towns all across the country: *some brains, nice enough guy but never quite had what it took to make it – married the first girl who was nice to him, had a couple of kids, got old, and died.* That description could have been written on nine-tenths of the tombstones in Mannville's cemetery. It didn't bother me that other people were thinking about me this way; but as soon as I realized I was starting to believe it, I panicked.

It wasn't that I lacked ambition. We Manns had plenty of that, or so I'd always been told. It was that most of my ambitions could be satisfied without ever having to leave my bedroom. A writer writes, and that was exactly what I was doing; there was no reason for me to be concerned with anything else. I had a house, I had enough money to live on, I knew everyone in town and everyone knew me. I saw no need for improvement in my life.

But the idea that my mother was out there somewhere had always eaten away at me, and by my nineteenth year it was starting to take bites too big for my own comfort. Every day that I didn't get a letter from her was a day she slipped farther away. Besides, I was about to lose the job I'd held for the last six years. The Grubers were both into their eighties now, and that spring they informed me that they were closing the store and selling out to Kwalitee-Mart, the corporation that had been buying up all the mom-and-pop stores in our part of the state and anonymizing them, cloning itself at a frightening rate in the process. I would have to find another job if I was going to stick around Mannville, but the very idea of working anywhere else was abhorrent.

'Kwalitee-Mart would probably hire you,' said Harold Gruber. 'They'll need clerks and stockboys and such.'

'I don't want to be a clerk or a stock-boy,' I said. 'I like delivering groceries, not stocking them.'

But Harold said, 'Kwalitee-Mart doesn't deliver. I already asked them. Can you imagine that? A town grocer that doesn't deliver?'

I could not imagine it at all. It was supposed to be in the nature of grocery stores to deliver things, and it struck all three of us – Harold, Emily, and me – as an ominous sign that Kwalitee-Mart refused this service. Progress was coming to Mannville, years after it had arrived everywhere else.

I was also saddened by the thought of all the lonely women in Mannville. My position as delivery boy was a highly privileged one – it was responsible for me losing my virginity, a fact for which I was unendingly grateful. I had once been defiled by an older woman, and I could hardly wait for the chance to defile myself again with someone else. There were a number of possibilities out there, widows and divorcées and such, which I hadn't had the nerve to take advantage of yet, but I could feel them slipping away from me, too, now, as the specter of Kwalitee-Mart loomed closer.

'Maybe Kwalitee-Mart could make you a manager,' said Emily Gruber.

'Hey, now there you go!' said Harold. 'You're responsible and trustworthy enough. Would you like me to put in a good word for you, Billy?'

'Are they going to change the store much?' I asked, thinking longingly of loneliness and the benefits it had almost conferred.

'Oh, you betcha!' said Harold.

'They're going to put a big red *M* on it,' said Emily. 'An *electric* *M*. They should have a *K* instead, but I guess that was already taken.'

'Goddamn thing will probably light up the whole town,' said Harold.

'I don't think I want to work here if you folks aren't going to be around,' I said. 'Thanks just the same.'

I didn't add that I didn't think I would be able to stand the sight of an electric *M* on the front of the store, instead of the hand-painted sign that had hung there for as long as I could remember. I'd been working for the Grubers since I was fourteen years old, and my father had worked for them, too, when he was in high school. By now it was sort of a family tradition. Working for Kwalitee-Mart was most definitely not any kind of a tradition at all.

'Well, what are you going to *do* then?' asked Emily.

'Yes,' said Harold. 'What are you going to *do*?'

★   ★   ★

That was a question a lot of people had been asking me lately. I was getting tired of hearing it and tired of answering it. Though I kept my stories themselves secret, I told everyone that I wanted to be a writer. Most people greeted this with some vague words of encouragement, though nobody really believed it meant anything. I could tell they thought I would grow out of it, and soon fall into a more sensible line of work. But writing was only half of it. What I really wanted more than anything was to find my mother, and that wasn't something I could explain to anyone. It was my secret. That way, if I failed, no one would be the wiser.

That was how I made the decision to leave town, and to leave behind the ancestral Mann farmhouse, which – since I was the last surviving Mann – was now mine. I would also leave Mildred to live in it.

It seems ridiculous to refer to a woman well into her sixties as somebody's girlfriend, but that's what Mildred was to Grandpa before he died – she was the second person living who knew what a good man Grandpa really was, underneath his facade of misanthropy and drunkenness, and as my adopted grandmother she had as much right to the old house as I did. To my relief, Mildred agreed to stay on after I left. Our house, with its broad, sweeping driveway flanked by majestic oaks and its endless hallways and cavernous parlors and bedrooms, was the last bit of proof that the Manns

24

had once been people of consequence. As long as Mildred continued to stay there, I knew the place was in good hands – and though the possibility seemed remote, I also knew that if the Manns were by some chance to rise again, we would always have somewhere to rise *in*.

Grandpa himself had taken up residence in the spring of 1988 in his new home, the little cemetery next to St Jude the Apostle's Church. 'It's not the cough that carries you off,' he used to tell me, 'but the coffin they carry you off in.' This was his style of humor – he used to say this every time I got a cold. Grandpa hadn't died of a cough, however. It was actually his liver that carried him off, one fine spring afternoon – he'd managed to quit drinking after meeting Mildred, no small feat for a man who had been drunk almost every day of his life since 1950, but his poor abused liver had already had enough by then, and it proved to be his undoing.

Mildred, brave but brokenhearted, was slow to recover from his death. Even now, two years later, she still consoled herself by sorting through his effects on a daily basis. She sat in his bedroom for hours sometimes, just smelling his shirts. I was growing worried about her.

'Come in here and put your nose to this shirt,' she would call to me. 'It's like he's right here in the room.'

'How could it still smell like him?' I said. 'It's been too long.'

'It's still there,' she said. 'Just barely, but it's still there.'

The female sense of smell, I've read, is so finely tuned that a blindfolded woman can actually sniff out her own baby from a whole roomful of babies, ten times out of ten. All she has to do is put her nose on its head for a moment. Mildred was remembering Grandpa the best way she knew how – through her nose. I refused to have anything to do with that, however. If Mildred wanted to conjure up the spirit of my grandfather through some kind of olfactory séance, she could go right ahead. As for me, I'd had enough of ghosts. My childhood had been full of them. Besides, I could still hear Grandpa's voice in my head. It was faint and querulous, as if he was confused at his shift from the earthly plane. But it was definitely him, and I was afraid if I smelled him, he would pop out of thin air and come back to life all over again. He was still that close to me.

So I left Mildred to her shirts, and I made plans to leave as soon as possible.

Since my junior year of high school, I'd been ignoring all the brochures that came in the mail from out-of-town colleges. I thought of college as merely a repetition of high school, which had been unutterably boring, and so pointless an experience the idea of going through it a second time gave me the jumping fantods. But Mildred had collected the brochures, cataloguing them in alphabetical order and cross-referencing them according to subject major. The most attractive of them had been appearing discreetly on my desk, where I couldn't miss them, for the last year. But I'd made no move to read them or to fill out any of the forms that were stapled to their middles.

'Your grandfather wanted you to go to college more than anything,' Mildred said. 'Don't you think it's about time you started filling out some of these forms?'

'I don't think so,' I said.

'You can't get ahead in life without an education,' she reminded me. 'You'll never get a decent job.'

'I don't want a decent job,' I reminded her in turn. 'I want to be a writer.'

'That's all very well and good, but how are you going to support yourself in the meantime?'

I had five hundred dollars a month coming to me from Grandpa's estate, which seemed like a fortune. If I'd stopped to add it all up, I would have realized that the money amounted to something like six thousand dollars a year, which is scarcely enough to support a dog. But I didn't bother with such details, and in my present situation I hardly noticed anyway: taxes were negligible, and the house had been paid for well over a century ago.

'I'll live cheap,' I said. 'I'll eat fried baloney.'

'You can't live on fried baloney.'

'I *like* fried baloney. I've lived on it this long. A few more years of it won't kill me.'

'Just apply to one or two,' she begged me. 'Just to give me some peace of mind.'

I grumbled and groused. I didn't see what *her* peace of mind had to do with it – it was my life, after all. But to humor her, I applied to St. James's College, which happened to be in Santa Fe anyway and which offered a program in creative writing. It was the kind of place I probably would have gone – had I wanted to go anywhere, that is. But I didn't, so I took pains to lie on the application, not to make myself seem better than I was, but worse; I was afraid they might accept me, and then I would *have* to go. So I deliberately lowered my grade-point average; told them my special interests were limited strictly to things such as taxidermy and professional wrestling; I spindled, ripped, *and* folded my SAT score sheet; and I filled out all the forms in pencil. Finally, I wadded up all the papers into one great big ball, put it in a box, and shipped it off a week after the deadline. That, I thought, took care of that.

To my amazement, in mid-July I received a letter from the college saying that they were pleased to welcome me into the class of 1994. There'd been some minor errors on my application, they said, but they would be happy to straighten those out once I arrived. In the meantime, congratulations, and enclosed I would find a copy of the reading list, which all freshmen were required to have completed upon their arrival.

'Oh, shit,' I said aloud.

'Ahem,' said Mildred, who took a dim view of profanity.

'Sorry,' I said.

'What is that? A letter?' she asked.

'Sort of,' I said.

'Who's it from?'

'St. James's College.'

She perked up. 'Really? What did they say?'

There was no way to hide it from her, so I didn't even bother trying. 'I've been accepted,' I said.

Mildred snatched the letter away from me and read it with joy. She clapped one hand to her mouth.

'Oh, Billy,' she said, her eyes shining. 'Your grandfather would be so proud of you!'

'Yeah, but Mildred—'

'All he ever wanted,' she said, 'was to see you do better than he did. Here's your chance! You're going to college!'

'But I—'

'We have to get you ready,' she said. 'You're going to need clothes. You don't have any college clothes. What are college students wearing these days, I wonder?'

I sighed. There was no getting around it. This was the first time I'd seen her happy about anything since Grandpa died, and I didn't have it in me to take that away from her. So I permitted myself to be dragged into town, where we went to Kaufmann's Department Store and I tried on suit after suit. Whatever college students were wearing these days, I didn't think it involved suits, but my objections fell on deaf ears. Mildred was in her element now. For what remained of the summer, I gave up trying to change her mind. I decided to go to college after all. I could, I reasoned, drop out whenever I felt like it; I would be far away, and she would never know. It was my life, anyway. And I had other plans, too. Not even Mildred knew that the real reason I was going to Santa Fe was to look for my mother, and that was just the way I wanted it.

About two weeks before I left, as part of her self-prescribed therapy after Grandpa's death, Mildred – always the organizer – decided to make an inventory of his books. Grandpa's library was extensive; he bought books compulsively, even those he knew he would never read, simply because they were books and he liked having them around. His bookshelves on the second floor were crammed full, and the overflow was stored in countless cartons in the basement and attic and wherever else he'd found a spot to stick them. One day she discovered a box full of feminist literature, which she hauled upstairs and began sorting. I came home to find her sitting at the kitchen table, immersed deep in a copy of *Our Bodies, Ourselves*.

'What's that?' I asked.

'Oh,' she said, her face coloring. 'Nothing.'

'Come on, let me see.'

I tried to grab the book, but she held it out of reach.

'This is a *woman's* book,' she said.

'So? What, is it in code or something?'

'It's not for young men to read.'

'Oh, *I* see,' I said. 'Dirty pictures?'

'Oh, stop it!' she said. 'They're not dirty. They're . . . medical.'

'What are all these other books?' I asked. The kitchen table was covered with them.

'Your grandfather was always full of surprises, wasn't he?' she said. 'I found these downstairs. Do you think he ever read them?'

'I doubt it,' I said. I'd missed seeing this box before. I picked up one of the books – the author was Camille Paglia. There was also Erica Jong, Betty Friedan, Gloria Steinem, all names unfamiliar to me.

'What are these?' I asked. 'Novels?'

'I'm not sure what to call them,' Mildred said. 'They're like instructions on how to be a woman. Things certainly have changed since I was young, I can tell you that. If my husband had ever caught me reading something like this, he would have . . .'

Mildred didn't finish that sentence. She didn't have to – I knew what she was going to say. He would have pulverized her.

Before she came to live with us Mildred had

had another life, with a husband and seven children. Now that her husband was dead, all of the children had put as much distance as possible between themselves and home, both because of their father's cruelty and because they blamed Mildred for allowing everything to go wrong. She rarely spoke of her children, but I knew she thought of them often. She was suffering silent heartaches of her own; and with Grandpa's death added to the picture, sometimes I feared for Mildred's general well-being.

But reading these books seemed to give her the peace of mind she sought, to soothe her in ways that I myself could not hope to understand. I didn't know it at the time, but Mildred had made the first step in what was to be a radical transformation. I would only see the effects of it later – I would never guess at the internal part of it, how she had reviewed her entire life up to that point like an accountant ticking off assets and debits, and then realized that, in the final analysis of her experience, she was greatly in the red. This would only be explained to me much later, by others who had grown close to her and who understood better than any twenty-year-old man could what trials she had undergone.

But the earliest signs of this transformation would manifest themselves immediately, even before I left home. The day before I was to leave, a strange girl appeared out of nowhere and, without notice or fanfare, took up residence in the old farmhouse as though she had every right to be there – a very pregnant girl, in fact. I came downstairs for breakfast that morning to find her sitting with Mildred, the two fo them drinking tea and eating toast.

'Morning,' I said uncertainly.

'Good morning,' Mildred chirped, as though all was normal, as though pregnant girls materialized in our kitchen every day of the week. The girl herself said nothing. 'Billy, this is Abby.'

'Hi, Abby,' I said. I poured myself a cup of coffee.

'Hi,' Abby mumbled. She kept her eyes on the floor.

'Billy,' said Mildred. 'Let's us have a little talk. Excuse me, Abby.'

Mildred motioned to me to follow her into the living room.

'I hope you don't mind,' she said.

'Mind?'

'About Abby staying the night.'

'Why would I mind?'

'Well,' said Mildred, 'because actually, she's staying longer than one night.'

'She is?'

'It's just that she has nowhere to go,' Mildred said. 'As you can see, she's very young, and this baby is somewhat of a . . . well, an accident, I guess you might say. She's Ethel Christie's niece. I told Ethel she should bring her by to visit, and if she liked it here she could stay. I'm afraid her father

33

is . . . well, he isn't being very understanding about the whole situation, the son of a bitch.'

I looked up, startled. I, who was not even allowed to say 'shit' in the house, had never heard Mildred talk that way about anybody before, not even her late husband.

'Excuse me,' Mildred said, as though she'd belched. 'Ah, the poor little thing. Anyway . . .'

'You mean she's going to *live* here?' I said.

Mildred nodded. A lightbulb went on in my mind.

'She's going to have the *baby* here?'

She nodded again. Suddenly many things made sense.

'What kind of an accident?' I asked – for I like to know the facts of everything, not out of nosiness but out of habit. Grandpa had trained me early in life to notice small details. But Mildred set her lips purposefully in a way that let me know she was sworn to secrecy. Suddenly I realized that it *wasn't* an accident that Abby was pregnant, or at least not an accident that was her fault; and whatever that accident had been, it was not only none of my business – it was too horrible to bring up.

'Given your own story,' said Mildred, 'I figured you would be sympathetic to her. Poor little thing,' she said again – though Abby was anything but little. I snuck another glance at her through the kitchen door. She sat gazing forlornly into her tea, her belly looking as if it might explode at

34

any moment. Bellywise, she was the biggest girl I'd ever seen.

'Sure. It's fine, Mildred,' I said.

'You're sure?' she said.

'Sure, I'm sure.'

Mildred put her hand on mine and squeezed. 'You're a good boy, Billy,' she whispered. 'I knew you would understand.'

I might not have understood the specifics of the situation, but I understood that Abby's sudden appearance had something to do with Mildred's books; and I was relieved beyond telling that she wouldn't be alone in the old house after I was gone. That thought had been tormenting me, for even though I couldn't let myself be held back from what I thought of as my destiny, I hated to think of Mildred all by herself. Now she had someone to talk to, and if the size of Abby's belly was any indication, very soon there would be a baby to take care of – another bastard in the Mann house, I mused, although I would never have dared to say such a thing aloud. It seemed the house was a magnet for unwanted children.

My leave-taking the next morning was brief and unceremonious. Abby was ill and unable to get out of bed, and she was so close to having her baby that Mildred was afraid to leave her alone, even for a moment. That was when I realized Mildred had not just meant she would 'have the baby here' in the figurative sense of living in the house but having the baby in the hospital, and bringing it home afterward; she meant she was actually going to give birth to it *right there under our roof.*

'Mildred,' I said, 'you have got to be kidding.'

'About what?'

'She can't just . . . deliver a baby. Not here.'

'And why not?' Mildred asked.

Her tone was so matter-of-fact that I was hard pressed to answer. But it wasn't that I objected to the idea of it – it was just that it seemed so primal, or something – so *dangerous.* But I also realized that Mildred certainly knew all this; she knew it better than I, and it was pointless for me to remind her. So I merely said, 'For one thing, think of the mess!'

'It's only blood,' Mildred told me. 'Blood, and water, and mucus – all things that people are made of.'

'But what if something bad happens? What will you do then?'

'I have someone coming over,' she said. 'A midwife. This is the way Abby wants to do it, Billy. She doesn't want painkillers. She doesn't want doctors, either. She wants to *feel* it. She wants it to *hurt.*'

'But – why?'

'Pain,' said Mildred, 'can be cleansing. That's why.'

'All right,' I said. Obviously, it was none of my business. 'Good luck.'

'Billy says good luck, Abby,' Mildred called.

'Gaaawd!' cried Abby.

'I better get going,' I said nervously – I didn't want to watch the baby arrive.

36

Mildred's arms barely reached around my middle. She grabbed me close to her and held me for a long moment.

'Sorry I can't walk you to the door, but she's going to start any time,' she said. 'Promise me you'll write.'

'I'll write.'

'And be good.'

'I will, Mildred.'

'Jesus fucking Christ!' screamed Abby.

I kissed Mildred. Then I went down the stairs and outside, started up my bike, and pulled out of the driveway, leaving the screaming Abby in Mildred's hands and feeling as though I'd picked a very good day to leave.

When it came right down to it, leaving home was as simple as that. I took one last nostalgic spin through town, passing the statue of my great-great-grandfather, greened with age and generously decorated by the pigeons; passing Gruber's Grocery and General Merchandise, closed and dark now, with the old sign gone but the new one not yet installed; even cruising up the hill to take one last look at Annie's abandoned house. Annie was my first what you'd call girlfriend, and the last, too. She'd run away a few years earlier. I still felt a pang every time I thought of her, made sharper by the fact that I didn't know if I would ever see her again – in fact, I was pretty sure I wouldn't. I thought of going into the place, of sitting in her old bedroom again just for a moment. But despite the anguish her memory caused me, I was too excited to stop, and in the end I didn't go in. I rode back down the hill and took the highway on-ramp in a great tire-screeching, body-leaning turn, and within seconds the spire of town hall, the only part of Mannville visible from the highway, had receded in my rearview mirror to nothing more than a tiny speck, and soon even that was gone.

I headed west on I-90, speeding through the fragrant vineyards of our corner of western New York State, into Pennsylvania and grazing the lake port of Erie, all the way to Cleveland. Nothing had changed yet. The same old Lake Erie was alongside me the whole way. I recited the names of small towns to myself as I passed them – Fairview, Conneaut, Ashtabula, Parma. Once at Cleveland I headed south, and now the land began to change little by little – it became flatter and more fertile, the domain of corn and wheat farmers. That first day I made it as far as the Illinois border, where I pulled my bike to the far edge of a rest stop and collapsed on top of a blanket, body aching and sore, bones still vibrating. The next day brought me as far as Missouri, and the next to Oklahoma. I was pulling marathon riding sessions on a daily basis. I felt unstoppable. By now the landscape was completely unfamiliar – red and dry, the earth crumbly and the sky somehow bigger. I emerged into Texas in a state of astonishment that I was actually doing this, that I'd left home and made it this far without mishap. For the first time in my life I saw cacti, tumble-weeds, roadrunners, once a bevy of prairie dogs whose heads turned in unison as I passed them and who looked, with their hands cocked downward at right angles to their bodies, as though they were praying for my safe passage through their territory. Texas was bigger than I'd imagined, nearly a thousand miles from end to end, and it took me two full days to cross it; by then my body was begging for relief from the ceaseless pressure of the wind, and my coccyx was bruised. But I kept on, past solitary shanties, past vast tracts of nothing, along stretches of road where it was just the sky and me and the occasional raven or crow, the odd solitary tree. Just when it seemed that Texas was all there was to the earth and that nothing else had ever existed, the land began to change again, to slope almost imperceptibly upward, and to change color once more. There was a breathtaking moment in which I had the sense that something was suddenly different, that I was in a new place, although I couldn't put my finger on what it was; and then I whizzed past a sign saying 'Welcome to New Mexico.'

It had taken me five days. Certain elements of the journey stick out more than others; I saw a majestic rainbow in Oklahoma, which still revisits me from time to time, the most splendid I'd ever seen; and one night in Texas I dreamed I danced with Indians around a fire, in honor of the eagle – the last dream I would have for months. I took the remaining miles between Tucumcari and Santa Fe with the practiced ease of a lifelong rider, passing mesas and buttes shaped by vanished rivers. Interstate 40 brought me to Albuquerque, and from there it was a trifling sixty miles to my destination: Santa Fe.

Compared to Mannville, Santa Fe was a strange and beautiful place – a symphony in Spanish brown, a town of mud houses, a cacophony of strange odors and unfamiliar plants and exotic street names, and behind it the tree-lined slopes of the Sangre de Cristo Mountains. The air was dry and as clear as spring water, the clouds lazy and regal, and the light fell so strongly from the cerulean sky that I could almost fel it pittering like rain on my jacket. From the highway, I took an exit that brought me to the very center of town, a large plaza filled with tourists and with Indians hawking handmade jewelry. Riding a bike is hard work; every muscle is tensed all the time, and I was hungry enough to eat a brick. I followed my nose from one restaurant to another. Restaurants were everywhere along the plaza, but from the menus posted in the windows I saw they were out of my budget, so I settled on a burrito from a vendor on a street corner. It was a great dripping concoction of beans, rice, and spicy meat that required my full attention and both hands. It had a number of new flavors, and one in particular that seemed to have a delayed reaction, setting my mouth on fire only after I'd wolfed down the whole thing. I danced around in pain until I realized the burning wasn't going to fade. I went back to the same vendor, who sold me a Coke. I drank it fast and ordered another.

'That's the green chile that's killing you. Take a piece of bread,' the man advised me. 'Drinking just makes it worse.'

He gave me another tortilla. I took a bite of it, and immediately the burning began to fade.

'Sorry, *ese*,' he said. 'I wouldn't of given it to you so hot if I knew you weren't used to it.'

'Why does drinking make it worse?' I said. 'I thought it was supposed to help!'

'You're an amateur,' he said. 'I can tell.'

'What the hell was in that thing, anyway?' I said, chewing the tortilla. 'Plutonium?'

'Green chile, *chile verde*,' he said. 'You never had it before?'

'No. Nothing like it where I come from,' I said. Sweat stood out on my forehead. I grabbed a handful of napkins and wiped my face.

'Where you come from?' he asked.

'Mannville, New York.'

He shrugged. 'Never heard of it.'

'Nobody has,' I said. I finished the tortilla and wiped my face again. 'Thank you,' I said.

'*Por nada.*'

I figured this meant 'you're welcome,' or something like it. 'By the way,' I asked, 'do you know where St James' College is?'

The man snorted in derision. He was dark skinned and black haired, his eyes a shining pair of onyx marbles. I wondered if he was Mexican or maybe an Indian. I'd never seen either one before, but I wasn't sure if it was OK to ask.

'What you want to go up there for? You going to be a Jimmy?'

'A what?'

'A Jimmy. That's what we call those *pendejos*.'

'Those *what*?'

'*Pendejos*. It means – well, are you going to be one?'

'No,' I said – because I had already made up my mind again that I was going to drop out.

'Good,' he said, 'because *pendejo* means pubic hair.'

'I'll have to remember that,' I said.

'You can see the place from here, almost,' he said, and he pointed up to the hills on the edge of town. 'Take that road out of the plaza and just follow it up. Turn left at the fork in the road by the liquor store. Then turn left again at the convent, go up past the seminary, and there it is.'

'Liquor store, convent, monastery,' I said. 'Got it.' I thanked him and went back to my bike, but as I was heading out of the plaza another question occurred to me. I rode up to the vendor again and killed the engine.

'You ever heard of anyone named Eliza McMeel?'
I asked him.

'Eliza Mc*Who*?'

'McMeel.'

He bit his lower lip and shook his head. 'I never
heard a name like that before, *ese*,' he said. 'What's
it mean?'

'I don't know,' I said.

This bit of ignorance appeared to concern him.
'My name is Julio, which means July,' he pointed
out. I waited for him to explain the relevance of
this, but after a moment I realized he was merely
introducing himself.

'Billy Mann, which also doesn't mean anything,
as far as I know,' I said. 'Nice to meet you.'

'Come back, you ever want another burrito,' he
said. 'I won't make it so hot next time.'

'Thanks,' I said. I pulled away once again and
pointed my bike out of town.

Following Julio's directions, I headed up towards
the hills, turning left at a fork in the road where
there was indeed a liquor store – even *that* was
made of mud walls, just like all the houses I'd
seen so far. Left at a sign that indicated Carmelite
Sisters lived there, straight up past a group of
low-lying pink earth buildings with a large white
cross, which was, I presumed, the seminary, and
then I had arrived at the campus of St James's. I
dismounted and looked around.

I was in the foothills of the Sangre de Cristos
now, a long series of hills dotted with large green

43

bushes and outcroppings of quartz and granite. The campus consisted of a handful of two-story buildings, again the same dun color of the earth, and a large fishpond, wherein cruised a single giant carp. In a sort of central area near the fishpond a number of students were hanging around, playing guitar, kicking a hackysack in a circle, or just sitting and talking. I asked one of them where I would find the admissions office; he was a slight, big-nosed fellow in a tweed jacket, and he pointed at a building with a bell tower on it.

'It's in there,' he said. 'But if you're going to ask about the new seminar schedule, don't bother. I already asked once and she practically bit my head off.'

'I'm not going to ask them about seminar schedules,' I said. 'I'm dropping out.'

He raised his eyebrows. 'Really?' he said. 'Good!'

I was startled. 'Why good?' I asked.

'No reason,' he said. 'Just – good for you. Freedom. Self-expression. Come on, I'll take you there. I'm Ralph Goldfarb, by the way.'

'Billy Mann,' I said. 'Nice to meet you.'

I offered my hand, but he was already marching toward the bell-tower building. I followed him inside and we entered a door marked 'Admissions.' A woman with glasses on a chain around her neck was sitting at a desk. She glared at us suspiciously.

'They're still not out yet,' she said. 'So don't ask.'

'He's dropping out,' Ralph Goldfarb informed her. 'His name is Billy Mann. Right?' he said to me. 'How do you spell that?'

'Two ens,' I said.

'Oh,' said the woman, reaching into a drawer for some forms. 'That's different, isn't it?'

'It certainly *is*,' said Goldfarb, with satisfaction. 'Good luck, sir. A pleasure to meet you.'

'Yes. Thank you,' I said, offering my hand once again, but he was already out the door.

I turned my attention to the secretary, who had picked up a pen and was poised to write. 'Reason for leaving?' she asked.

Ralph Goldfarb's words came back to me. 'Freedom of self-expression,' I said.

She peered at me from over her glasses. 'You may think you're being clever,' she said, 'but you'd be surprised how many people say exactly that.'

I left the campus and headed back down to the plaza. It was time to find the address at which I knew my mother had lived once, more than twenty years ago. I pulled up in front of the same corner and looked around for Julio of the burrito stand, hoping he could give me directions, but he was gone. It was now late afternoon. He was probably at home, I figured, putting his feet up and relaxing with a burrito so hot it would burn right through the stomachs of ordinary mortals.

I'd have to find it on my own, then.

I removed a letter, typed on light-blue stationery, from my wallet.

This letter was the most important link in the search for my mother that I possessed. I'd received it while trying to find out where my father's personal effects went, after he was vaporized. I knew that most families of men killed in action got boxes of things sent back to them: clothes, toothbrush, razor blades, socks; the poignant reminders of the smallest details of a man's life. But for some reason, Grandpa'd only gotten a telegram, nothing more.

A couple of years ago I'd driven to Buffalo to talk to a man who'd served with Eddie in the air force, to see if he could help me figure out who my mother was. His name was Henry Hutchins, and he'd met my mother once, the same night she'd met my father – Henry and Eddie had been on leave, and they'd been out wandering the streets of Buffalo together in the hours before my conception. Henry Hutchins asked me if I'd searched my father's belongings for some clue about her. Grandpa didn't get any belongings, I told him. Henry told me they must have gone *somewhere*. It would have been up to my father where they were mailed – it depended on who he listed as next of kin. It was strange, we agreed, that it wasn't Grandpa. Eddie must have wanted them sent to someone just as important, if not more so. Find out where they went, Henry Hutchins told me. If the address belonged to someone named Sky, I was on the right track.

So I wrote to the air force and asked them where my father's things were sent. Months later, I received the letter I was holding now. It gave an address in Santa Fe, as well as a name: Eliza McMeel. That was how I learned my mother's true identity. I already knew that Sky wasn't her real name; but it was how she would have introduced herself to Eddie because it was the name she went by in those days, and perhaps still did. *That* fact I had gleaned from old Doctor Connor, who'd delivered me and who'd known my mother for a few short weeks. My mother had sworn him to secrecy concerning the details of my birth. She didn't want my grandfather to know who she was, she said. It was as if she wanted to make a clean getaway. Connor considered himself bound by his Hippocratic oath not to tell, but he also believed that his oath was dissolved once he himself was dead. So his last words to me were in the form of yet another letter, delivered after his death, which revealed everything he knew about the pregnant young woman who'd showed up in his office one day in 1970: that her real name was Eliza, that she went by Sky, and that she was from somewhere to the south and west of here.

The address was the first real lead in the case of her whereabouts – my *only* lead, in fact. Back in Mannville, it had seemed like the news event of the century, but standing on a street corner almost two thousand miles from home, it suddenly seemed very slim indeed.

The typewritten words were nearly illegible after constant reading, folding, unfolding, and rereading, but it didn't matter. I had committed the contents of the letter to memory. The address it gave was 125 South Blossom Street.

I stood there with the letter fluttering in my hand and looked around. Indian women knelt on blankets in a line stretching around the length of the plaza, rows of handmade silver-and-turquoise jewelry spread out before them. Tourists wandered back and forth in a disorganized herd. I stared at the women – they looked like the people I'd danced with, in the eagle dream I'd had in Texas.

I began to peruse the blankets, pretending to look at the jewelry but really looking at their faces. The people had rounded chins, high foreheads, and an almost Oriental cast to their eyes. Their hair was jet black, worn long by men and women alike. The men were in jeans and cowboy boots, the women in long, colorful skirts, sometimes adorned with beadwork. They chatted to each other in a strange language. I listened, but I couldn't make sense of a single word.

Out of the corner of my eye, on one of the blankets, I saw something that stopped me. It was a silver pendant in the form of an eagle, not the sort of full-on view that is the emblem of the United States but an eagle streaking forward in profile, its one visible eye sharp and keen. It was the precise image of my dream. I bent down and looked at it more closely. The eagle was enclosed within a circle of silver. If I closed my eyes I could see the fire, and us dancing around it, and I could hear the hypnotic drumbeats in my head.

'How much?' I asked the man on the other side of the blanket.

The man leaned forward and inspected the pendant closely, as if he'd never seen it before. A long black braid flopped over his shoulder.

'That?' He frowned. 'What do you want that for?'

It was an odd question from someone who was supposed to be selling his jewelry, not casting doubt upon it.

'I just like it, that's all,' I said. 'Did you make it?'

He laughed – or rather, he grunted, his shoulders heaving once. 'Yes,' he said. 'I made it.'

'Can I try it on?'

The man leaned forward with a long metal rod, which after a moment I realized was the antenna from a car radio. He lifted the pendant from the blanket and held it toward me, dangling it from the end of the antenna. When I put it around my neck, the silver was cool and heavy on my chest.

'How much?' I asked again.

'Ninety-five dollars,' he said.

I took it off and put it back on the blanket.

'Too much?'

'Sorry,' I said.

'It's pure silver,' he said.

'I'm sure it's worth it. I just can't afford it.

Thanks, anyway.' I began to move on down the sidewalk.

'Why do you want it?' he called after me.

I turned. He still wouldn't look at me directly, and I took advantage of this to study his face in greater detail. I was struck by the familiarity of it, even though I also knew I'd never seen him before.

'I dreamed it,' I said.

If I'd told anyone in Mannville that I wanted to buy a pendant of an eagle because I had dreamed of it, they'd have thought me more than odd; they would have thought me crazy. But I wasn't in Mannville anymore, and the man accepted this without comment. He remained silent for a time, thinking deeply. Then he picked up the pendant again, this time with his fingers. He gave it back to me and our hands brushed slightly as he did so. It was a warm day, but his skin was cool and dry.

'You can have it for fifteen,' he said.

'Fifteen? Really?'

He heaved his shoulders again. Wondering what was so funny, I handed over a ten and a five.

'Don't take it off,' he said.

'Why not?'

'It's medicine,' he said. He unbuttoned the throat of his shirt and pulled out a little skin bag. He showed it to me quickly, then tucked it back in again.

'I don't understand,' I said.

The man did not appear in the least surprised

that I didn't understand; he looked like someone who was never surprised by anything. He thought for a while longer.

'Medicine helps you go,' he said finally.

I waited for some moments, but that was all he was going to say. He folded back into himself, fixing his eyes on the ground before him once more.

'Thanks,' I said. I fastened the pendant around my neck again and headed back for my motorcycle.

A cop told me that South Blossom Street was only a few blocks from the plaza, across the main ditch that ran through town – the Acequia Madre, the mother of all irrigation ditches, whose silvery offspring crisscrossed the town as if in a sort of Southwestern Venice. I found it within five minutes, and soon I was parked in front of number 125. I hit the kill switch and knelt next to my bike as if there was something wrong with it. I lifted up the seat and removed the little toolbox I kept in there to make it look like I was doing repair work. Meanwhile I stared at the house through the gap between the carburetors and the front fork.

It was empty: that much was clear right away. The house was small, only one story, with a tiny, crumbling porch in front. The stucco on the walls had peeled off in large patches, revealing a layer of chicken wire and cement underneath. It wasn't real adobe; it was only made to look that way. One window was broken. The yard was brown and dead, a depressing moonscape of gravel and dried-up weeds. If my mother had ever lived there, she was gone now and had been for a while. I could see why all my letters had come back to me.

'Shit,' I said.

I looked up and down the street. It was quiet, humble, the houses small and made of the omni-present adobe. Here and there along the curb were cars that hadn't run in a long time; the tires were flat, and there were large pools of oil underneath them, with stray parts littering the ground. Dogs barked, a cat groomed himself unconcernedly on a nearby roof, strings of dried red peppers swung from porches in the slight breeze. I smelled deli-cious cooking. There were no people visible. It was a poor neighborhood, I could tell, but mostly a quiet one. Number 125 seemed to be the only abandoned house. I wondered what had happened there to make everyone go away.

Then I noticed a sign on the house directly across the street from 125: it said, in large red letters, 'For Rent – call Mr. Martinez,' and below gave a phone number.

I pursed my lips and considered my options. Dropping out of school meant I had to find a place to live, since I wouldn't be in the dorms. It had crossed my mind briefly to live in the mountains as a sort of modern wild man, coming into town whenever I needed supplies. The mountains were alluringly majestic; I had felt them beckon me almost immediately. But with a tinge of regret, I had to admit I wouldn't get much writing done if I

52

was living in a cave, or something equally as primitive. Writing required enough electricity to make coffee, and also a desk. But I thought might have just enough money left over to pay a month's rent on this place – if the rent wasn't too high, of course, and if I ate only once a day until the next check came from Grandpa's estate. And if my mother had really lived here in this neighborhood, then it made sense, poetically speaking, for me to live here, too. Some of the neighbors might remember her. Maybe she would even come back. I memorized the phone number on the 'For Rent' sign and got back on my bike to look for a pay phone.

CHAPTER 2

THE LAND WITHOUT RUST

The next day, after yet another night of roughing it in a campground on the out-skirts of town, I made an appointment from a pay phone with the owner of the house, one Mr Martinez. Mr Martinez showed up an hour later, driving a near-mint-condition 1939 Chevy pickup painted robin's egg blue, moving in anachronistic splendor down the street at twenty miles an hour. He pulled up in front of 124 and disembarked with dignity, like a general.

Mr Martinez was ancient and stooped. He wore a brand-new straw fedora; his mustache was a meticu-lously trimmed line of gray; and like his truck, he himself seemed to have a top speed that was just a notch above standing still. The military analogy was apt, for one of the first things I learned about Mr Martinez, besides his name, was that he'd served in the war – the Great War, that is. But he hadn't been a general. As he cheerfully admitted, he hadn't even been an officer. He was proud that he'd served in the trenches, and this piece of information was delivered so smoothly that I could tell it was a standard part of his introduction to strangers.

'I did my training in New Jersey,' he told me. 'I know an Easterner when I see one. This place is filling up with you folks pretty fast.'

Mannville was not, strictly speaking, an East Coast town, lying as it did less than a hundred miles from Ohio, which considered itself the heart of the Midwest – but I wasn't interested in arguing with Mr Martinez. He was too old. It had taken him nearly a full minute to walk from the street to the porch, and he waved off with indignant pride my offer of a helping arm as he attempted to mount the single step. He had to make three tries. Once he'd succeeded he leaned against the wall, catching his breath, a gnarled and trembling hand pressed to his chest.

'That's a beautiful truck,' I told him.

'I just wash it and polish it, that's all. Nothing ever rusts out here,' he said. I could tell he was pleased I'd noticed. His voice was high and reedy, and he gave off the odor of starch and freshly laundered clothing; despite the exceedingly wrinkled state of his skin, he was a well-pressed man. 'No humidity. Well, let's get down to business. You got a dog?'

'No, sir.'

'Good. No dogs allowed. No cats, either. A bird would be okay. Come on in.'

He unlocked the front door, and I followed him into the house. From the outside it was a small and undistinguished place, but there was nonetheless something about it that set it off from

55

the other houses on South Blossom; it was thick walled and squat, a solid dwelling built to survive any kind of weather – an ageless, ancient place. Inside there were five rooms, all small, already sparsely furnished, and there was a cast-iron stove in the living room. The floors were hardwood, the walls thick and whitewashed, the doorways low and their edges smooth and rounded. It was a house without corners, like the interior of a seashell. The floor curved into the wall, and the walls gradually became the ceiling; everything had been smoothed over with plaster, patted into shape by knowing hands, like a house of mud – which was exactly what it was.

'My great-grandfather built this place,' Mr Martinez told me. 'You couldn't knock it down with a bulldozer. You know 'bout 'dobe?'

'No, sir.'

'Well,' he said, 'first you got to find the right kind of dirt. Not too much sand, not too much clay. Then you got to mix it with the water. Sometimes you need straw, too. Then you pour it into your forms, and you let it dry. You let it sit a week or two. Then you got your bricks.'

'Doesn't it wash away?'

'This place is almost two hunnert years old,' Mr Martinez said. 'If it was gonna wash away, it woulda done it already. You just put stucco on the outside, and do it again every couple of years. No rain can hurt this place. 'Dobe keeps you cool, too. Not like that fake cement shit they put up now.'

'How much is the rent?'

'I was nineteen years old when we declared on them Germans,' he said, as though he hadn't heard. 'How old are you?'

'Twenty,' I said.

Mr Martinez looked me up and down with that same dubious expression I'd come to expect from men his age – and much younger, too – men old enough to have fought in wars ended long before I was born. There was always an element of scorn in their faces, as though they were trying to figure if I'd survive or not, if I had what it took to kill or be killed. I stood up a little straighter and tried to look brave.

'Back in my day we never had hair like that,' he said – my hair was long, reaching nearly to my shoulders, and he reached out now and gave it a disapproving tug, but a gentle one. 'Two fifty a month.'

I was relieved – I had two hundred seventy-five dollars to my name, right there in my pocket, and I figured I could live easily on twenty-five dollars until my next estate check came at the end of the month, just a week away. But I couldn't help wondering whether the rent would have been lowered if I agreed to get a haircut.

We shook on it – Mr Martinez didn't believe in contracts, he said, because they reminded him of lawyers, and if a man's word wasn't good enough then what the hell was the world coming to, any-way. I counted out the money, and he departed in his museum piece of a truck, leaving me alone in my new home.

The first impressions of the neighborhood I'd gotten the day before proved to be accurate: it was humble, sleepy, and quiet – during the day. Night was a different story. After the sun had gone down behind the Jemez Mountains to the west, and the Sangre de Cristos had shed their robes of royal purple and sanguine red, the street came alive with music and revelry that sometimes lasted far into the night, regardless of the day of the week. For some people in Santa Fe, apparently, every night was Saturday night. There was shouting, breaking glass, the throbbing of car stereos, the ropy smell of marijuana. It was not a general sort of party – the noise seemed to have a single source. A crowd of men congregated nightly in front of number 123, next to the abandoned house that had or had not been my mother's, and directly across the street from mine. I watched them from behind the curtains of my living room window. There were usually ten or twelve of them, a tough-looking crowd with bandannas on their heads and gold crucifixes around their necks, which glinted under South Blossom's sole streetlight; their flannel shirts were buttoned only at the neck, and they flapped loose at their sides in upside-down Vs, revealing grimy T-shirts and potbellies. The men drank from large plastic bottles of cheap booze and howled like wolves at each other's jokes instead of laughing, so that the general impression I got was of a pack of wild animals that grew more and more disorderly as the night wore on. They spoke only in Spanish. The rhythm of their words was as rapid and musical as rainfall, and of course completely incomprehensible to me. When they were out, I stayed in. I had seen some of the other neighbors in passing and was already acutely conscious that mine was the only white skin in the neighborhood; I didn't want to attract any attention to myself until people had had a chance to get used to me. These guys looked like the kind of people who would want to know what I was doing there, and I wasn't sure I could explain my presence in a way that would suit them.

This went on for a few days, during which I gathered my thoughts and tried to come up with a plan. As the sun came up, things quieted down again, and after trying without much success to sleep with pillows pressed against my ears I woke early and sat down at my typewriter.

The other half of my plan was to write a novel, which I intended to work on during those times when I wasn't actively seeking out my mother. This was nothing new – I'd been trying to write a novel for several months now, but it was giving me a great deal of trouble. My head had always been well populated with imaginary people, so coming up with interesting characters was not the problem. It was that there were too *many* of these characters. I was like a crowded theater with only one exit, and everyone clamoring to get out at once. I tried to give them some semblance of order, to pick and choose which among them was worthy of being set down on paper – but they were an unruly mob, paying me no attention, and still I didn't even know what the story was to be about. I had only the vaguest notions of how novels were made, but I knew that something important and interesting had to happen in them that people would remember afterward. Not enough had happened in my own life, I reflected glumly, for me to start making up the things that happened in other people's. Maybe I was too young to write a book. Nevertheless, the only way to learn was to try, and it wasn't going to write itself. So I pounded away for a few hours every morning, writing whatever came to mind. Most of it was nonsense, not worth keeping – like a literary kind of exploratory surgery. But I knew from experience that sooner or later a story line would emerge. The surgery would reveal something vital, and then I would expose the guts of the whole thing – that was the only way I knew how to do it.

After each morning's work I ate a frugal lunch, revisiting my friend Julio at his burrito stand in the plaza – breakfast consisted solely of coffee and cigarettes. Then I spent a few hours poking around the older parts of Santa Fe, sticking my head briefly into the centuries-old buildings from which the

Spanish had once governed their territory. But besides those and a seemingly excessive amount of art galleries, there didn't seem to be much to the town. I hardly noticed the lack of things to do – compared to Mannville, it was a cultural mecca – but I wasn't much interested in either history or art, and I found myself spending a lot of time simply sitting on a bench in the plaza, observing the tourists and the Indians and allowing my burrito to be digested.

I was growing very interested in chiles. It was harvest season, and the smell of roasting chile peppers hung over the town in a mouth-watering fog. Everywhere there were things called chile roasters, with long lines of people waiting to purchase their yearly supply. By now I had deduced that chiles, in all their various forms, were highly regarded in New Mexico; next to beans and rice and tortillas, they were the most integral ingredient of New Mexican cooking, especially the roasted green variety. They were to New Mexico what soy sauce is to Japan. Chiles were used in burritos, soups, stews, cheeseburgers, salsas, and casseroles. In every menu I'd gazed at longingly so far, in every restaurant I couldn't afford to enter, green chile was the prominent feature, the star of every gastronomical show. My bowels had been in a state of uproar for two days after my first experience with Julio's burrito, but despite the pain, there was something about the scorching heat, the earthy and delectable flavor of the chile itself, that left me wanting more.

And it was this urge for heat that would give me my next real lead in the case of my missing mother.

Across the street from my house, in the yard of 123 – the site of the nightly street parties – a solitary man was tending a roaster of his own. A chile roaster is a cylindrical cage, large enough to hold a half-grown child; it rotated, and propane flames shot out of the bottom. It was therefore a machine, and I understood machines; I felt an immediate kinship with anyone who was operating one, and moreover it gave me an excuse to go talk to this man. I parked my bike at the curb and approached him.

The man gave no sign that he saw me coming. He wore a filthy, worn camouflage jacket and a pair of mirrored sunglasses that reflected the flames of the roaster, giving him a diabolical expression. He stood unmoving, contemplating the action of the roaster, his long black hair falling over his shoulders and his thick beard hiding much of his face. He was one of the rip-roaring howlers I'd seen as I spied out my window at night.

'These chiles for sale?' I said.

He jumped. Then, looking at me, he turned a deathly pale.

'Jones?' he said.

'No. Mann.'

'*Hijo*,' he said. 'Where did you come from?'

'Sorry,' I said. 'I just moved in across the street. I didn't mean to scare you.'

He stared at me, mouth ajar, until I grew uncomfortable. Then he appeared to collect himself.

'I thought you were someone else,' he said. 'You look like . . .'

I waited, but he didn't finish that thought.

'Never mind,' he said. 'My mind is playing tricks on me. You're the new guy, huh? I was wondering when you was gonna introduce yourself.'

'Billy Mann,' I said. He didn't offer to shake hands, so I kept mine in my pockets. He didn't offer his name, either.

'You a friend of Señor Martinez?' he asked.

'Sort of. I'm renting the place from him.'

He grunted. 'Well, these chiles are *not* for sale,' he said. 'I got a piece of a little farm down in Hatch. I get a delivery every year and I give them out for free. To my *friends*,' he said pointedly.

'That's all right,' I said. 'I just wanted to come over and say hello.'

'Where you from? Not from around here.'

'New York.'

'New York City?'

'New York State,' I said. 'Mannville.'

'Never heard of it.'

'Nobody has,' I said.

He gave me the once-over again. I pretended to ignore him, meanwhile checking out the roaster. The cage was turned by an electric motor, and propane jets underneath were roaring up and scorching the peppers inside. The man stopped the roaster and pulled out a chile. 'Here,' he said. 'Try this.'

63

I took the pepper by the stem, waited for it to cool, and nibbled tentatively at the bottom. The man laughed – a hoarse, raspy sound, like gravel pouring out of a bucket.

'You gotta peel it first, Jones,' he said. 'Don't they have no chiles where you come from?'

I wondered if he'd already forgotten my name, but if he wanted to keep on calling me Jones that was fine with me. The blackened parchment of the skin came off easily in my fingers, exposing the flesh of the pepper. I took a large bite. Once again came the fire, the burning throughout my mouth, but I was already getting used to that. Soon the heat of the pepper was surging throughout my body.

'That's the way,' he said approvingly. '*Mira* – they call me El Perrero.'

'El what?'

'El Perrero.'

'El Pear Air Oh,' I said.

'*Ay, Dios mio,*' he said. 'You gotta roll the r's like you mean it. Don't you even know how to speak Spanish?'

'No,' I said. 'What's it mean?'

He shrugged. 'I used to keep a lot of dogs,' he said, 'before I went crazy. It means like a . . . well, a guy who keeps a lot of dogs.'

'You don't keep dogs anymore?'

'Nah. Too much work. Plus I went crazy, like I said.'

'I see,' I said, wondering what kind of crazy he meant. 'You lived here a long time?'

64

'*Aquí?*' He blew a great puff of air through his lips. 'I'm forty years old, *ese*,' he said, 'and I lived here all my life, except when I was in 'Nam.'

'My father was in 'Nam,' I said.

His manner changed abruptly; he stared at me again, longer this time.

'What was his name?' he whispered.

'Eddie,' I said. 'Eddie Mann.'

'*Dios mio*,' he said, 'Your dad a marine?'

'He was an air force pilot.'

'A pilot,' he said. 'What kind of plane did he fly?'

'F-four,' I said.

'A Phantom.'

'Yeah.'

'You have *any* relatives in the marines?'

'Not that I know of,' I said.

'Well, I guess it's just my imagination.' He gave a heavy sigh. 'I was not no pilot, Jones,' he informed me. 'I was in the marines, too. I was a sniper.'

'A *sniper?*'

'That's right, homes. A hardcore badass mother-fucker. I killed eight people. That's why I'm crazy,' he added, as if that would explain everything. 'What do you do?'

'I'm a writer,' I said.

'A writer,' he said. 'I never met no writer before. And now I got one living across the street. What do you write?'

'I'm writing a book.'

'What about?'

'I'm not sure yet, to tell the truth,' I said. He laughed again and slapped me on the shoulder.

'He writes books, but he don't know what about,' he wheezed. A coughing fit came over him. He removed a small bottle of vodka from deep inside his jacket and took a hearty swig. He offered it to me, but I waved it off politely.

'Don't you worry,' he said, replacing the cap and stowing the bottle back inside the jacket. 'Don't you worry about that. You'll think of something sooner or later. Hee-hee-hee! A writer who don't know what he writes about!' He fell to laughing again and then suddenly grew serious. 'I only read two books in my life, the Bible and the manual for the Remington .700,' he said. 'Now *those* are the only two books a man really needs to get by.'

'What was a Remington .700?'

'That was my weapon in 'Nam,' he said. 'My rifle. Big black barrel, heavy as a motherfucker. You ever kill anyone?'

'No, sir,' I said.

'Ha,' he said. 'You just haven't had to yet, that's all.' He gave me the same look I'd gotten from Mr Martinez, that appraising once-over. Then he snorted dismissively. I chose not to pursue the subject. I pointed to the abandoned house next door.

'Did you ever know anyone who lived there?' I asked. 'There was a friend of my father's who used to live around this neighborhood. I think that was the house.' I was acting casual; I didn't want him to know how badly I wanted to know.

66

'That place?' he said. 'It's been empty a long time.'

'It was a woman,' I said. 'Her name was Eliza.'

He shook his head. 'Nope.'

'She changed her name to Sky later,' I said.

'Oh, yeah. Sky. Hee! I remember her. How could I forget?'

A thrill shot through me and rooted me to the spot.

'Do you know where she is now?' I croaked – thinking, or rather hoping, that my quest would be solved this easily after all. But he said: 'She's gone, homes. Long gone.'

'Gone? You mean – dead?'

'No, gone like in gone. Vanished like smoke. She ain't dead, not that I've heard.'

'Thank God,' I said. He looked at me curiously.

'What you wanna know about her for?'

'She was a friend of my dad's.'

'You already said that.' He thought for a moment. 'Your old man come home from the war?'

I shook my head.

'Aha,' he said. 'Trying to track down his old friends?'

'Something like that,' I said. But I changed the subject. I didn't want him knowing anything about why I was really asking. I had a lead now, and I was elated, but with a couple of questions I steered him back to chiles. El Perrero explained how they were best prepared – peeled, then chopped and cleaned, which meant removing the stems and as many of the seeds as you felt like getting rid of – it was the seeds that made them hot, he said, so if you wanted your chiles mild you scraped all of them out, and if you wanted them thermonuclear you left all of them in. After that you could do whatever you wanted with them, he went on – most people froze them, and that way you had them all year long.

He produced a plastic grocery bag from one of his pockets and filled it half full of the chiles.

'You take some home with you,' he said, pressing it on me. 'You eat that stuff a couple times a week, which is all I recommend for a white guy, no offense, you'll never get sick. Ever. They're full of vitamin C.'

I stuck my head inside the bag he gave me and inhaled. It was heavenly and overpowering.

'Thanks,' I said.

'Don't forget to peel them,' he said.

'All right. Listen, I better get going. Nice to meet you.'

'Later,' he said.

I turned and headed back for my house.

'Hey, Jones!' he shouted, when I was across the street. 'You like to party?'

'Sure,' I called. 'I guess.'

'Come on over one of these nights. Me and my homies like to get together and drink a little booze.'

'Yeah,' I said. 'I sure will.'

'Welcome to the *barrio*!' he said, and he threw back his head and howled like a wolf.

★   ★   ★

I put my chiles in the freezer, a rickety old model that looked like it dated from Mr Martinez's early adolescence. Then I sat down in front of my type-writer and thought. She was gone, he'd said; long gone, but not dead. I hadn't thought to ask him when was the last time he'd seen her. It could have been years, I realized; this thought was so depress-ing it sparked the beginning of a dull headache. He was forty, and he'd lived here his whole life – she'd last lived here for sure nearly twenty years ago, and it was possible 'long gone' meant she hadn't been seen around here since that time. I didn't want to appear too curious about her, not in front of him. He liked me, I thought, at least enough to give me a bag of chiles; but he wasn't the kind of person I wanted to know about what was going on inside me. It was none of his business. It was none of anyone's business.

I decided instead to start looking things up. There would be property records in city hall, wher-ever that was, and if she'd owned the house, that fact would be set down on paper; there would be phone books in the library, too. Those were the only places I could think of to check, but if El Perrero knew her, then perhaps others did, too. I could ask people who'd been around for a while.

I got back on my bike and found city hall. A clerk wanted ten dollars for the privilege of looking through the files, which I handed over with a heavy heart. This reduced my worldly finances to a pocketful of change and some crumpled singles, and I still had a week to go before my next check came. *Don't worry about that now*, I told myself. *There's always government cheese, and white bread is always on sale somewhere. You're getting closer every moment.*

The clerk let me into a room filled with file cabinets and stood by while I read the file he'd pulled out. According to the records, 125 South Blossom Street had indeed once been owned by an Eliza McMeel, but in 1980 it was reclaimed by the city for back taxes and had been empty ever since. I wondered what had happened, why she couldn't pay the taxes. There was a phone number listed on the deed, which I tried later just for the sake of thoroughness, but it was disconnected. A trip search through some old phone books in the public library gave me the same number.

Gone. *Long* gone. Nine years gone – but not dead.

Then where was she?

I went back home. El Perrero's chile roaster stood empty and cold, and he himself had left the yard. I thought of knocking on his door, but I didn't – he seemed unstable, maybe even a little on the far side of paranoid. And it would seem odd to him that I was so intent on finding a woman who I'd already claimed was only my father's friend, nothing more.

A week passed, a week of pondering my next

move, of rising at 5:00 A.M. and pounding out my thoughts on my typewriter. My check from Grandpa's estate came and heralded the end of my period of extreme starvation. I celebrated by buying a whole chicken, some potatoes, carrots, onions, corn, and garlic, and along with a handful of the chiles El Perrero had given me I made green chile stew, according to a recipe he'd described: I boiled the chicken until the meat fell of the bones, chopped everything else up and threw it in, and cooked the hell out of it for another couple of hours. When the stew was ready I ate until I couldn't hold any more. It marked my first serious sojourn into the culinary world, and I was impressed with myself. Nobody in Mannville, I was sure, had ever eaten anything as good as that chicken stew. I was so pleased I filled a bowl and took it over to El Perrero's house.

He answered the door in long underwear. Even indoors, he still wore his sunglasses.

'Eee,' he snarled. 'What do you want?'

'I made some stew,' I said. 'You want to try it?'

'Listen, Jones. Next time you wanna talk to me, stand outside and whistle, like this.' He stuck two fingers in his mouth and blew a deafening blast – *fweet!*

'I don't know how to whistle like that,' I said.

'Well, just yell, then. Only cops come to the door. Gimme that.'

He took the bowl and a spoon from me and drank some of the broth. The soup had been

71

boiling only moments earlier, but he didn't even flinch. He smacked his lips and thought.

'This tastes like shit,' he said. 'What did you do to it?'

'Just what you said,' I told him.

El Perrero sifted through the bowl with the spoon, scanning the contents with a practiced eye.

'First of all, you forgot to take the stems off the chiles,' he said. 'Stems don't belong in no stew. Did you wash these potatoes before you put them in?'

'I guess I forgot,' I said.

'Did you even peel these carrots?' he demanded.

'No.'

'You need *seasonings*,' he said. 'Salt, and pepper, and shit like that. Sheesh. And cilantro. Put a little bit of cilantro in, but only after it's done cooking. A little cilantro goes a very long way. What is all this lumpy stuff in here?'

'Flour,' I said.

'*Hijo de la madre*,' he said, rolling his eyes. 'Whoever told you to put flour in? Not me, that's for sure. What were you *thinking*?'

All I knew about cooking I had learned from watching Mildred, and it had seemed to me that there was always flour involved, no matter what she was making; her hands were always covered in it.

'Right,' I said. 'No flour. Thanks.' I held my hands out for the bowl, but he hung onto it.

'I am pretty hungry,' he said. 'I'll eat it, but . . . Jesus.'

I said, 'By the way, I was wondering – I mean, is

72

there anyone around who might know where your neighbor went? Someone I could talk to?'

He stared at me impassively for some moments, the steam from the stew rising up around his face like fog.

'You *sure* you're not a cop?' he asked.

'Yeah, I'm sure.'

'What neighbor you asking about?'

'The one I asked you about before. Sky.'

'Listen, Jones,' he said. 'There's one thing you gotta understand. Strangers come around asking questions about neighbors, it makes me wonder why they want to know. You gotta be careful. You're gonna make people nervous.'

'Sorry,' I said.

'It's all right. I trust you. You wanna ask her about your dad, huh?'

'That's it.'

He chuckled. '*A la verga,*' he said. 'If you're so interested, why don't you go talk to her daughter?'

'She had a *daughter*?' I said.

'Sure. Sophia, her name is. She works just up the street at the Cowgirl. She's a waitress.'

'Thanks,' I said. 'I think I will.'

'Thanks for the stew, Jones,' he said. 'I'll get this bowl back to you when I'm done.'

'No hurry,' I said, knowing somehow I would never see that bowl again.

I knew the place he was talking about. The Cowgirl Hall of Fame was a bar just a few blocks away. My heart was thrumming like a V-8 at full throttle. If Sky had a daughter, that meant that I had a half-sister. She wouldn't be a Mann, but she shared some of my blood with me; more important, that blood was from the side of the family that I was so desperate to learn about. It was *better* than finding another Mann. I already knew all about the Manns.

I wouldn't tell this waitress who I was, either, not right away. Grandpa's warnings rang in my ears: my mother, whoever she was, had probably had a very good reason for giving me up, and I shouldn't assume that I would be doing her any favors by reappearing in her life after all this time. And this Sophia, my half-sister, would be sure to tell her mother if someone showed up out of nowhere and claimed to be her brother. I would play it cool. I would not betray my hand until the time was right.

CHAPTER 3

THE GIRL WHO SANG MAGIC SPELLS

It was easy to figure out which waitress was Sophia – she was the only one on duty that night, and she wore a name tag pinned to her chest with her name in bold black letters. I sat at the bar, watching her in the mirror as she danced between tables, a tray in one hand and a cluster of beer mugs in the other. She wore a stained apron tied around her waist, a pen behind her ear – the uniform of waitresses everywhere. Her jet-black hair was cropped just below her ears, and her eyes were the same shade of midnight as most of the eyes in this town – I realized, with a jolt, that she was Latina. She was full figured, a little on the chunky side, with skin the shade of dusk and lips set in a grim, purposeful line. Her jaws worked as she chewed a massive wad of gum.

She must be only half Latina, I thought, *because the other half is the same as half of me.*

But I didn't care about that. It was unimportant. What *was* important was that she seemed to have my nose.

It was a Tuesday, and Tuesday was Dollar Pearl Night – Pearl Lager, that is, fresh from the heart of Texas, normally two-fifty but tonight offered for only a single buck. Even with my check from the estate lately deposited in my brand-new bank account, I couldn't afford to be drinking beer, not even the cheap pig swill. However, I couldn't just sit in there and not drink anything. So I sat with my back to the tables and nursed the same mug of Pearl for an hour, watching her meanwhile in the mirror, struggling to name the complex surge of emotions that she evoked. *I am looking at my own half-sister*, I thought. *My blood. Sophia.*

She came around suddenly to the end of the bar, not three feet from me.

'Ordering,' she barked.

'Hi,' I said.

'Hi.' She didn't even look at me. 'Franco! Ordering!' Her voice went up an octave. She blew a bubble, popped it, and sucked it back in expertly.

'I heard you,' said Franco, the bartender. 'I'm not deaf.'

'You act like it,' she said.

Franco winked at me. He was in his late thirties, a stocky man with a barrel chest and a number of tattoos on his arms, barely visible through the thick coat of hair that seemed to cover his entire body.

'I *wish* I was deaf,' he said, to nobody in particular. 'They can hear that voice in Albuquerque.'

'Shove it,' Sophia said, not cracking a smile. She gave him her drink orders and he moved away to fill them.

So she wasn't exactly sunshine and lollipops.

Still, I had to speak to her, to introduce myself. But nothing came to mind. To my surprise, my palms were sweating, my face hot. *Say something – anything*, I ordered myself.

'I'm Billy,' I said.

'I'm sure you probably are,' she said, snapping her gum. She didn't even look up from her order pad.

Well, that was that. She thought I was hitting on her. How do you explain to a strange girl that you're *not* hitting on her, that she's actually your half-sister, that you'd like nothing better than to sit and talk for a while? It was impossible – there was no graceful way to do it. I was too shy, for one thing; and for another, I wanted to be careful. Grandpa's warnings were still ringing in my ears, though they'd had more to do with my mother: he'd reminded me that I had no right to barge into anyone's life and expect to be welcome. I very well *might* be welcome, he'd said, but then again I might not. It was better to move slowly. I turned my attention to my beer again. Franco brought the drinks and Sophia whisked them away on her tray, all efficiency.

'Don't waste your time, pal,' Franco said. 'That's the Ice Queen there.'

'No, no,' I said. 'I wasn't – I mean, I was just saying hi.'

'Yeah,' he said, winking again. 'All us guys wanna do is just say hi.'

I couldn't even begin to explain. I ordered

another beer and watched her some more in the mirror, but now Franco was watching me watch her, so I looked away.

'How old are you, anyway?' he said, as though the question had just occurred to him.

I'd forgotten one had to be twenty-one to drink, and I didn't have a fake ID. There was a sign above the bar, which I hadn't noticed, written in large red letters:

THE PURCHASE OF ALCOHOL
BY MINORS
STRICTLY FORBIDDEN
UNDER STATE LAW

And under that, in smaller letters:

PUNISHABLE BY $500 FINE
SUSPENSION OF DRIVER'S LICENSE
OR BOTH

I knew the law, but I wasn't going to let a little thing like the minimum drinking age come between me and my sister. Now, however, I was invaded by panic. I was just thinking up a lie when a hand fell on my shoulder and a voice said, 'Don't worry about him, Franco. He's okay. His beer is on me, and you may bring me one for myself, whenever the mood strikes you.'

Franco shrugged. 'If you say so, Ralph.'

It was the small tweed-jacketed fellow I'd met on the campus of St James, the one who'd shown me the way to the admissions office.

'Ralph Goldfarb,' he said, offering me a hand. 'Remember me? From school?'

'Sure,' I said. 'Nice to see you again.' As Franco turned and reached for a fresh mug, I leaned over and whispered, 'Thanks. I owe you one.'

Ralph Goldfarb winked, pulled up a stool, and sat. 'You don't have to worry about Franco,' he said in a low tone. 'He doesn't really mind us being underage, as long as we keep out of trouble.'

I took a closer look at Ralph Goldfarb. He was about my age, but already he'd lost most of his hair, and he had two very large front teeth and a nose all out of proportion to his body. He didn't speak again until our beers came; then he buried his prodigious snoot in his mug and drained the contents of the glass in one go.

'Cow piss,' he gasped when he was done. 'The brew of bovines. But you can't beat the price. Franco, my good man—'

'Way ahead of you, Ralph,' said Franco, sliding another mugful across the bar. Obviously, Ralph Goldfarb was a regular.

'Now *that* is the way a bar should be tended,' said Ralph admiringly. 'Never understimate the value of a really good bartender, Mr Mann. The best ones are telepathic. All one needs in life is a bar, and a bartender who anticipates your every need, even before it is spoken aloud. Am I right?'

'I'm actually not much of a drinker,' I said.

'Probably a good thing, overall,' Ralph said. 'Drink has brought many a better man than me to the brink of ruin, and beyond. By the way, I couldn't help noticing – do you fancy our young Medusa of a waitress here, the always elusive Sophia? Because if you do, I'd recommend you go stick your hand in a blender instead. The experience would be much more satisfying.'

'I was just saying hi,' I said again, but this time it sounded lame even to my own ears.

'Oh,' said Ralph, his tone knowing. 'Wait! Excuse my manners. I should have cheered you earlier. Here's to you – cheers.' He held up his mug and we clinked glasses. Then he drained his beer again. Franco was ready with a third.

'I don't always drink this fast,' Ralph said, when he'd finished that one. 'The first for thirst, the second for taste, I always say. I just happen to be rather thirsty today. How's the dropping out going?'

'Excuse me?'

'I mean, how is life after dropping out? I've always wondered.'

'It's going fine, I guess.' Sophia brushed by behind us; I could smell chewing gum and patchouli.

'You mind if I ask why you did it?'

I forced myself to stop watching her in the mirror. 'I never really wanted to go to school in the first place,' I said. 'I was doing it more for . . . other people, I guess.'

'Tell me about it,' said Ralph. 'My parents are like that, too. Pressure, pressure.'

'It's not my parents.'

'It's not? Usually it's—'

'I don't *have* any parents,' I told him.

'Oh – I'm sorry.'

'It's okay,' I said. 'I never actually knew them.'

'Were you brought up in an orphanage?'

I had to laugh at that. 'They don't have orphanages any more, as far as I know. My grandfather raised me. He was it for me, as far as family goes.'

'Was?'

'He died last year.'

'Jeez,' he said. 'I'm *really* sorry.'

'I'm not looking for sympathy,' I told him. 'I was just telling you how it is.'

'I have more family than I know what to do with,' said Ralph. 'And my parents drive me nuts. I came out here to get away from them, to tell the truth.'

'Where are you from?'

'New Jersey. *They* wanted me to go to Princeton. That way I could live at home. You wouldn't believe the scenes we had over me coming this far west. My mother almost had to be tranquilized.'

We paused and sipped our beers.

'Ah, well, family,' Ralph said philosophically. 'When you have one, you can't stand them, and when you don't, you wish you did. What do you do with yourself now?'

'I'm trying to write a book,' I said.

81

Ralph raised his eyebrows. 'You don't say. What kind of a book?'

'A novel.'

He whistled through his large front teeth. 'No fooling? A real novelist, right here in the Cowgirl?'

'Not a real novelist,' I admitted. 'Not yet. I'm still not sure what it's about.'

Unlike El Perrero, Ralph didn't find this amusing. He seemed to understand.

'Keep plugging away at it,' he said. 'You know what Edison said – genius is one percent inspiration and ninety-nine percent perspiration. It must be awful hard work. I respect novelists, I must say.'

'Do you know any others?'

He turned and indicated the roomful of students with a sweep of his arm. 'Half the people in here want to be writers,' he said. 'They all go to St James's, and they're all enrolled in the same writing classes. They put out a monthly student magazine.'

'Any good?'

'Atrocious. They deliver it for free to all the bathrooms on campus. That's the only way they can get people to read it – on the crapper.' He sniggered. 'It's sort of a literary shit-house outreach program.'

I started laughing and accidentally snorted beer into my nose. Ralph handed me a napkin.

'Good one,' I said. 'I was going to be in that program, before I dropped out.'

'Trust me, you're better off on your own. They

seem to have a little assembly-line thing going on. They read the same stuff, they soak up the same opinions from the same teachers, they turn out the same boring nonsense. I'm in the *other* department.'

'What other department?'

'There's just the two – writing and Greek. I'm in Greek.'

'*Greek?*'

'Homeric,' he said. 'I'm a translator, but not the kind at the UN. I study a kind of Greek no one speaks anymore, except for a few scholars. You know Homer?'

'Heard of him.'

He looked at me with concern. 'But you haven't read him? The *Iliad*? The *Odyssey*?'

'Nope.'

'Oh, dear,' he said. He picked up a plastic swizzle stick and swirled it around in his beer. 'Oh no, that won't do,' he said, worried. 'Listen, Mann. Ordinarily I never tell people what to do, but if you're going to be a writer, you have to read Homer.'

'Why?'

Ralph froze, the way a grade-school teacher might stop in horror at hearing a nasty word. Then he put down his swizzle stick with care and turned to face me.

'Listen,' he said, 'I don't know much about writing, but I do know that Homer is the greatest storyteller this side of the Euphrates. Who's your favorite writer?'

'I don't know,' I said. 'I read a lot of Hemingway, mostly because I wasn't supposed to. My grandfather said it was mind poison.'

'He said *what*? Why?'

'War,' I told him. 'My father died in Vietnam, and Grandpa blamed Hemingway. He said Hemingway gave my father the idea that war was great.'

Ralph sagged on his barstool.

'I can't even begin to tell you in how many ways that offends me,' he said. 'But I'll let it drop for now. Your grandfather had a point – war is not as glorious as some writers would have you believe. But historically, war was the proving ground for a man's courage. That's when you really find out what you're made of.'

'Have *you* ever been in a war?'

'Of course not,' he said. 'Look at me – I'm a nerd. If I was in a war movie, I'd be the brainy guy who never shuts up. I wouldn't last ten minutes. I'm talking in a *literary* sense,' he said. 'That's one of the reasons why Homer is so important. He talks about virtues that have fallen out of style. Courage and bravery and loyalty.'

'Since when are courage and bravery out of style?' I asked.

'They have been for years,' he said. 'Where have *you* been? I don't know why. People got disillusioned, or something.'

'I guess,' I said.

'Look – I'm going to turn you on to some really good stuff,' said Ralph. 'I think you were wise to

84

drop out, but you have to have some direction. Some focus, you know?'

'Sure,' I said. 'Focus.'

'Stick with me,' said Ralph. 'Maybe you're going places, but you're going to need a little outside influence. And if we hang around here long enough you just might get lucky with herself over there.'

He indicated Sophia with a nod. He'd deliberately said it loud enough for her to hear. She didn't look up from the credit card she was processing; she only extended her middle finger, casually – at both of us. I winced. Things were not off to a good start with her.

'That's what I love about you, Sophia!' said Ralph. 'Your charm!'

'You're gonna get cut off, Ralph,' said Sophia.

'Are you talking about my service or my manhood?' he said.

She rolled her eyes, sighed in exasperation, stomped back to her tables. I thought I detected a glimmer of moisture in her eyes.

'You shouldn't tease her, Ralph,' said Franco, who'd been listening. 'She's on a short fuse these days.'

'I forgot,' said Ralph. 'I'll apologize. I was only fooling around.' He turned to me. 'See what I mean?' he said. 'I never know when to shut up.' He excused himself and went over to her.

I turned to watch him, but my eyes went past where Ralph was making his apologies to an aloof Sophia and settled on the band that was setting up their equipment in the corner. There were two very large men wrestling with an amplifier, a much smaller, older man sitting in a chair with a guitar in his lap, and a young woman standing off to one side, watching them, her face partially hidden in shadow. It was the woman who had attracted my attention. She looked like a gypsy in her brightly colored dress, a shawl thrown over her thin shoulders. I tried to get a glimpse of her face, but she remained hidden.

Ralph finished talking to Sophia. He went past me and said, 'Bathroom. Back in a minute.' Sophia came by again with another drink order and waited impatiently for Franco to fill it. Her eyes were red rimmed; she really was upset about something, but I didn't think it actually had anything to do with Ralph. What could it be? I wondered. Boy-friend? Work? Money? Life? I decided to try one more time.

'You from around here?' I asked her.

'You could say that,' she said. Still she didn't look at me. Would she see some resemblance if she did? I brought one hand up to my face and covered my nose. We didn't look enough like each other so that it was startlingly obvious – you would have to know we were related before you saw it. But I, of course, saw it.

'I just moved into the neighborhood,' I said. 'I live on South Blossom.'

That seemed to touch her somewhere. Her face softened for a moment and then iced over again.

86

'I know South Blossom,' she said, but that was all she said; then she was gone again with her tray load of drinks.

Franco smirked at me, but he didn't say anything. Ralph emerged from the bathroom and resettled himself on his stool.

'I'll have to go again in about thirty seconds,' he said. 'I have the bladder of a mouse.'

'What's the matter with Sophia?' I asked.

'Family problems, or so I hear,' Ralph said. 'I don't know much about it.'

I was desperately curious to find out more, but at the same time I couldn't stop looking at the woman in the bright dress.

'You know what band this is?' I asked. 'Or who that woman is there?'

'Jeez, you don't waste any time, do you?' said Ralph. 'You're back in the air only moments after getting shot down. I like that. I think I'll call you the Red Baron.'

'I'm just asking,' I said. 'And I'm *not* interested in Sophia. I was really only making conversation with her.'

'Okay, okay,' said Ralph Goldfarb. 'I think her name is Chimichanga or Hoochy-Coochy or something.'

'It's *Consuelo*, for Chrissakes,' said Franco, who'd been listening. 'It's not like it's that hard to say, Ralph.'

'I can't remember Spanish names to save my life,' Ralph told me. 'Greek, no problem.'

87

'What does she do?'

'She's the singer,' said Franco. 'You should stick around and listen. She's really something.'

'Do you play darts?' Ralph asked me. 'You wanna throw a game of cricket?'

I had never played darts before, but we went to the board in the back room and Ralph taught me the rudiments of the game. I kept straying to the doorway to look at Consuelo the singer. She took no notice of me; she was too far away, and I still couldn't see her face. The band had begun to warm up. One of the huge twins was sitting behind the drums, and the other now had an accordion strapped to his chest. The old man had moved his chair up onto the stage and was tuning his guitar, holding his ear close to it; under the single spot-light, he looked even older than he had before, and his guitar was like him: ancient, weathered, beaten. But for all his advanced years, his fingers danced nimbly up and down the neck of the instrument like those of a much younger man.

'Your mind's not on this game,' said Ralph from behind me. 'Do you still want to play?'

'Yes, yes,' I assured him. 'Sorry.'

'Well, it's your turn,' he said, handing me the darts.

But I paused in the doorway again, for the woman who had been standing off to the side in the shadows had just come onto the stage. It was nothing more than the simple act of stepping upward, planting one booted foot on the boards and lifting herself into view. Yet there was much more to it than that. She moved up as though she'd been lifted there by unseen hands, ascending with an uncommon lightness, and suddenly she was standing there in the center of the spotlight – she looked like she had *floated* up, and there was something immediate and commanding and even permanent about her presence. Surely no stage in the history of music had ever been taken as definitively and professionally as that. We were only in a small bar in a small city in one of the least-populated states in the country, but at that moment it seemed to me that she was on the stage of the world. And suddenly I found it hard to breathe, because now I could see her face.

It was not the sort of face one would describe as classically beautiful. She had a long, thin nose and glittering obsidian eyes set slightly far apart; her ears stuck out from her head just enough to call attention to themselves, and yet they were small ears, delicate. She smiled at the audience. Hers were not American teeth – they were uneven, and like Ralph she had a gap between her front incisors, but quite unlike Ralph the effect was somehow arousing. Her chin was small and pointed, almost elfin, and her cheekbones, which were perhaps the only part of her face that could be called perfect, were high and well defined, like in the impassive faces of the Navajos I had seen in the plaza.

Not a beautiful face, when reduced to its

components; but when taken altogether, it somehow produced the shortness of breath I was experiencing. My eyes traveled downward to her slender shoulders, to the fragile lines of her collarbones, past her slight fist-size breasts and her narrow hips to the laced-up high-heeled boots she wore. She was magnetic.

But at that moment I became aware of Sophia in my peripheral vision. She was standing over by the bar, arms folded in front of her chest and one leg stuck out and rocking to and fro on its heel. Her eyes were narrow, her lips pressed tight in disapproval.

'All right,' said Ralph from behind me. 'You forfeit. I win.'

'Okay,' I said. 'I think I want to go sit down again.'

'Suit yourself, Romeo. I'm going to keep playing.'

My spot at the bar had been taken, so I slid into an empty chair at a table. An expectant hush fell over the crowd, which by now was composed of about fifty people, most of them Jimmies. The lights dimmed and the spotlight grew brighter. Then Consuelo began to sing.

There was no accompaniment at first. She sang alone, a high single tone, sustaining it for an impossibly long time, somehow keeping it going even when she was breathing in. Then the guitar followed her into the song, tentatively in the beginning, then more boldly; the accordion entered in unison with the drums, and then the song had come alive. So had the crowd, who'd begun to clap in steady rhythm. As if by some prior agreement, the room was divided in half – some clapped on the downbeat of the song, the rest on the upbeat, and the music settled into a steady, rapid gait. They had done this with her before.

I couldn't take my eyes away from her, and by chance our gazes locked for just a moment. I shivered. At the same time, she put one hand to her head and stopped singing. Pain showed in her face, and for a moment I thought she was going to faint. So did others – a few people toward the front got up as if to help her, but she waved them off and resumed the song. She didn't look in my direction again.

Sophia came over to my table. 'You wanna sit here, you have to order something,' she said.

'Another Pearl,' I said. 'And look – I'm sorry about before. It was a misunderstanding.'

'Whatever,' she said. 'Anything else, big spender?'

I gave up on her. 'No,' I said. 'That's it. Just the beer.'

She lingered by the table for a moment. 'She won't talk to you,' she said. 'So don't even bother.'

'*Who* won't?'

She indicated Consuelo with a toss of her head. 'She thinks she's too good for everyone,' she said. 'Whenever I try to talk to her in Spanish, she answers me in English.'

'So?'

Sophia looked at me with contempt. 'I guess *you* wouldn't understand,' she said. 'If you were Latino, you would, though. It's *rude*. It's an *insult*.'

I was growing irritated – she'd read my mind, for I'd been plotting some way to talk to that singer. I'd stick around all night if I had to. But Sophia had deliberately burst my bubble, with an almost malicious pleasure. And she was right about me not understanding this Spanish-and-English business; who cared what language Consuelo spoke, as long as she talked? Sophia was beginning to strike me as the kind of person who thrived on drama. I didn't say anything. She left and came back with my beer.

'A dollar,' she said. I paid her and she drifted off again, but I thought I could feel her eyes on the back of my head. I turned quickly and caught her looking at me; she glared at me in anger and stomped away.

Ralph came out of the back room and sat down. 'I just beat the guy who won the city finals two years ago!' he said, exultant.

'That chick is weird,' I said.

'Who? Sophia? She's got issues, my friend.'

'I guess she must.' I wondered again what those issues were; I wondered a lot of things about her, such as who her father was and what she was doing here, working as a waitress; most of all, I wondered where our mother was. I would have liked to sit down with her and talk for hours, but it was too late for me to make a good impression on her. I would have to get to know her another way.

'Aren't you going to congratulate me?' Ralph asked.

'For what?'

'For beating the former champion of Santa Fe!'

'Good job,' I said. But my heart wasn't in it. The band was already into their second song, and I focused my attention on the singer again. I forgot about Ralph completely. I forgot about everything. We stayed for hours, with me sipping that beer and then another one as slowly as possible. During an interlude in the music, Ralph said, 'If you can forgive a personal question, there's something I've been meaning to ask you. Why do you dress like a biker?'

'I am a biker,' I said.

'You mean a real one?' He looked alarmed. 'Like a Hell's Angel?'

'No, not like a Hell's Angel,' I said. 'I'm not in a gang or anything. I just like to ride.'

'How'd you get your motorcycle out here?'

'I rode it,' I said. 'How'd you think?'

'All the way from New York? How long did *that* take you?'

'Five days or so,' I said.

Ralph was impressed. 'You think you might take me for a ride sometime?' he asked. 'I've always wondered what it's like.'

'Sure,' I said. 'We can go tomorrow, if you want.'

Ralph grew excited. 'I know the perfect place,' he said. 'You want to swing by campus tomorrow and pick me up? I'll show you where it is.'

'Sure,' I said.

'Great!' He was exultant. 'I can't wait.' He finished his beer and stood up. 'I ought to get a little studying done tonight, if I can,' he said. 'I'm in Uppers, in the Terpsichore building. Room 111. Think you can find it?'

'No problem,' I said. 'How about after lunch?'

'After lunch it is,' he said. He picked up his mug as if to toast me again and saw with regret that it was empty. He put it down with a sigh. 'Oh, well,' he said. 'No more for me tonight. See you then, Mann.'

'See you,' I said. He headed for the door, passing Sophia, who ignored him.

The crowd had begun to thin around eleven-thirty or so. It was now nearing one, and there were only about fifteen people left: a couple of die-hard drinkers at the bar, and several other guys who also seemed suspiciously interested in Consuelo. By this time I had begun to spin a story in my mind to explain her existence: she was a gypsy who had spent her childhood traveling the world in a caravan, and she'd learned to sing from her grandmother, who'd also taught her magic spells. And she used those spells to weave webs of enchantment around the hearts of men like me.

Consuelo finished the last song, the band stood up and bowed with her, and one of the other swains was immediately on his feet and heading for her with a bouquet of roses in his hand. I couldn't tell if she knew him or not; she accepted the roses graciously, with the same smile she gave to the crowd in general.

Shit. I couldn't compete with roses. Within moments she was surrounded by men. Obviously, I wasn't the only one who wanted to talk to her. All right, forget about it, I told myself. Last thing you need is to get mixed up with some woman, anyway.

I finished the last of my beer and stepped outside. There was an outdoor patio that had been stripped bare for the coming winter season, but the picnic tables had been left out. I sat on one of them and looked up at the waxing moon, clear and close in the chilly air. Winter came early in the mountains. A few dried leaves skittered along the bricks. The last few people came out of the bar and headed down the sidewalk together, talking loudly. Soon I saw the man who'd given Consuelo the roses; he came out by himself, without noticing me. He headed glumly onto the street, hands in his pockets, and started heading east, but I saw him stop about twenty yards away and lean against a car.

Moments later Consuelo came out with Franco. They didn't notice me, either.

'It's okay,' she said to Franco. 'He's gone.'

'You sure?'

'I will be fine,' she said. 'And you have no jacket. Go back inside, Franco.'

95

'If you say so,' said Franco. He went back into the bar. She came pensively down the walk; then she noticed me sitting there.

'Oh,' she said, startled.

'Hello,' I said. 'Sorry to scare you.'

I could see her face in the artificial glow of the few streetlights on Guadalupe Street. She was wearing a thin coat now, and she was shivering.

'Who is that?' she said. 'Were you waiting for me?'

'No. Just looking at the moon.'

'Oh,' she said again. She relaxed and looked upward. 'It *is* a very good moon,' she said.

'Sure is,' I said.

She hummed a few notes of something.

'I really liked your music,' I said.

In the half-light I saw her teeth flash. 'Thank you,' she said. 'You are a musician?'

'No. I don't play anything.'

'What is your name?'

I told her.

'Mine is Consuelo,' she said.

'Yeah, I know. You feeling all right? You looked kind of sick for a minute up there. Like you were going to faint.'

'It was nothing,' she said. 'Sometimes the blood rushes to my head all at once. I did not eat enough today.' Again she hummed a few notes. Then she said, 'May I sit down there, too?'

I was too surprised to answer. I moved over to make room for her, and she settled herself on

96

the other end of the table. We looked upward together. Suddenly I couldn't concentrate on the moon anymore; she was a few feet away from me, but I could feel heat coming off her in waves – heat, or some other kind of energy. Whoever this Consuelo person was, she was *full* of energy; it came flooding out of her in all directions. I felt buffeted by it, like a small sailboat in the wake of a speedboat.

'I was avoiding someone,' she said presently. 'I thought you were him.'

'If it's that guy who gave you the roses, he's still over there,' I told her, pointing to where he lurked by the car. 'I think he's waiting for you.'

'Oh, brothers,' she said.

'Does he bother you?'

'He is not a bad person,' she said. 'He's not dangerous. I just don't feel like talking to people after I sing, and he always is wanting to walk me home and ask me crazy questions.'

'You're talking to me,' I observed.

She looked at me and smiled again. '*Sí*,' she said. 'That's true. But talking to you doesn't make me tired.'

'Well, that's good,' I said.

'Could I ask you some favor?'

'Sure.'

'Can you walk with me, just down to West Alameda?'

Nothing would have brought me greater pleasure than to walk her to West Alameda, or to the moon, or anywhere she'd wanted to go. We got off the table, and to my astonishment she slipped her arm through mine and we went down the steps to the sidewalk.

He was still leaning against the car, a young guy in a turtleneck and sport coat. We went by him quickly, and I glanced at his face. He had his mouth open as though to speak, but we were moving too fast, and he was surprised to see me with her. We were gone before he had the chance to say anything. Consuelo was tense now, her arm rigid in mine. When we got to the corner of West Alameda I turned and looked behind us.

'He's still there,' I said. 'In fact, he's following us.'

'*Ay, mierda*,' she said. There was a note of panic in her voice now. I wasn't worried; I was bigger than him. But I could tell she was more than annoyed. She was scared.

'You want me to keep walking with you?' I asked her.

'If you don't mind,' she said. 'I should have asked Franco to stay with me. I don't like people knowing where I live.'

'I understand,' I said. 'I can leave you here. You want me to say something to him? Just to hold him up?'

'No,' she said. She looked at me again, longer this time. 'I don't know why, but I trust you. You can know where I live. It's okay. Just stay with me.'

'Okay,' I said.

We kept walking several more blocks, turning once onto a side street. There was no traffic this late. When we got to her house we'd lost her stalker, or maybe he'd just given up. She began fumbling in her pockets for her keys.

'I am embarrassed that I had to ask you to do this,' she said. 'Now you will think I am helpless.'

'I don't think that,' I said.

'Well, good. Because I am not helpless.'

'I believe you,' I said.

'You are very nice,' she said.

'Thank you.'

She leaned forward and kissed me on the cheek. Then she went up the walkway to her front door and let herself in.

'*Buenas noches*,' she called.

'Good night,' I said.

It took me a few moments to recover from that kiss. Her strange scent lingered in the air for a scant second and then was gone, but I knew I would recognize it again: some kind of smoke, like incense, and also the smell of her hair: honey, bread, milk.

I was less than a half mile from my house. I headed back the way I'd come. I saw a figure sitting on the corner of West Alameda and Agua Fria – it was the rose bringer. When he saw it was me he lifted his head.

'How's it going?' I asked.

He didn't answer me. He just sighed.

He didn't have to say anything. I knew just how he felt about her.

CHAPTER 4

THE MIRACLE OF CENTRIPETAL FORCE

The next afternoon, Ralph and I set off on our first excursion into what was – to me, at least – an unknown land.

We roared down Cerrillos Road, weaving through stop-and-go traffic, in a hurry to escape the concrete desolation of strip malls and shopping centers in that part of town. Cerrillos Road was modern and straight, six lanes of asphalt with a median down the middle, and always clogged with traffic. The interesting parts of Santa Fe were hidden, far from the malls and the parking lots. Ralph told me there was a joke that said the streets of the old town had been designed by a drunk Spanish priest, riding backward on a donkey. They certainly seemed like it, with their crazy angles and unpredictable turns. Few of the streets led anywhere directly, and often it was impossible to fit two cars on them at the same time; they'd been laid out centuries before there was such a thing as an automobile. But once one left the old Spanish neighborhoods, with its hobbitlike dwellings and narrow, donkey-wide streets, Santa Fe was just as anonymous and commercialized as any other American city, except that the storefronts were made of fake adobe. Real adobe was hardly awe inspiring, as marble was, for example; nonetheless, it gave the buildings a soft, comfortable look, and the houses blended in perfectly with the landscape. But somehow fake adobe was even more depressing than plain cinder block.

Yet when we came to the edge of town, the desert opened up again: miles of gently sloping hills and valleys, rock in infinite shades of red and brown, and countless acres of piñon bushes dotting the landscape in thumb-size smudges of dark green. There was not a single human dwelling visible ahead of us, not a plane in the sky, nothing to mar the beauty of it. We stopped at the last traffic light before freedom and waited for it to turn.

'Screw this. Stoplights are un-American,' said Ralph. 'Just go straight.'

'Where are we going?' I asked. I gunned the engine, and we soared through the empty intersection and into the wilderness.

'We're on a mission of truth and justice!' he yelled as we picked up speed. 'That's all you need to know!'

Ralph had told me about a two-lane highway called the Turquoise Trail, which previously he'd seen only by car. I assured him that the world was a much different place when you didn't have a window between you and it. If I went for only one more ride in my life, he told me, the Turquoise Trail ought to be the one; also, there was something he wanted to show me. He was tight-lipped about just what that was, but he promised I would love it.

'It will be an inspiring day,' he'd said. 'A day that will make you glad to be alive.'

So far he was right. It was a beautiful ride, and we had the road practically to ourselves. Ralph clung to the sissy bar on the rear of the bike and hooted in delight as we swooped and dove around curve after curve, driving on the wrong side when we felt like it, picking up speed on the straightaways and slowing to below the speed limit only once, when we passed a state police cruiser.

'Wave hello to the fascists!' Ralph screamed in my ear.

We waved. The trooper grinned ear to ear and waved back; it seemed to me that everyone was in a good mood today, as if they were sharing my elation at being on the road and also at having been kissed on the cheek by an exotic singer whom I'd saved from the clutches of a desperate maniac.

Well, maybe it hadn't happened quite that way. But *something* had happened, something magnificent; with a shock, I realized I was falling in love. I recognized the symptoms: loss of appetite, inability to sleep, a boundless optimism that under ordinary circumstances would have seemed ridiculous. After walking Consuelo home I'd been unable to sleep a wink. I was tormented by surges of adrenalin, and it hadn't helped that El Perrero and his band of wild revelers were at it again across the street. At 3:00 A.M. some of them had started pounding on my door and yelling in Spanglish, a curious blend of Spanish and English, of which I understood exactly half. They'd wanted me to come drink with them, but I pretended I was asleep until they went away. Around sunrise I finally managed to drop off, but when I awoke I had one of Consuelo's tunes running through my head, and it was there still.

Consuelo's music was strange and otherworldly, mostly Spanish sounding but with an odd twist of what I imagined might be gypsy music. I'd never heard anything like it before. Whatever it was, it was the perfect accompaniment to the countryside unwinding on either side of me. Rock formations, sculpted by eons of wind and rain, graced every portion of the road like statues carved by some inscrutable race of beings. It was as though we were in an outdoor museum, and the sky was so clear it was made of glass. It seemed as if I could see nearly to the upper reaches of the atmosphere, where light blue became deep blue and then black, and the sunlight fell harsh and clean and dripped off the smooth rock faces, puddling here and there and warming my back through my leather jacket. We went on like this for thirty miles or so, yelling at each other to point out interesting things, and sometimes just yelling for the sake of it. We passed a small forest of cholla and the flyblown corpse of a coyote lying on the side of the road. Then we rounded a sharp bend in the road, and suddenly we were in a town.

I slowed to twenty miles an hour. 'This is it?' I said. 'This is our mission of truth and justice?'

'Keep an open mind, Mann,' said Ralph. 'There are wonders in the world as yet unheard-of.'

'This is just a ghost town,' I said.

'No, it isn't. It's a very *small* town, and there could very well be ghosts in it. But for the most part everyone is alive.'

'What's it called?'

'Madrid.' He pronounced it with the emphasis on the first syllable rather than the last: MAD-rid.

'Don't you mean Ma-DRID?' I asked.

'That's just the way they say it around here,' said Ralph. 'Say it the right way and nobody will know what you're talking about.'

However one pronounced it, Madrid was on the edge of extinction, nothing more than a handful of empty buildings from the last century with a few newer dwellings here and there. There was no adobe in evidence, fake or otherwise; it was an Anglo town, made entirely of wood. There were a couple of small crafts galleries, a drug-store advertising a real soda fountain, a diner, an old burlesque theater, which according to a sign was still in operation. That was about it. It looked like the set of a Wild West movie. Set in the middle of everything was a bar with a broad porch and swinging half-doors. A sign above it read

THE OASIS OF TRUTH AND JUSTICE

'See? I told you,' said Ralph. 'Mission accomplished.'

'This is just another bar,' I said, disappointed; I hadn't known what to expect, but a bar certainly wasn't it.

'This is anything *but* just another bar, my friend. In a minute you'll see why.' We parked and dismounted, stretching our legs.

'What kind of name is that, anyway?' I asked.

'The owner is an old Jimmy,' said Ralph. 'A Greek major, just like me, but he was way before my time. Greek philosophy is all about truth, Mann. What it is, where to find it, and so on. See? You're already learning something. Come on in and I'll introduce you.'

The Oasis of Truth and Justice was vast, considering the size of the town – the whole population of Madrid could have fit inside. But for the moment, it was empty of people. The floor was covered with wood shaving and peanut shells, and there was an old piano over in one corner. The bar itself was at least fifty feet long. We seated ourselves on a couple of stools, and I studied the wall facing us. It was decorated with elk and deer antlers, as well as specimens of various indigenous wild animals: the heads of a bobcat, a lynx, a mountain lion, and a coyote; a whole jackrabbit; a turtle shell; an impossibly long snakeskin. There was also an impressive collection of antique six-shooters nailed up there, most of them, like Mr Martinez's truck, free of rust and in surprisingly good condition. Set on a shelf above the cash register was a large glass jar, filled with a tawny liquid. Something unrecognizable floated in it.

'What's in that jar?' I asked.

'See for yourself,' said Ralph.

I stood up and peered at the hand-lettered card taped to it. It read

ONE-HANDED JACK'S OTHER HAND

'Jesus!' I said. 'There's a *hand* in there?' I looked more closely. I could just make out the shape of a fingernail pressed against the glass, and part of the finger to which it was attached. The rest of the hand was obscured by the murky fluid.

'Rub the jar, if you want. It's good luck,' Ralph said.

'No, thank you,' I said. 'Who was One-Handed Jack?'

'Ask Bob yourself. He tells it better than I do,' said Ralph. 'Here he comes.'

A man was just coming out of the back. He had long, silver hair that fell well below his shoulders, and a handlebar mustache of the same color and

106

nearly the same length; he wore jeans and boots that clunked and jangled on the floorboards – stifling the urge to laugh, I realized he was wearing spurs. Pinned to his vest was a silver star.

''Lo, Bob,' said Ralph.

'Howdy, Ralph,' said Bob. 'Long time no see.'

'My friend here was just asking about old Jack.'

'Howdy, friend,' said Bob.

'Er – howdy,' I said.

Bob leaned casually against the bar and said something to Ralph in a language I didn't recognize. Ralph answered him in the same language, and the two conversed for a few moments. Then Bob drifted away to pour us a couple of beers.

'What was that?' I whispered.

'Greek,' said Ralph. 'What else?'

'I thought you said nobody spoke Greek anymore.'

'I said "hardly anybody speaks *ancient* Greek,"' Ralph told me. 'You really must learn to be more precise with your words, Mann. There's only a very few of us in the world who still understand it. We're the heirs to a lost kingdom. We have to practice when we can.'

Bob came back with two chilled mugs of beer, alarmingly close in color to the liquid that preserved One-Handed Jack's remains. He waved off a five-dollar bill from Ralph.

'First customers of the day always drink free,' he said. 'Don't tell anybody, though. Otherwise I'd have a line of people here at sunrise.'

'Thanks, Bob,' Ralph said. We toasted him and drank.

'Ain't you got class today?' he asked Ralph.

'Skipping,' said Ralph shortly. 'Weather's too nice.'

'It is that. Out ridin' yer scoot, are ye?' said Bob to me.

'My what?'

'He means your bike,' said Ralph.

'Yessir,' I said. I hadn't noticed it before, but Bob wore a pearl-handled six-shooter in a holster on his belt. I looked from it to the star and back to his face, sun wrinkled and seamy. I wondered how many tourists made it this far south of Santa Fe; probably a fair amount. Likely he put on some kind of Wild West act for them, I thought. As if on cue, he went into his spiel.

'You was askin' about old Jack there,' he said, nodding at the jar. 'He was the very last feller to be hanged in this town. Horse thief. Cattle rustler. No-account card-cheatin' bully. My grandaddy was sheriff back then. He was the one what hanged him, so he saved his hand for posterity.'

'You mean he cut it off?' I asked.

'No, not exactly,' Bob said. He began to chuckle, and he winked at Ralph. 'He more like *shot* it off. There was a little gunplay before they got Jack once and fer all, and his right hand, which was the only one he had left, got knocked off'im. Granpop figgered he'd hang onto it. Used to show it to folks for ten cents a gander.' Bob wheezed with

108

laughter. 'So by the time they buried him, he was really No-handed Jack!' He slapped the bar and guffawed. Ralph laughed, too. I could only manage a weak grin.

'Is that why you wear that fake star?' I said. 'Because of your grandfather?'

Bob stopped laughing. 'It ain't fake,' he said.

'Careful, Mann,' Ralph whispered. 'He's actually the sheriff.'

'Sorry,' I said. 'No offense, Bob.'

'None taken,' he said; but he fingered his star and gave me a stern look.

The doors swung open then, and three men in cowboy hats entered and sat down. Bob jangled off to serve them.

'I thought that getup was a tourist stunt,' I said.

'Nope. Not Bob. He's the real thing.'

'Is this what you brought me down here for? To show me a hand?'

'I brought you down here for the experience of it,' said Ralph. 'Writers need experiences, you know. The more the better.'

'Thanks,' I said. I couldn't look at the jar; I felt as if poor One-Handed Jack's privacy was being violated. I decided to change the subject. 'How can Bob be the sheriff if he's also the bartender?' I asked.

Ralph shrugged. 'If you stand on the porch, there's no part of this town you can't hit with a rock,' he said. 'Besides, people keep themselves under control here. Bob hasn't arrested anybody in years.'

'And he speaks Greek, too? A Greek-speaking sheriff in spurs? With a hand in a jar? He ought to sell tickets to himself.'

'He's working on his own translation of the letters of Paul to the Corinthians,' Ralph said. 'Been at it for twenty years.'

'Twenty *years*?'

'Well,' Ralph said, 'Bob's never been in any hurry. It took him twelve years just to get his Ph.D.' Ralph picked up a napkin and began shredding it carefully. 'Listen, Mann, I've been thinking. I want to buy a motorcycle.'

'You can probably get a used one pretty cheap,' I said. 'I can help you look, if you're serious.'

'I'm serious, all right. I never knew there was such a feeling.'

'I know,' I said.

'The wind, and—'

'Yeah.'

'Gravity. Inertia. Centripetal force.'

'Well, I never thought about it *that* way,' I said. 'But I see what you mean.'

'God, it feels *good*,' he said.

He reached out and grasped my shoulder, giving it a hard squeeze. His eyes were glistening with emotion, and he said: 'Thank God I met you. You might very well have saved my life.'

'Let's not get carried away here,' I said, embarrassed. I wasn't used to being touched like that, not by another male; in Mannville, men kept their hands to themselves. 'How do you mean, saved your life?'

'I mean that I might have gotten to be an old man without ever knowing what it was like to ride a bike,' he said. 'And that would have been very sad indeed.'

We sipped our beers and considered the tragedy that had been narrowly averted.

'My mother would never have let me get on a motorcycle,' he said. 'She never let me do *anything.*'

'She was probably just looking out for you. They're pretty dangerous, after all,' I said.

'My mother's a neurotic,' he said. 'I can't stand her.'

'You shouldn't talk like that.'

'Why not?'

'Because she's your mother. At least you knew her.'

Ralph helped himself to a cigarette from my pack and struck a match on his zipper. 'Sorry,' he said, coughing as he exhaled. 'I guess it seems kind of childish for me to complain about my parents, when you didn't have any.'

'You don't have to apologize. All I mean is, you should be grateful,' I said.

'Do you remember her at all? Your mom?'

'No.'

'Were you pretty young when she died?'

'I was kind of exaggerating when I said I was

111

an orphan,' I said. 'I don't know for sure that she's dead.'

He paused in mid-drag, his eyes widening in surprise.

'You mean she might still be around somewhere?'

'Might be. She gave me up when I was a baby.'

I hadn't intended to tell anyone about my mother until I knew for sure where she was. But even though I barely knew Ralph, I trusted him; he'd brought me all the way down here to see a severed hand, which I supposed in his own weird way was a gesture of kindness, and also to meet one of probably only two people in New Mexico fluent in Homeric Greek. I was still uncertain what that was supposed to mean to me, but it was something, at least. Ralph was trying to edify me; from the moment in the Cowgirl when I first told him I was working on a novel, he'd believed without question that I would be a writer – believed it even more than I did, in fact. What was more, he wanted me to be a *good* writer, one with interesting stories to tell. I appreciated that. Other people just laughed at me when I told them about my dream. But Ralph hadn't laughed. He'd taken me seriously.

Besides, I had to tell *someone* what I was up to. I needed an ally. I couldn't talk to El Perrero, who was a self-proclaimed lunatic, and I sure as hell couldn't talk to Sophia, at least not until I figured out what her problem was.

'Any idea where she might be?' he asked. 'You ever think about going to look for her?'

I decided then and there that if there was anyone I could trust, it was Ralph, and if I was going to trust him, it might as well be now.

'Sure,' I said. 'That's why I came to New Mexico in the first place. She used to live in Santa Fe. She might still be there, for all I know.'

I started back at the beginning and told him everything: about my father, Eddie, about my mother, about Grandpa. I told him about Mildred, too, and the old farmhouse. I even told him about Sophia. When I got to that part he spluttered and choked theatrically on his beer, spilling a good deal of it.

'She's your *sister*?' he echoed in disbelief. '*That?*'

'Hey, now,' I said. 'I know you don't like her, but—'

'Sorry. She's just so . . . *weird*. And it's not that I don't like her, Mann. She won't *let* me like her. She won't let *anyone* like her.'

'I noticed,' I said. 'She has the personality of a tank.'

'I take it she doesn't know who you are?'

'No. And I don't want her to, not yet.'

'Why not?'

'I don't know. It just doesn't feel right.'

'You know best,' he said. 'You don't know what she'd do if she knew who you were. She might have to hug you or something, and that would probably kill her.'

'I only have El Perrero's word for it that we're related,' I said. 'I don't know for sure.'

'Who's El Perrero?'

'A neighbor of mine,' I said. 'Another head case.'

'Santa Fe is full of head cases,' Ralph told me. 'It's one of those places where strange people just seem to end up. A city of lost souls. You met any crystal gazers yet?'

'What's a crystal gazer?'

'One of those New Age types. You'll meet one soon enough, if you stick around. They believe Santa Fe is the center of some kind of harmonic convergence. An energy spot, like the Bermuda Triangle.'

'Do *you* believe that?'

'It would certainly explain why all the freaks end up there,' he said. 'Who knows? Maybe they've got it right, and the rest of us have our heads up our asses. But no, I don't believe it. I'm too much of a rationalist.'

'Listen,' I said. 'Don't tell anyone about Sophia. All right?'

'I don't blame you,' Ralph told me. 'I won't say a word. It's a hell of a story, though.' Abruptly he sat up straight and snapped his fingers. 'Listen,' he said. 'You just reminded me of something.'

'What?'

'Remember when I told you Sophia was having some kind of family problem?'

'Yeah?'

'I just remembered what it was,' he said. 'Franco mentioned it to me a while back, but I wasn't really paying attention, which is why it just came to me now.'

'What is it?'

'It's her mother,' he said.

A nasty sense of foreboding came over me. Suddenly the mood of the day was ruined. 'What about her?' I asked.

'Well, I'm not totally sure,' he said. 'But I think he said she's sick.'

'How sick?'

'I don't know,' he said. 'Sick enough to worry her, I guess.'

'But – that's *my* mother,' I said. 'Sophia's mother is my mother, too.'

Ralph winced and looked down into his beer. 'I know,' he said. 'I'm sorry.'

'What's wrong with her?'

'I never heard, Mann. I would tell you if I knew. Honest.'

'Is she going to get better?'

'I—'

'Is she *dying*?'

'Look, I—'

'I have to get back,' I said. I pushed my beer back across the bar; I'd barely tasted it anyway. 'I want to go, Ralph. Come on.'

'Look, Billy, even if she is dying, it's not like *today* is going to be her last—'

'How do you know?' I demanded. 'How can you say that for sure?'

Ralph mumbled something unintelligible; he'd spoken without thinking.

'See? You don't know!' I said. 'It *might* be her last day! I came all the way out here to find her, Ralph, and if there's something wrong with her I want to know what it is! And I want to know right now!'

'All right,' said Ralph. 'I didn't mean to upset you. We're going.'

'You boys headed out?' called Bob.

'Good to see you, Bob,' said Ralph. I didn't say anything. I was suddenly in a great hurry to leave. I pushed through the swinging doors, but not before I heard Bob's parting line to Ralph: 'Come on down more often, young feller. I always like to keep my hand in. Get it? *Hand* in?'

His laughter trailed me out onto the porch, where I waited impatiently for Ralph. In my state it sounded like mockery. I hadn't come all this way just to lose her again. I had to talk to Sophia now, no matter what the consequences.

I dropped Ralph off on campus. He told me Sophia wasn't likely to start her shift until around six o'clock, which meant I had a couple of hours to kill, so I went home first. If my mother was in the hospital, I thought, it should be easy to find her – there was only one in Santa Fe. I called the switchboard and asked if they had a patient named

116

Eliza McMeel, but there was nobody listed under that name. It was the same with Sky McMeel; same with Eliza Mann, which was a wild guess, and Sky Mann, at which point the switchboard nurse hung up on me. I didn't think she'd be under my father's name, since they'd never been married, but I had to try. But no luck. Unless she'd changed names again, she wasn't there.

By this time it was four-thirty. I was debating what to do with myself until six when there came a knock at the door. It was El Perrero, wearing his standard army fatigues and sunglasses.

'Hey there,' I said. 'How's it going?'

'All right, Jones,' he replied. He stood there several moments more, not speaking.

'Well, that's good,' I said finally. 'I was just on my way out.'

'Don't go yet,' he said. 'I brought you something.'

'What is it?'

He waited again, but when I showed no signs of inviting him in, he opened his jacket.

'We gotta look out for each other around here,' he said. 'You understand? It's kind of a rough place sometimes.'

'Okay,' I said.

'This is for you,' he said. 'A little present.' He reached into an inner pocket and pulled out a pistol, holding it out to me butt first. 'Go on,' he said. 'Take it, Jones. You know how to shoot?'

'No,' I said.

'You should learn,' he said. He was still holding the gun out. 'Take it, *ese*,' he said. 'Don't be scared of it. You have to make it obey you.'

I took the gun gingerly. It was old and battered, and the grip was wrapped with duct tape. I held it pointing down. 'What is this for?' I asked.

'For protection,' he said.

'Is it loaded?'

'Of course it's loaded.'

'All right. Well, thanks,' I said. I wished he would take those glasses off so I could see what he was thinking. What the hell was he giving me a gun for? For a moment, when he'd pulled it out, I thought he was going to point it at me, and my heart was still racing with fear. I didn't like guns. I'd owned a .22-caliber rifle back in Mannville, but that was nothing unusual – a lot of boys my age got a .22 as soon as they were old enough. I had used mine to shoot at cans and bottles. But this was a pistol, and a pistol was different.

'Let's go down to the arroyo,' he said. 'I can show you how it works.'

'Won't someone hear us?' I didn't want to go down to the arroyo, not now – not ever. The arroyo was the gully at the foot of the street, built to hold spring runoff from the mountains. It was dry now, but it was still a dangerous place. The cement walls were covered in graffiti, which meant gangs hung out there, and the one time I'd poked around in a mood to explore, I'd found a used syringe. *That* was the kind of place the arroyo was.

118

But El Perrero said, 'Naw. Long as there's no cops around, we'll be fine. Come on, Jones. Just for a few minutes.'

I sighed and put my jacket back on. After some deliberation I stuck the gun in the inside pocket. Then I locked the front door behind me, and we walked down the street together in silence. I was keenly aware of the weight of the gun at my side. I was also nervous. If he was going to pull something funny, at least I was armed, although for all I knew he had another pistol in one of the many pockets of his fatigues – and if he was going to hurt me, the last thing he would do beforehand was give me a gun. Nevertheless, it crossed my mind that it was stupid to go with him. It was stupid to take the gun in the first place. What did I need with a gun? I wondered if this had something to do with that guy he'd known in Vietnam, the one who looked like me – maybe he was having a flashback.

But still he said nothing. We scrambled down the bank and stood in the soft sand of the arroyo. I was trembling a little. The feeling of anxiety that had overtaken me earlier, when Ralph told me my mother was sick, had by now increased to plain old-fashioned fear. I realized that I did not like El Perrero, nor did I trust him. It was a very strange thing to give someone a gun. Maybe I was just learning one more new rule in a land of strange customs, but I didn't think so. There was something else going on.

The banks of the arroyo were high, nearly twenty

feet. I hoped they would be enough to muffle the sound of gunfire from the traffic speeding by above us, on West Alameda. If a cop happened to be passing by, we'd be in big trouble. But El Perrero showed no signs of concern. He hunted around in the weeds until he'd found several rusted cans and a few unbroken bottles. He set them in a row in the sand about fifty feet away and then came back to where I stood.

'All right,' he said calmly. 'Get 'em.'

'You want me to shoot at those?'

'I said get 'em,' he repeated. There was soft menace in his voice now.

I took the gun out of my jacket and clicked the safety; in that respect, the pistol was the same as my old rifle back home. I leveled it at the left-most bottle.

'Use both hands,' he said. 'Put your left one under the butt.' I did as I was told. 'Now relax your shoulders,' he said. 'Breathe.'

I squeezed the trigger, and the gun leaped in my hands. I was unprepared for just how loud it would be. It was a great shout of rage, a thunderclap. I was so startled I didn't even see where the bullet hit. But the bottle I'd been aiming at sat unscathed.

'Too high,' he said. 'You got to compensate for the kick. Here, watch.'

He grabbed the gun from my hands and fired, hardly taking the time to aim. He shot twice, and the bottle disintegrated. My ears rang again.

'Someone's going to hear us,' I said. 'This is crazy.'

'Here,' he said, handing it back to me. 'You do it. We ain't leaving until you get it right.'

'Why are we doing this?' I asked him. 'Will you just tell me?'

He looked at me, but again he didn't answer. His lips under his mustache were tight with impatience. I turned back to the bottles and aimed. My next shot missed, too, but I was beginning to get the hang of it now. My third shot hit the second bottle from the right. It wasn't the one I was aiming at, but I chose not to mention that. I fired three more times, this time hitting my intended target, and the gun was empty.

'There,' I said. 'Good enough?'

'Reload,' he said. From the arsenal of his pockets he produced another clip. He showed me how to pull back the top part of the gun so that the empty clip dropped out of the handle. 'Fire,' he said.

I dropped to one knee and aimed again. This time I squeezed off the whole clip, nine shots in a row, and when I was finished the bottles were all dead and the cans had been gravely wounded. El Perrero seemed satisfied. He handed me a box of ammunition, and I thought he was going to tell me to reload again, but instead he said, 'That's good. You learn quick.'

'Thanks,' I said. Concentrating on my aim had removed the edge from my nervousness. I felt better now. I hefted the gun, testing its balance. I had to admit I liked the way it felt in my hand.

'What caliber is it?' I asked.

'Thirty-two,' he said. 'Cop gun. Don't ask where I got it. Come on, let's get out of here.' We climbed back up the bank and walked down the street toward our houses. There he stopped and turned to me.

'You know the sniper's rule?' he asked.

'No.'

'One shot, one kill,' he said. 'You do it right the first time. You know when you're supposed to shoot someone?'

'No.'

'Before he shoots you,' he said. 'Someone's ever aiming at you, you don't wait to find out if he's going to shoot or not. You take him out. Don't think. Just do it. *M'entiendes*?'

'Got it.'

'All right, then,' he said.

'Perrero,' I said. 'Why are you doing this?'

Again he wouldn't answer. He only stared at me, and once again I saw myself in his lenses, distorted and rounded and doubled. Then another strange thing happened. He put his arms on my shoulders, and I wondered if now he was going to teach me how to wrestle; but instead he hugged me. It was quick but hard, almost paternal. I was too astonished to react. Then he stepped back, turned, and went into his house, leaving me standing there in the street.

I went back into my own house and sat on the couch for a while, holding the gun. There was no denying that it felt good; it made me feel powerful. I loaded the two empty clips from the box of ammo he'd given me and pushed one of them into the magazine. It slid in easily, like a well-made piece of equipment was supposed to, and clicked home with a sound that was immensely satisfying. That was all a gun was, when you thought about it – just a machine.

I made sure the safety was on and took out the clip again so it wouldn't go off accidentally. Then I practiced twirling it on my finger. It was too short to twirl well. I imagined Sheriff Bob's long pearl-handled revolver was made for twirling, like I'd seen cowboys do in movies, but this gun wasn't designed for show. It meant business. I spun it around, trying to catch the grip neatly in my palm, aimed and ready to go. What the hell was I going to use it for? I had no business with a pistol. But I kept twirling it, and then I heard the barest *snick* as the safety fell into the off position, just as my finger happened to be on the trigger. The gun went off again, this time pointed at me.

If it had sounded loud outside, inside the house it was purely deafening. In my mind's eye I had a sudden image of myself as a very young boy, playing alone on the shore of Lake Erie. The picture shifted suddenly to me wandering through the old mansion in Mannville, again alone. I'd spent my entire childhood alone, I realized. I'd

123

grown up like a hermit, like a prisoner. A feeling of sadness overwhelmed me. People weren't meant to be alone, I thought, especially children. It was unnatural.

Then I realized my life was passing before me, and I knew that meant I had been shot; I was going to die. But there had been no pain. Cautiously I felt my head, and then my upper body. There was no blood, no wound. I turned and looked at the wall behind me. There was a ragged hole in the adobe, about an inch deep. The bullet itself had vanished. I'd felt the heat as it sizzled by my face, I remembered now, but I was too stunned by the noise to register what it was. I'd taken out the clip, but I hadn't know there was still a round in the chamber – I had been playing with a loaded gun. I wasn't going to die. I had merely *almost* died, and that was enough to trick my mind into saying good-bye to the world.

I came to my senses then. I wrapped the gun, the two full clips, and the box of ammo in a towel. Then I stuck the bundle under the kitchen sink. There was no fear, no nervousness, as one might expect after a narrow brush with death. I felt oddly calm. I went to the front door and opened it a crack, peeking out at El Perrero's house. He hadn't heard the shot. Nobody else had, either. That crazy fucker, I thought, suddenly angry. Why was he doing this to me? If I had shot myself, it would have been his fault. I'd just been minding my own business when he came out of nowhere and presented me with an instrument of murder. And why was he acting like he was doing me a favor? Like the gun was something I needed?

All right, I thought. I'd just received my first glimpse of my own mortality, and I was still here. I knew I should have been scared, but instead I felt invincible. The bullet had missed me because I had a purpose in life. I was not meant to go this early. I had great things to accomplish; that was what it all meant. I'd seen my life, or part of it, in review, and that was a perspective usually only granted to those who were dying. I felt as though I'd been presented with a gift, as if I'd gained a new wisdom from almost blowing my head off, in what would have been my greatest blunder ever. But I didn't think about everything that had almost happened, about my life that had nearly been lost. I only thought about the fact that I was still alive. I was feeling calm and centered. I'd just come through something important and was still in one piece; I felt good, like Superman.

I was still in this mood when I headed up to the Cowgirl an hour later to talk with Sophia. She wasn't there yet, so I sat down at the bar and said hello to Franco.

'What happened to your face?' he said.

I looked in the mirror behind the bar. There was a spattering of tiny red marks along my right cheek – particles of gunpowder, I realized. 'Oh,' I said, 'I was riding without a helmet. Must have gotten hit with some little pebbles, or something.'

He accepted this. 'Beer?'

'Coke,' I said. 'You from around here, Franco?'

'Born and raised,' he said. 'Lived here my whole life.'

'You speak Spanish?'

'Sure.'

'So you understand what Consuelo's songs are about?'

He smiled. 'Not really,' he said. 'She sings in a dialect.'

'Really? What kind?'

'Some old version of Spanish,' he said. 'I think it's Andalusian. I only catch a word here and there. It's the language the old man speaks – he writes all her songs.'

'The guitar player?'

He nodded. I was disappointed to learn that she didn't write the songs herself; somehow it made her a little less interesting. But what he said next piqued my interest again.

'Consuelo's the only one who can even talk to the old guy,' he said. 'He doesn't speak English, and he doesn't even seem to understand regular Spanish. At least not the kind we talk around here.'

'Is New Mexico Spanish different?'

'Sure, it is,' he said. 'It's kind of like the difference between American English and British English. We have our own words for some things, and the accent is different. But they speak a whole other kind in Cuba, and also in South America – there's as many different kinds of Spanish as there are countries that speak it. But Esteban – that's the guitar player – he talks almost like Shakespeare would talk, if he was Spanish.'

'Like how?'

'Really formal,' he said. 'Almost a completely different vocabulary. I can't understand him at all.'

'Where did you say he was from?' I asked. But before be could answer, the door swung open, tinkling the little bell that was attached to it, and Sophia came in.

She trailed cold air in after her, and though the sight of me seemed to surprise her she didn't say a word. She headed back to the kitchen and came out a moment later without her coat. Then she tied her apron on and smoothed it with her hands. She looked at me, and then at Franco, and then at me again.

'Hey,' I said.

She sniffed. 'Hello,' she said, looking down.

'Amy already did the silverware this afternoon,' Franco told her. 'You want to check the glasses?'

Sophia went into the other room off the bar, where the non-smoking tables were. I got up and followed her; it was now or never, and though I was nervous again I was still feeling good.

'Where you off to?' Franco said.

'Be right back,' I told him.

She was standing in the waiters' station at the back of the room, counting racks of water glasses. I cleared my throat as I came up behind her so I

127

wouldn't give her a scare. She ignored me; she just kept counting.

'Excuse me,' I said.

'Twenty-one,' she said.

'Beg pardon?'

'Twenty-two, twenty-three, twenty-four. What is it?'

She turned and faced me. She still wouldn't look at me; she kept her eyes on the ground.

'Listen,' I said. 'There's something I have to tell you.'

She raised her eyes from the ground and looked directly at me. There was something hungry about her, I thought, something searching in her gaze. She was reading me, trying to guess what I was talking about.

'This is kind of tricky,' I said. 'I mean, I—'

'Can it wait?' she said. 'I'm kind of busy.' But she said it without conviction, as though she only wanted me to believe that she was busy. Her voice had lost its edge, and it was like she was doing her best to maintain a tough exterior that didn't fit her. My courage grew. I didn't have to be afraid of her, after all. She was my own flesh and blood. Once she knew that, too, everything would be fine between us, and I could find out what was wrong with my mother.

'This is really important,' I said. 'Can I please talk to you now?'

Her face twisted into an expression of grief, or perhaps something else – some kind of a longing.

I was unprepared for what she did next. I was just forming the words I'd planned when she stepped forward and threw her arms around my neck. Does she already know who I am? I wondered. But that question was answered a moment later when I felt her lips suddenly connect with mine, mashing together hard, and her tongue forced its way inside my mouth and probed it, hot and insistent.

We were alone back there, out of sight of the bar. I pushed away from her and wiped my mouth with the back of my hand. She backed away until she ran into the wall.

'Oh, Jesus,' I said. 'Oh no.'

'I'm sorry,' she said. 'I thought you—'

'Sophia,' I said.

She covered her mouth with her hands and stared at me.

'That wasn't what you wanted?' she said.

'I – I don't even know where to—'

'Okay,' she said. Her voice was shaking. 'Forget it. You don't have to say it.'

'You don't even know what I was going to say!'

'Well, I thought I did,' she said.

'Listen—'

'No. Don't say it now.'

'Sophia, please.'

She put her face in her hands. 'I can't take it,' she said. 'Whatever you're going to say, I can't take it. You're going to tell me why you don't like me. Well, I'm sorry. I made a mistake.'

'It's not what you think,' I said lamely. But she was right, though she didn't know it – I couldn't tell her now. There was obviously something really wrong, and though I knew now that it was about her mother, our mother, I couldn't tell her that I knew – I couldn't tell her she was my sister. Not after this. And I saw now that she was fragile, scared, on the edge of a breakdown. Whatever was going on, it had worn her almost to the breaking point. If I told her she'd just kissed her own brother, what effect would that have? Would she go mad right there, or would she slowly crumble into pieces over the next few days? I didn't want to risk it.

'All right,' I said. 'Forget it.'

She was crying now, silent, her shoulders shaking. She slumped down against the wall into a kneeling position, her face still hidden by her hands. I knelt down next to her and put a hand on her shoulder.

'Will you at least tell me what's wrong?' I said.

'I can't,' she wailed. 'I don't even know you!'

'Who cares?' I said. 'Maybe I can help. I'm not such a bad guy.'

'But you don't like me!' she said, sobbing.

'I do like you,' I said. 'In fact, I like you a lot. Just not like that.'

She tried to get herself under control. I handed

her a stack of napkins. She wiped her face and blew her nose.

'Shit,' she said. 'You ever feel like you do things that you have no control over? Like, you know they're stupid, but you can't stop yourself?'

'Sure,' I said, thinking about my shooting lesson with El Perrero. 'Sometimes.'

'I'm just under so much pressure,' she said. 'I don't know how much more of this I can take. I swear, if just one more thing happens . . .'

That was when I made up my mind: I was definitely not going to tell her.

'I know I'm acting like a total bitch these days,' she said. 'It's like I can't help myself. You let people close to you, and then they go away. So I just push everyone away.' She blew her nose again. 'I used to be a really nice person,' she said.

She smiled – only halfheartedly, but I was encouraged. 'You're still nice,' I said. 'You can't keep things locked up, though. Sometimes you have to talk about them.'

'I know,' she said. 'It's – it's my mother.'

So Ralph was right.

'How sick is she?' I asked.

Sophia looked puzzled. 'How did you know she was sick?'

'I just guessed,' I said.

'Well, she is sick,' she said. 'Really sick.'

I waited for her to go on, but she began to cry again. I kept my hand on her shoulder.

'Where is she?' I asked.

'Albuquerque,' she said.

'Is anyone down there with her?'

'No,' she said. 'She's by herself.'

'Why don't you go stay with her?'

She sniffled. 'We had a fight,' she said. 'A long time ago. I know it seems stupid now, but she . . . she threw me out of the house. We still haven't gotten over that one. We haven't gotten along for a long time. Even now, it's like we can't even be in the same house.'

'What'd you fight about?'

'Everything,' she said. 'You name it. Like my curfew.'

'You were mad because you had a curfew?'

'No,' she said. 'I was mad because I didn't have one. She never seemed to care whether I came or went. It used to drive me crazy. She never cooked, she never cleaned, she never did any of the stuff moms are supposed to do. It was like she just didn't care.' Sophia was talking fast now, on a roll, letting it all out.

'We used to have these bake sales at school, where we were supposed to bring in stuff our moms had made, like cookies and brownies and whatever. She would never make me anything. I don't think she even knows how to bake, so I just didn't go to school on those days. I couldn't play sports because she would never have picked me up after practice, and I knew she wouldn't even make it to my games. This kept on right up through high school. Then I'd had it. It wasn't like she was mean on purpose. Like, being mean to somebody involves thinking about them, and that was her real problem. She never thought about me. Never. I told her one day she was a lousy mother, and she said if I felt that way about it, I could just take care of myself from then on. So that's what I've been doing. Before she got sick, I'd hardly talked to her for two years.'

'Is she in the hospital?'

'No,' she said. 'She's at home.' She was under control now. 'There's nothing more they can do, except give her pain medication,' she said. The transition from upset to calm had been a little too fast to be natural. It was forced. She was wound as tight as a watch. 'I try to get down there when I can. I feel like it's important for us to make up, now that she's going to . . . now that she's sick. But as crazy as it sounds, we still don't get along. You'd think we would now, but we don't. And when I do have time to go see her, I'm dead tired. I've got all these books I wanted to give her, but I'm not off until this weekend. And I wish . . .'

I waited. She was starting to cry again.

'I wish we could get along!' she sobbed. 'I wish we'd never fought! I feel so bad, you know? I feel guilty!'

I thought fast. 'Will you let me do something for you?' I asked.

'Why would you want to do something for me?' she asked.

'Just because,' I said. 'You don't have to ask why. Just because.'

'What do you want to do?'

'Will you let me take those books down to her? Will that at least give you a little peace of mind, if she has some company?'

She nodded again. 'It would, a little,' she said. 'I mean, I guess. But why—'

'Don't,' I said. 'I'm not sure I can explain it. Just tell me. Will you let me do it?'

Her face was swollen and tear streaked. We were still kneeling together in the waiters' station, surrounded by coffeepots and racks of glasses and stacks of plates. She looked doubtful.

'If it makes it any easier, I have to go down there, anyway,' I said. 'To see a . . . knee doctor.' It was the first thing I could think of.

'All right,' she said. 'If you don't tell anyone I kissed you.'

'I won't breathe a word,' I said.

'Billy?' she said.

'Yeah?'

'It's not because I'm fat, is it? That you didn't want to kiss me?'

'Come on. You're *not* fat,' I said. 'It's just that I'm – sort of into someone else.'

'Consuelo,' she said.

I nodded.

'I knew it.' She sighed.

'But I think you're very pretty,' I said.

It wasn't exactly true, but it wasn't a lie, either.

She was not unattractive, in a general way. But the point was moot for me; she was my sister. I felt a great wave of tenderness wash over me as I looked at her crouched in the corner, her face a mess, miserable. She was my little sister, I was the big brother, and I was supposed to take care of her. Even if I never told her who I was, I would always act that way. I wanted her to trust me. But I knew I would tell her, someday – when this day was long behind us.

'You're just saying that to be nice,' she said. But she brightened.

'You shouldn't worry about how you look,' I told her. 'You should worry about how you feel.'

She rolled her eyes. 'Jesus,' she said. 'If *that* isn't the biggest high-school health-class self-esteem bullshit.' But she smiled.

'How do you feel?' I asked her.

'Better,' she said.

'Keep feeling that way,' I said. 'Everything's going to be all right.'

I didn't know if it was true, and I didn't think she was going to believe me. Who was I to her, after all? But I acted like I believed it, and it worked on her, for the moment. We stood up and she took my hand.

'Thanks,' she said. 'Sorry about—'

'Don't,' I said. 'We don't have to talk about it anymore.'

'All right,' she said. 'Thank you.'

★   ★   ★

The next morning I took the interstate to Albuquerque. At eighty miles an hour I made the trip in about forty-five minutes. I took the ramp onto Coal Street, where I found the address Sophia had given me. I parked in the street and took a stack of twine-bound books from my knapsack. Then I crossed the yard of the house and rang the bell.

It took an eternity for someone to answer. The door opened a crack, and I could see an eye looking out at me.

'Yes?' said a woman's voice.

'Are you Sophia's mom?' I said.

The door opened completely, and she stood before me.

The woman was tall. Her eyes were steel gray, her nose sharp and Roman and well defined. There was a handkerchief wrapped around her head, but a few strands of long brown-gray hair had escaped and fallen to her shoulders. She wore a bathrobe, which she clutched in front of her. She pushed open the screen door.

'Come in quickly,' she said. 'It's chilly out there. Are you Billy?'

'Yes, ma'am.' I stepped inside and was greeted by the smell of medicine and uncirculated air. She pushed the door shut behind me.

I hadn't known whether she would recognize me instantly or not, whether there was some kind of magical bond between mother and child that would cause the previous twenty years to vanish like a veil of tissue paper. It appeared now that there was not. She merely smiled at me in a tired way, took the books from me and set them down, and then sat on the couch.

'I'm sorry,' she said. 'I don't seem to be doing very well today. But I can make some tea, if you like.'

Her eyes were sunken deep into her skull. There were great black circles around them, as though something was slowly beating her to death from the inside. Her skin was dry and hung in loose folds about her face, as if she'd lost a lot of weight.

'No, no,' I said. 'It's . . .'

'Perhaps you could make it instead,' she said. 'I would hate not to offer you anything after your trip. It's just that I'm very . . . tired.'

I took off my jacket and hung it on a closet doorknob. I couldn't speak.

'The kitchen is back that way,' she said.

I went into the kitchen and found the kettle. I set some water to boil and found a pot and some teabags. Then I gripped the countertop with both hands as hard as I could and struggled to get myself under control.

'Are you finding everything in there?' she called.

I pushed it all back down inside me. 'Yes,' I said. 'Do you . . . do you have any milk?'

'In the fridge.'

Of course it would be in the fridge. I was just trying to find something normal to say. What would I say to her if I wasn't her son, if I was

137

just some person? I would ask where the milk was, that was what. I took the carton out and poured a dash into a couple of mugs.

'Sugar?' I called.

'In the cupboard above the sink,' she said. 'Just give me one lump.'

I gave her one lump and myself two, and when the water boiled I poured it into the pot with the teabags and took everything out into the living room on a tray. I set it down on the coffee table and pulled up a chair.

'We'll let that steep a moment,' she said. 'I'm sorry I'm not dressed. I'm sure Sophia must have told you I was sick.'

'Yeah, she did,' I said. 'Sorry to hear it.'

She smiled wanly. 'What's your last name, Billy?'

'It's, uh – Shumacher,' I said.

'You're not from around here, I take it?'

'No. Pennsylvania.'

'I see. What have you brought me to read?'

'I didn't even look at them, to tell the truth.'

She tried to untie the twine around the books, but her fingers fumbled uselessly with the knots. After a moment she said, 'Can you do this for me, please?'

I took the package from her and untied it.

'What a silly girl my daughter is,' she said, looking at the books. 'She thinks I like the same things she likes. She forgets romances make my stomach turn.' She smiled again, and I laughed too loudly.

'It's not every day a handsome young man appears in my living room,' she said, arranging some pillows behind her and leaning back into them. Her tea sat untouched in front of her. 'Tell me about yourself.'

'I don't – I mean – what would you like to know?'

She closed her eyes. 'Anything,' she said, in a voice that said *It doesn't matter – I'm too tired to listen, anyway.* 'You decide.'

'I'm an orphan,' I said, surprising myself. But it was the lie I'd begun, and now I had to stick with it.

She opened her eyes again – she was surprised, too. *Idiot,* I thought. *She's going to think you're looking for sympathy.*

'Really,' she said. 'How terrible.'

'It's okay,' I said quickly. 'I never knew my parents.'

'They died when you were young?'

'My father died before I was born,' I said. I saw a twitch cross her face then – what was it? Had I jolted a nerve?

'How did he die?' she asked.

'A car accident.'

The twitch passed. 'And your mother?'

'Childbirth,' I said.

'You don't hear of that happening often these days,' she said. 'Still, I suppose it must, from time to time.'

We sat quietly for a few moments. I thought the

silence was growing uncomfortable, but she was only thinking. She said, 'I was lucky. I knew my parents pretty well.'

'Where are you from?' I asked.

'I grew up in San Francisco. In the houseboats. Have you ever heard of Sausalito?'

'No.'

'It's a little floating community, sort of near the Golden Gate Bridge,' she said. 'It was a wonderful place then. We had our own society, more or less. We made our own rules, and we were pretty self-sufficient. It was a great place to be a kid. It's good for kids to be around water, I think.'

'I grew up around water, too,' I said.

'Really? Where?'

'Lake Erie.'

Again the twitch, and again it passed. 'Lake Erie is a pretty big lake, isn't it?'

'Huge,' I said. 'Hundreds of miles long.'

'I suppose a lot of people live near it.'

'Yup.'

'I see.'

She was struggling hard to keep her eyes open.

'I'm sorry,' she said. 'I'm taking a lot of medication, and it wears me out.'

'Maybe I should go,' I said.

'Sophia was right,' she said.

I put down my teacup. 'About what?'

'She thought you looked familiar. You look familiar to me, too.'

'I do?'

140

She'd closed her eyes again.

'Yeah,' she said, and then her breathing had suddenly changed – it was light, rapid. She was asleep.

I put my jacket on again and stepped closer to her.

'Sky?' I said.

No answer.

I cleared away the teacups and washed them out in the sink. When I came back into the living room she was still asleep. I leaned over and kissed her on the forehead. Her skin was moist and cool, clammy. Whatever was wrong with her, it was serious – it wasn't just the flu or a cold. She'd had the same look in her eyes that Grandpa'd had when he first became seriously ill, that glassy, almost disinterested look.

I was certain my mother was dying.

I let myself out, making sure the door was locked behind me, and rode back up the highway to Santa Fe.

CHAPTER 5

CONSUELO SINGS

My name is Consuelo Constanza Maria Bachicha y Gonzalez, and I tell my story in the form of a song instead of on paper, because I'm not as gifted in the art of writing as I feel would be necessary to tell it right. On paper, like so many people, my words come out all wrong, confused, falling over each other. When I sing, however, my words are perfect, as flawless as diamonds – singing is the one way in which I never fail to express myself, in exactly the way I want.

I saw him staring at me from the back of the room last week, this new face I didn't know on the young man with long hair. He sat alone, at the very last table. There were many unfamiliar faces there, of course, but his leaped out at me across the tables, over the heads of the other listeners. It was distracting. I didn't know why my attention was drawn to him. He was not outstandingly handsome, although he is good-looking enough – not that that has ever been my main concern with men. I like men who are strong, and have a sense of humor, like my father. But I had trouble concentrating after I noticed him. Not because of the way he looked at me, but because of the prodding I received at that moment from my angels, who had also noticed him and who had suddenly grown excited.

Ordinarily, the angels are quiet when I sing. They know they have to let me concentrate. Sometimes I can hear them singing along with me, their tiny voices raised in unison with mine, but for the most part they try to stay quiet. The night I saw the long-haired young man in the back, though, there was pandemonium in the air. All eleven of them were thrown into an uproar.

'That's the one!' I heard them saying. 'Him! You must talk to him!'

I tried to ignore them. I sent them a silent reminder that I was onstage, in the middle of a performance. But they paid me no mind.

'We found him!' I could hear them chanting to each other, as though they were dancing around in a circle. 'Finally! He's here!'

I could no longer hear myself over their voices. I lost my focus, had to stop and try to concentrate. *Shut up*, I thought fiercely. *All of you, just shut up. You're ruining it!*

They fell silent then, but it was too late. Everyone had noticed. I heard a murmur running through the audience. I must have looked like I was going to faint, because several people got up as if to assist me. But I was not going to faint – I was merely trying to silence the voices in my head. I smiled to conceal my irritation and resumed the song. It was a close call; it was the only time the angels had ever interfered with my outside life, and afterward they were apologetic. They had broken their own rule, which was never to do anything that would keep me from singing. The whole reason they were with me in the first place was to help me sing. But it was not their fault; even angels can lose their heads when it comes to matters of the heart.

Between songs, I asked them: *What are you carrying on about?*

They answered: *He will wait for you outside.*

I don't tell many people about my angels. They tend to think I'm crazy, which is not true, or that I'm strange, which might very well be true. Who are the angels? people may wonder. Do angels still appear, in this day and age? Certainly they do. It is not even a matter of debate. They came to me when I was young and have never left me since. And they have a story, just like everyone. Their story is tangled up with mine, so I may be excused, perhaps, for telling them both at once. It begins when I was a small child.

When I was young, I was the most famous female tightrope walker of any circus in the western world. I was famous precisely because I was young – there are many grown women who can walk the wire, but very few small girls. In those days I performed in front of huge crowds without an ounce of nervousness. I was very good, and I was too young to understand that what I was doing was unusual. I just assumed that most little girls were tightrope walkers. It was a great shock to me to learn that this was not true. And most of the time the circus was nothing more than a lot of hard work – practicing my juggling, practicing my high-wire act, practicing my unicycle. I was always practicing something, always tired and sore, and most of all I can see now that I was not happy.

I was born in Chihuahua City, the youngest of five daughters, but I don't remember very much of it because we never actually lived there. I remember a great church – a cathedral – and outside of the cathedral was a flock of short, dark Indian women in brightly colored clothing, each in turn tending a flock of children. The women made their living by sending the children into the street to beg coins from passersby. I admired the clothing of the Indian women very much, because it was so pretty, but I felt sorry for the children, who were thin and tired looking and hungry, and most of whom had lice. Come to think of it, I must have looked much like them, although my mother was too diligent with the soap to allow our hair to become home to parasites. Children in Mexico are much smaller than the children here in America, who seem to me far too large and pale and and overfed – almost like grubs. This is a land of fat people, plump children. I suppose when you have all the food you want it is normal to be too fat. I wouldn't know. I did not grow up like this – we always had food, but it was never enough. There were too many mouths to feed, and not enough money.

These Indian children never bothered to ask me or my sisters for coins. They could see by our clothing that we had nothing to give. They begged instead from the chubby Anglo tourists who had come down from El Norte, who wandered around looking sick and hot, their cameras hanging around their necks. This was in the days before my parents signed us on with the Strawberry Family Circus in San Francisco, when we still went from town to town in Mexico in our school bus and performed for the people, and we were very poor. Really, we were not much better off than the Indian children who begged in the street. We ate more often than they did, perhaps, though not much more, and we had somewhere to live, even if it was only a bus. But the children looked at us and knew that there was nothing to be gotten from our pockets, so they left us alone.

Whenever we came into Chihuahua during our travels, my parents would tell me, 'This is the city where you were born. This is your home.' But I didn't think of it as home, because the school bus was our home. Home, to me, was a large yellow box on wheels. I couldn't imagine what it would be like to live in a house that stayed in one place all the time. Before I was born, my father bought the bus, removed all the seats, and installed two rows of bunkbeds along one wall. It was in one of these beds that my mother gave birth to me. Inside the bus my father put a kerosene stove, and on the outside he painted a mural of Nuestra Señora de Guadalupe, Our Lady of Guadalupe, in bright greens and yellows and reds. When people saw this mural they were to understand by it that we, La Familia Gonzalez, were dedicated heart and soul to the Virgin and that it was for her we performed our various acts.

It's difficult to explain this kind of dedication to Americans. My American friends seem to think that my father was maybe performing a lifelong penance for some terrible sin he'd committed in his youth, or that we were a sort of evangelical family group. I have since seen an American family like this on the television, a family of evangelists, on a station that is entirely devoted to Christian programs. They sang and played their guitars together, which I thought was nice, but they also seemed intent on converting me to their own particular brand of Christianity – me, whom they did not know and never would – so I changed the channel.

This was not the case with my family. We were not interested in making anyone believe anything in particular. In Mexico, if you have a dream that matters to you more than everything else, you dedicate your life to the Virgin or to one of the saints, which means that you're doing the thing that is most important to you in their name.

It's much easier to be successful that way, because then it's the Virgin or the saint who is getting all the credit, not you, and you don't become conceited and think perhaps you're doing it without any help at all from above. This would be a fatal error to commit. As a result, it's much easier for people to take you seriously. They don't think to themselves that you're interested only in money or in fame. They understand that you have a calling, that you've abandoned all else in favor of this calling, and moreover that the call came from something – or someone – divine.

At first I slept with my mother in the bus, but when I was big enough I was given a little bed of my own near the floor, so that if I rolled out I wouldn't have so far to fall. Later, when I was no longer a small child, I was allowed to have one of the higher-up beds near the ceiling. That was a great day for me. I lay there very solemnly, thinking about the fact that I was a big girl now and about how my view of the inside of the bus from up high was so much different than it had been from near the ground. My father warned me before I went to sleep that first night that I should not fall out of bed and hit my head on the floor. I should think straight and level thoughts, he said, and in that way I would be safe. That night, of course, I had a nightmare, a crooked dream instead of a straight one, and I fell out of my bed and hit my head a great crack. I woke up screaming and terrified. But my father, after comforting me, put me right back in the same high-up bed.

'You have to learn not to fall,' he told me, gently rubbing the sore spot on my little skull with one of his great paws. 'Next time you feel yourself going over, remember what it felt like to hit the floor. That will keep you up there.'

This, of course, was probably the most important advice I have ever been given in my life – it applies not only to beds, but to almost every situation one can think of. It was not my fault that I fell. I was accident-prone, and it seemed there was nothing anybody could do about it. I could juggle with three balls by the time I was nine years old, but I was incapable of walking from point A to point B without tripping over every physical object in my path, and some other objects that were completely imaginary.

When I was eight I began learning to walk the wire. My other mother, my father's second wife, trained me in this by putting up a practice wire and walking alongside of me, holding my hand all the while. The wire was only a couple of feet off the ground, and I learned quickly without falling more than is common, but still while walking on the flat earth I fell constantly, and my stepmother saw that unless drastic measures were taken I would be doomed by my own clumsiness to fall one day from the wire and meet an untimely death. Not from the practice wire, of course, but from the real high wire, which she hoped I would be walking one day in the big circus.

'You were not born for this earth,' she used to tell me, sighing.

I didn't understand what she meant by this. When I pushed her to explain, she said: 'You are more comfortable up high with the angels than you are down here on the ground with the rest of us. The air is where you belong, *chamaca*. That's where you were meant to be.'

I pressed her further, but that was as much as she would tell me.

Another thing people don't seem to understand about my family was why my father had two wives. They say nothing to my face, but I can see that privately they think he was a bigamist, and therefore a lecher. But it wasn't his idea to take a second wife. It was my mother's. Five daughters, she protested, were too many for her to train, feed, keep clean, and educate. Furthermore, she lived in mortal fear of another pregnancy – my birth had nearly killed her, and if she were to have another baby, she would need to go to the hospital, which of course we couldn't afford. Also, she needed company; she would appreciate having another woman to talk to on our endless voyage around and around Mexico, instead of five silly young girls and my mostly silent father. Finally, she knew it was unfair to deprive my father of the pleasures of a woman simply because she herself didn't want to have any more babies. These were all very good and practical reasons; she had thought the matter through completely. She even knew the perfect woman for the job: Claudia Atondo, a former acrobat who lived in Guaymas, whom my mother had known for many years. Claudia was pretty, but because of childhood measles she would never bear children, and it was for this that no man wanted to marry her. This was sad, because Claudia wanted children very much.

My father thought the matter through carefully. According to the Church, it was a sin for a man to have two wives. But my father, though he had painted the mural of the Virgin on the bus, and though he prayed to her daily along with the rest of us, was not, if the truth be told, a believer.

'Sometimes, you have to make your own rules,' he used to tell me. 'The laws of the Church were made long ago, when things were different. And just because the Church is the Church doesn't mean they know what's best for *me*.'

Though almost completely without any formal education, my father had taught himself to read when he was twenty years old and, since then, had spent a great deal of time reading and thinking about everything it was possible to read and think about. He was a natural philosopher and an intellectual, and though he did not follow the word of the Church down to the letter, he believed in doing the right thing. Furthermore, if he did not actually marry Claudia, then no sin would have been committed, because as I said it was my mother's idea in the first place – my father would not even be guilty of bigamy. Finally he agreed, and the next time we passed through Guaymas we added Claudia to our number. She took over my training and the training of my next eldest sister, Celestina. Just like that, I had two mothers, my father had two wives, and my mother's burden was cut in half – a very practical arrangement.

It was Claudia who decided to cure me of my clumsiness. She took me to the *curandera*, an old lady who specialized in herbs. I remember this old woman clearly because I was so frightened of her. The *curandera* was ugly and smelled strange, and she lived in a dark little house – where this was, I don't remember – and she burned plants and chanted incantations over me for hours. That was the day I learned about my angels. Most people had only two or three, the old lady told me, but I had no less than eleven; they'd been waiting for the proper time to make themselves known. I had to do nothing more than welcome them into my life, as long as I was willing. I liked the idea of having angels around me, and I said of course I was willing. So the *curandera* taught me the right prayers to say. I said them, and from that day on I no longer tripped over imaginary objects, nor did my feet become tangled up for no reason, nor did I fall out of bed, and I was able to walk along as simply as snapping my fingers. And I could feel, from time to time, the touch of tiny, invisible hands supporting me, helping me stay upright, keeping me level and true.

Soon after that we came to the United States, to work with a real circus, and things got a little better for us. We ate three times a day and I was allowed to go to school. I thought always of Mexico, and at first I missed the old school bus horribly, and my bed high up by the ceiling, and the Indian women in the brightly colored clothing that I admired so much. But now I had my angels with me, and they helped me feel less homesick. At first I tried to tell the others about them, but nobody listened. My mother ignored me, my father smiled indulgently, and my sisters teased me. I learned that they were meant to be a secret. When I found someone who believed in them unquestioningly, that was how I knew that that person was a good one. But for the most part I didn't say any more about them to anybody – not for years.

It is perhaps not true that I was never nervous before walking the wire. There was always just a hint of fear – not of falling, but of performing. As I grew older, Claudia used to tell me that the day I stopped getting nervous was the day I should stop my act. Otherwise, I would be cocky and self-assured and would not feel the proper reverence one ought to feel before performing in the name of the Virgin. She was right, too: the day of my big fall, when I was seventeen, I remember clearly and distinctly that I felt nothing before I went on, not so much as a twinge or a flutter. I

153

didn't tell Claudia about this, because it was a bad sign. But she knew. I could see the foreboding in her eyes. Yet we did not discuss it, as though there was an unspoken agreement between us not to bring it up.

There was such an agreement, in a way. At seventeen I was already a woman, old enough to take my destiny into my own hands, and Claudia knew this. She had stopped directing me. By then she was merely helping me practice. I no longer needed her, but she was there, anyway. And most important, she believed in my angels; she was the one responsible for introducing them to me, after all.

I was a woman, but I still had never had a boyfriend. My mother used to say, 'Never let a man know you're interested until you are absolutely sure of him. And you will never be absolutely sure of him, because he is a man. So never let him know.'

I didn't always understand the things my mother said when I was a girl. She started giving me advice about men when I was still too young to need it. Later she explained this by saying that the sooner I heard these things from her, the more they would make sense when the time came.

'The time for what?' I asked her.

'You'll know when you're big,' she would say. 'When you're old enough, you won't need to ask me what I mean.'

She was right, of course. When I finally realized

what my mother was talking about, I didn't need to ask her anymore. It was obvious. She was talking about *el sexo*. And I knew she knew, because she stopped making her mysterious pronouncements, and instead she just sat back and watched me with the same tight-lipped smile with which she greeted everything the world had to offer. It was not a happy smile; it was cynical, mistrusting. There were very few men in the world with the bravery to approach me after a performance with my mother sitting there in plain view, staring at them scornfully. Those who did try to talk to me usually did not realize at first that the iron woman with the crossed arms and the fixed gaze was *mi madre*, because she always stayed slightly removed, like a tiger ready to pounce; but they realized soon enough who she was when she stood up and asked them, point-blank, what their intentions were with regard to me, her daughter, and who did they think they were speaking to me without introducing themselves to her first?

A thousand apologies, profuse apologies – I meant no disrespect, *señora*, I only wished to offer my congratulations for a fine performance – a job well done, truly well done – ah, excuse me, my brother is calling me, I must go, a pleasure to meet you both. Good day. Go with God in your travels.

As often as not, after one of these encounters, I would reproach my mother. How on earth was I supposed to meet anybody interesting with her standing guard over me like an old watchdog? And she would say: 'When you meet the man who is not afraid of me, then you will have met someone worth talking to. Until then, don't waste your time. They are as transparent as windows, these *cabrones*. And about as deep, too.'

I remember that the very next day after my great fall I told *mi madre* I was quitting the circus, and as if I'd fallen not just from the wire but also from the grace of God, she snapped her mouth shut and stopped speaking to me altogether. From that moment on she pretended I'd ceased to exist in her eyes, not only as a performer but also as her crazy youngest daughter who claimed to speak with angels. If we met in the little hallway leading from the living room to the bedrooms, I had to make way for her; she brushed by me as though I were a phantasm, and would have knocked me to the ground if I hadn't flattened myself against the wall. She also stopped making meals for me, though she continued to cook for my sisters and father and Claudia. I was left to do my own cooking, and to eat – like a servant – after everyone else had left the table.

My father, who seemed unaware of my quitting the circus or of my mother's sudden and silent rage at me, said nothing. Since we'd abandoned the old school bus in Mexico and moved north some years earlier, life had become safer, simpler, and more predictable, and Papi's role had changed from driver and protector of our virtue to mere vague fatherly presence. The fact was that very little was required of him anymore, and this is death to any man's spirit. Men need to be needed, or they wither and fade. But Mami was in charge of things now. Papi accepted his new role without comment or complaint, and even though he was still physically present I had somehow come to miss him, as one might miss a person who's vanished mysteriously in the night. Later I would realize that the poor man, without friends or male children, must have been very lonely – it wasn't that he had stopped talking to us, but that we had stopped talking to him. In a home with seven women there was always one emotional episode ending and another just beginning, and since nothing Papi did or said made any difference, anyway, he must have learned to ignore us as a means of saving himself.

My sisters, all of them older than me and absorbed with their own problems, also paid me no attention – I'd left their world, the circus, of my own volition, after all, and if I chose to ruin my life by chasing empty dreams it was no affair of theirs. To them I was the one who'd refused to abandon her childhood beliefs, and therefore I was not to be trusted. Claudia was sympathetic but busy. As if by magic, the world as I knew it came screeching to a halt, and I found myself in limbo.

Instead of enduring my mother's stony silence, and because the routine of my life had been so disrupted, I started going for comfort every day to the trailer of Lucinda the Bearded Lady. Lucinda was a great friend of mine. She had been in the circus since she was a teenager herself. She came from a small town in the state of Ohio, the second eldest in a huge brood of farm children, and had lived a normal life until she hit puberty and it became obvious to everyone that she was not, in fact, going to be normal at all. In those days circuses traveled more than they do now, and freak shows were still a respected part of the attractions. Farmers and their families came from miles around to see hermaphrodites, two-headed calves bottled in formaldehyde, and living people with unborn twins fused into their own bodies. One day in the 1950s, Lucinda's mother marched her down a long dirt road to a field where some tents had been erected and a few dispirited and hung-over clowns were practicing their pratfalls.

'This is my daughter,' she'd said to the man in charge of things there. 'How much can she make with you?'

This was all the introduction that was necessary, for one had only to look at Lucinda to see that she belonged in the circus. She stood nervously looking down at the ground, warned beforehand not to speak. Her beard had already begun to grow with a fullness that would have been envied by boys her age if she'd been one of them, if she hadn't been such a freak of nature. Everyone had heard of women with beards, but nobody in that Ohio

158

town had ever seen one before, and her life had become a nightmare. Neighbors, unannounced, brought out-of-town guests to the house just to see her. Lucinda's mother would lead her out onto the porch while these strangers gaped and made rude comments about her. She ate her lunch alone in a corner of the schoolyard, and she hurried home as fast as she could at the end of each day to avoid the stones, both verbal and physical, which the children flung at her. Her mother had decided to give her to the circus as a last resort. Not, however, to save her daughter from torment, but because she realized she'd been showing her freakish child all this time for free.

The ringmaster had never seen a bearded lady before, either, but only because he had not yet been so lucky. He did not react with the mixed revulsion and fascination common to ordinary people. Instead he was overjoyed.

'I can give you twenty dollars for her now,' he said, 'and she'll make five dollars a week.'

'Will she go to school?'

The man shrugged. He pointed out a tall, lanky clown with a bulbous rubber nose and red frizzy hair. 'That fellow used to be a teacher,' he said. 'If she wants, she can ask him to help her keep up with her numbers and letters.'

'It's a deal,' said Lucinda's mother. She took two wrinkled ten-dollar bills from the ringmaster and tucked them into her dress. Then she handed Lucinda a small cardboard suitcase containing her few clothes and her shoes. 'Make the most of what God gave you,' she told her daughter, 'and come home when you're rich.'

'She sold me,' Lucinda told me later. 'My own mother flat out sold me to the circus! In this day and age! And I didn't even get a percentage!'

Needless to say, Lucinda never went home again. She spent the next quarter-century moving from place to place, heading down South in the winters and back up North where the money was when it was warm. The clown with the red frizzy hair had been more than just a former schoolteacher; he was a Shakespearean scholar and the scion of an old New England family, sent away in disgrace for falling in love with his cousin. Only a natural ability to juggle and to make people laugh had saved him from the gutter. It was he who taught Lucinda the poise and control he'd learned as an actor and which she put to good use in the sideshow, adding, she said, 'a touch of class' to what would otherwise have been a rather boring and depressing career. And it was because of the clown's training that she was eventually able to get a job with better and more established circuses, instead of that rickety, rusty old carnival, which consisted mostly of a troupe of aging pickup trucks, a few Airstream trailers, and a homesick Indian tiger with mange.

Lucinda befriended me soon after my family came to San Francisco, helping me to improve my English and telling me stories of what her life had been like in the old sideshow days. Once, she had been married to the Shortest Man in the World, but he'd died years ago – of what, I did not know. Dwarves often suffered serious health problems, but the Shortest Man in the World was not a dwarf. He was simply very, very small. I got the impression that as a logical result his life span was shorter, too. Although I never knew the Shortest Man, Lucinda spoke of him so often and with such reverence that I felt he was an old friend of mine.

'He may have been tiny in body,' she told me, 'but he was tall in spirit. One hundred percent man. And not *all* of him was so small, you know,' she added, leering at me so that I giggled and blushed.

I liked Lucinda because she treated me as an adult instead of a child, and I could speak with her about matters that my mother refused to discuss rationally. I liked her also because she believed in my angels. I had known instinctively that I could trust her with my secret; she, too, had guardians, she whispered to me, though she never told anyone about them. That made us closer, like accomplices. I didn't have to explain to her why I wanted to leave the circus – that it was not because my fall had scared me, but because it was time for me to move on. Lucinda understood that, too.

'Believe me,' she said, 'if I had any other talents, I'd use them. But all I'm good at is prancing

161

around in a bikini and letting people stare at my beard.'

'What if I'm not good enough to make it, though?' I said. 'What if all I'm good at is walking the wire?' After only a few days of freedom I was feeling desperate; my earlier bravado, which had made me bold enough to march into the ringmaster's office and quit on the spot, had already deserted me, and in its place were feelings of uncertainty and fear. I was afraid of what I'd created for myself.

But Lucinda was a bastion of fortitude, a rock of consolation. 'You are far too young to know yet what your limits are,' she said. 'You're doing the right thing. Later on, maybe, if it doesn't work out, you can come back to the wire. But for now, remember that you're *young*. You owe it to yourself to try everything you can think of. Within reason, that is. What do *they* say?'

I knew what 'they' meant – the angels.

'It was their idea,' I told her. 'They want me to be a singer.'

Lucinda raised her bushy eyebrows. 'A singer? Not a circus performer?'

'No.'

'Listen to them,' she said. 'Even if it doesn't make sense yet, listen to them. They always know. Mine do.'

Lucinda had a little electronic keyboard she let me play with. The keys were tiny, only as big as my little finger. She showed me where middle C was and how to play the C-major scale. When I became proficient at that we progressed to C minor, and then to D, E, and F major, minor, diminished, seventh. I was learning about music.

'Don't practice too much on this little thing,' Lucinda said. 'Or else when you finally get your hands on a regular one it will seem too big.'

Privately I wondered if this was not advice that Lucinda herself might have been given about her husband at one time. But as weeks went by she told me how she'd been completely in love with the Shortest Man in the World, whose name was Derek, and that his diminutive size hadn't mattered to her in the slightest. She never regretted marrying him, she said – not for a moment. From this simple declaration I learned a great deal. Even though it had been my mother's idea for my father to take a second wife, their relationship had suffered because of it; they treated each other more like business partners than lovers, and I could not remember the last time I'd seen them touch each other. Thus it was Lucinda, and not my parents, who first taught me what true romantic love is like, the kind of love so strong that it turns a blind eye to physical shortcomings.

'When you meet him,' Lucinda told me, 'when you finally meet the man who's right for you, you'll know right away. You won't be able to sleep because of it.'

'What do you mean?'

'Butterflies in the stomach,' she said.

163

We were sitting on her couch, and Lucinda was clutching her wedding photo to her chest – I'd already seen this picture many times before. It showed Lucinda looking radiant in her wedding gown, her beard plaited with white ribbons for the occasion. In one arm she holds a bouquet of flowers, and in the other she holds her husband, who despite his unbelievable stature was in every other respect normal looking. In the photo he seems to be smaller than the bouquet by at least one or two inches. He is wearing – what else? – a tiny, child-size tuxedo.

I thought Lucinda was beautiful. Strangely enough, her beard, always neatly trimmed and brushed, did little to detract from her femininity. She was shapely and petite, and onstage she gave off a sort of come-and-get-me sexiness that often confused the men in the audience. Most of the people who came to stare at her were men, and they didn't know whether to be attracted or disgusted. Lucinda didn't care either way. She had fine-tuned her abilities to the point where all eyes were drawn to her whenever she took the stage, and she knew she was good at what she did. I admired her for her confidence and loved her for the friendship she'd shown me; it was difficult to imagine any man having power over her, especially one as little as her deceased husband.

'You'll feel like you just ate a cake of soap,' she went on, still on the subject of love. 'You'll find yourself acting like an idiot around him, and you

164

won't even know why at first. Then, when you realize you're hooked, you'll hate him for making you feel that way. But *then* you'll see that you really don't hate him at all. Haven't you met anyone who makes you feel that way?'

'No. Not yet.'

'What about Baxter?'

I rolled my eyes. Baxter was the ringmaster's son, a gangly boy of sixteen with pimples who was all elbows and kneecaps. He stared at me constantly. Everyone knew he had a crush on me, but I couldn't stand him.

'Not Baxter,' I said. 'No way.'

'Not even a little?'

'Baxter is nice, but he doesn't give me butter-flies.'

'Has he asked you on a date?'

'Yes.'

'And what did you say?'

'I said no.'

'You don't have to be in love with someone to go on a date with them,' Lucinda said. 'Maybe you should try it once, just for fun.'

I didn't see the point in going anywhere with Baxter, but Lucinda made me realize something; when the time came and I met the right man, I would need to have some experience in dating so that I wouldn't make a complete fool of myself. I knew he would ask me out again. He was always asking me out. The next time he did, I resolved that I would say yes, just for the practice. And sure enough, just a few days after that conversation with Lucinda, Baxter asked me in his wheedling way if I would go to a movie with him. To the great surprise of both of us, I agreed.

The next day I made a great show of getting ready. I put on some makeup and spent half an hour or so fixing my hair. My mother chose that moment to start speaking to me again:

'And what do you think you're doing?' she asked.

I said nothing. I hummed to myself as I put on eyeliner. I was not in the habit of wearing makeup and putting it on was very tricky.

'I asked you a question,' she said. 'What are you doing?'

'I have a date,' I said.

'A . . . you have a *what?* Over my dead body.'

'Baxter asked me to go to a movie with him,' I said, 'and I said yes.'

'Without consulting your mother?'

'You mean my mother who hasn't spoken to me in three weeks?'

'Your mother who brought you into this world, even though it nearly killed her, and who has fed and clothed you ever since.'

'I am seventeen years old,' I said, 'and I worked for everything that has ever been given to me.'

'You think you're so old and experienced? Let me tell you something. You know nothing about what he really wants. You can't trust him. You know nothing about men in general. You're not going.'

'I will never know anything about men as long as you treat me like a child,' I said. 'And I *am* going. I'm old enough to make up my own mind about these things. I'm a woman now.'

My mother grabbed me by my shoulder, spun me around, and slapped me. It hurt, but I turned around again and kept putting on my makeup as though nothing had happened. This only served to infuriate her even more.

'What do you mean, you're a woman now?' she spat. 'You are nothing of the kind. You're still a child. You still talk to those little fairies at night, just like you did when you were a girl.'

In my family, we have never made any great fuss about modesty. With eight people crammed into the bus for all those years, one or another of us was constantly in some state of undress. I say this to explain what I did next. It was highly uncharacteristic of me, for I am not generally prone to such actions. But my mother had hurt me, and I wanted to shock her. So I turned around again, unbuttoned my blouse, and showed her my breasts.

'Do these look like they belong on a child?' I asked her calmly.

I did not then and do not now have much in the way of a bosom, but it had the effect I'd intended, anyway. It shut her up. She stood there with her mouth opening and closing, like a fish.

I buttoned up my blouse again and proceeded to finish my makeup. My father, who was sitting at the table sipping a cup of coffee, began to choke with laughter. Coffee went everywhere.

'She's got you there, *Mamacita*!' he said, snorting with glee.

My mother was speechless with rage. She turned on him and knocked his cup to the floor.

'How dare you mock me!' she screamed. 'How dare you let her behave like a common tramp!'

My father stopped laughing. He wiped his mouth with the back of his hand.

'Woman,' he said sternly, 'watch your tone. Remember that I am your husband.'

'And *you* remember that this is my house, that I am her mother, and I have been training these girls all their lives! I will not have this one whoring around like some kind of—'

'Oh Sainted Mother of God who lives in heaven,' my father said, 'she is *not* whoring around. She is going on a *date*. With a nice boy. I know Baxter. *You* know Baxter. He's shy and quiet, and he's not going to hurt her. Come to your senses.'

'And now you take the name of the Virgin in vain!' my mother screamed. 'What next? Disaster! Catastrophe! Earthquakes!'

My father rubbed his face with his hands. 'You're making me tired,' he said. 'Be silent, do you hear?'

'Damn you to hell, you worthless lump of flesh!' she screamed. 'And the same to you, you harlot!' she said to me. Then she stomped out of the house.

I sat down next to my father at the table. Only then did I allow my sadness to show. I buried my face in his shoulder and cried for a long time, and all the makeup I'd put on so carefully was ruined. Most of it ran onto his shirt, but Papi didn't mind. He put his arm around me and hugged me until I was done.

'Your Mami loves you as much as all her other girls,' he said. 'And you are the baby. She's protective, that's all. Never mind. She'll get over it.'

'I wish she could let me be who I am,' I wailed.

'She'll get over it,' he repeated. 'Just do what you need to do. We can't all live our lives the way other people plan them.'

Even in the throes of my misery that gave me pause to think. It seemed at that moment that Papi was not just talking about me, but also about himself. It had never occurred to me that Papi hadn't always wanted to be a circus father. Not once had I asked him what ambitions he might have had for himself in his youth. Certainly I would have been astonished if he'd told me his highest goal had always been to be head of a house of seven women, and all of them in the circus to boot. What sane man would want such a thing? The Virgin had guided my parents throughout their lives, or so they said. It was in her name that we performed. But my father was not as devoutly religious as my mother – I say this not to condemn him but merely to explain – and I found myself wondering if perhaps my father saw Our Lady as simply one more meddling woman who had altered the course of his life irrevocably, without bothering to check with him first. I am aware that this is sacrilege. I would never say such a thing aloud. But it is safe here in my head, and I know She forgives me.

'Papi,' I said. 'When you were my age, what did you want to do?'

'What did I want to *do*?'

'I mean, what was your plan? For your life?'

He smiled. 'When I was seventeen,' he said, 'I wanted to be an aviator.'

'An aviator?'

'A pilot.'

'Did you ever fly in a plane?'

'I have never left the ground in my life. Not even once, except the time I was being silly and was jumping on the trampoline and fell off and sprained my ankle. You remember that?'

'Yes.'

'That was the only time,' he said. 'And I had the feeling that God didn't want me to leave the ground at all, which was why he made me sprain my ankle. To remind me that my place is here on earth with my girls.'

'But why didn't you go to pilot school?'

'Because there was no money for such a thing.

And soon after that I met your mother, and we started having babies. Then there was *really* no money, and no time, either. I had to forget about it.'

'Do you still think about it?'

'Do I still . . . no. I haven't thought about it in many years.'

'Are you sorry?'

Papi rubbed my shoulders. 'If I had become a pilot, I would not be the father of five beautiful girls whom I love very much, even though they drive me crazy,' he said. 'Now listen. These are different times. We are in the United States now, and you can do anything you want here. I don't waste my time thinking about how things could have been for me. I'm just happy that you have your whole life ahead of you. If you want to quit the circus, I don't blame you.'

'Thank you, Papi.'

'But don't go flashing your tits at your mother anymore. It's not respectful.'

'You laughed!'

'I shouldn't have laughed. And you shouldn't have done it.'

'I'm sorry.'

'You have a right to be happy, *chamaca*,' he said. 'And she'll get over it. Don't worry.'

'Papi,' I said. 'I have to tell you something.'

'What is it, *niña*?'

'My angels, the ones nobody believes are real?'

'Yes?'

'They're real.'

Papi was silent. He looked at me thoughtfully.

'I have to leave soon, Papi. They're telling me to go.'

He still didn't say anything. He gave a slow nod.

'I don't know where I'm going yet,' I went on, 'and I don't know what I'm going to do when I get there. But I'm going, anyway.'

'Yes,' he said. 'I knew it would happen some-day.'

Outside, a car honked. I winced – it was Baxter. It wasn't that he didn't have the decency to come to the door, I knew. It was that he was too shy. I stood up and kissed my father on his head.

'I'll be back early,' I said. 'Good night, Papi.'

'Good night, *niña*,' he said. 'Have a good time.'

I remember almost nothing of that date, except that Baxter was utterly silent the entire time. I was quiet, too – I was busy thinking about where I was going to go, and when, and why. It took me four more years to figure out where: Santa Fe, the City of Holy Faith. It was not my idea to go there; I was just following the instructions of the eleven tiny beings in my head. But now, I see that they were right.

I wonder what my mother would think of the long-haired young man who sat in the back of the bar that night, listening intently to me sing. I wonder also what she would say if she knew I had let him walk me home, pretending to be scared of the other man who waited for me outside. I was not scared of him; I am not scared of anyone. I only wanted to find out who this person was who had the power to disrupt my singing without lifting a finger, whose presence caused such an outcry among the angels. Such a thing has never happened before. Perhaps it should be cause for alarm, but again I do not worry. I only hope I see him again soon.

CHAPTER 6

A LETTER FROM MILDRED

Dear Billy,

Well, you have been gone for some time now. I wish you would write more than you do, but I guess you must be pretty busy, what with your studies and all. I am very proud of you going off to college, and I know your grandfather would be, too, God rest his crotchety old soul.

There have been some changes around here since you left, which I thought you ought to know about. Even though you're not around, officially you're still the man of the house. You remember Abby, the girl who was in trouble who came to stay with me right before you left? Well, she had her baby all right, a healthy little girl. For a few days things seemed fine, but one day she was just plain gone, and she took the baby with her. I found out later that she left the little one at the hospital and disappeared. Nobody knows what happened to her.

Abby didn't owe me anything, but it hurt me that she would leave like that without saying good-bye. Maybe she thought I was going to try and stop her from doing whatever she needed to do. Her life is in a terrible mess, anyway, and she is the only one

174

who knows what must be done to fix it. But I got to thinking that there were probably more girls like Abby out there who didn't have anyone to turn to and who could use a chance to start over. And I was right. It turns out there are even more girls in trouble than anyone could have guessed, not just in Mannville, but in other towns nearby, too.

To make a long story short, I've opened up the house to anyone who needs a safe place to stay. Those books of your grandfather's I found in the basement have been giving me some interesting ideas, and I decided to put them into action. There are too many girls in this world who don't get a fair shake, and to be plain, I was one of them. I think every young lady ought to have a choice about what becomes of her future, and not leave it up to the men in her life to decide. You grew up without any mother or sisters, so you might not know about that – but then, there was your friend Annie who I heard so much about, and I know how you felt for her, so maybe you do understand, after all. The way I heard it, she didn't get much of a fair shake, either.

Anyway, I put the word out to some of the ladies who work at the hospital and in different shelters, and soon enough they came. I won't put down all the details here, mostly because I don't have time. But when you do come home again you're going to find the house a good bit more full of people than it was when you left. I don't think you would mind – they're all nice girls, and their babies are just as

175

darling as can be, of course. But fair is fair, and the fact is, this place is not mine to do with as I please. I hope nonetheless that all this is okay with you.

Do drop me a line please, Billy, and let me know what you think of it all, and let me know how you're doing in general. No doubt you're having great adventures and learning all kinds of new things out there. I want to hear all about it. How are your grades? I think of you every day and pray for you before I go to sleep at night. And everyone here is dying to meet you when you do come home.

Love,
Mildred

CHAPTER 7

DOING IT COLD

Mildred was right – I *was* learning a great deal. She might have been horrified, however, to discover exactly what my subject was: a continuing study of the operation of small arms.

My next shooting lesson with El Perrero took place up in the mountains, behind the campus of St James's. He didn't bother explaining why we were going there and not to the arroyo again, but I assumed it was for reasons of common sense. Someone must have complained to the police about our target shooting, and perhaps they'd come around asking questions. On the other hand, the sound of gunfire wasn't unusual in Santa Fe. I'd heard it as Consuelo and I lay in bed together, she sleeping, me staring at the ceiling and wondering how things had worked out so that the most exotic and beautiful woman in the world was also my lover.

Consuelo was already used to it; gunfire, I mean. 'Machismo,' she explained. 'That's what it's all about. Who can make the most noise. Who has the biggest gun.'

'You mean they're not shooting at each other?'

'Probably not,' she said, unconcerned. Nothing seemed to concern her, not even on those nights when it sounded like the opening of deer season back in Mannville. Santa Fe was a rough town, a lot rougher than the fake adobe facades and the countless tourist traps would have you believe. But if she said they weren't shooting at each other, then I believed her. In some ways, she said, Santa Fe was not so different than Mexico, where she'd grown up.

Machismo was a funny thing; I was only just starting to figure it out. There was a whole new set of rules to learn about how a man should comport himself in public. If you looked too long at a guy whom you didn't know, he'd bristle and stare back at you, waiting for you to flinch first: that was machismo. If you happened to be in traffic, he would gun his engine and peel out when the light changed, hoping you would race him: more machismo. It was also macho to fly into a jealous rage – I had already learned the hard way that it didn't do to gaze too appreciatively at a pretty woman if she was on another man's arm. This had earned me a couple of 'What the *fuck you* lookin' at?'s. In fact, it was macho in general to lose your temper, as if the farther south one went in the world, the hotter one's temperament became. And to top it off there was also the whole low-rider phenomenon, which I didn't follow at all.

A low rider was a decked-out car installed with

immensely powerful hydraulic shocks, which could be raised and lowered with the touch of a button. When the driver of a low-rider saw a couple of attractive girls walking along, he would jack his car up until it was a couple of feet above the ground. Sometimes he would even make it hop up and down by pressing the button fast. This was supposed to get their attention, and even though I thought it was one of the stupidest things I'd ever seen, to my surprise it often worked.

But Consuelo was not impressed by machismo, and maybe that was what she liked about me. One night before my next shooting lesson with El Perrero, I'd walked her home again, and this time she'd invited me in. We sat in her living room, listening to records by Mercedes Sosa, and she translated the lyrics into English for me while we drank wine. Outside it had begun to snow. Ordinarily, I hated snow – I couldn't ride in it, which meant I was condemned to traveling on foot until the streets had cleared. But that night she'd looked out the window and informed me that the weather was too bad for me to walk home. I might get sick, she said. I should stay over. I acquiesced. I didn't mention that I'd never been sick a day in my life.

We finished our wine and she made up a bed for me on the couch, but when she leaned over to give me a good-night peck on the cheek again, I turned my mouth to hers. It was a bold move, but she didn't hesitate – she let me kiss her good night that way, instead. Encouraged, I pulled her onto the couch with me and kissed her good night again and again.

'Look at me here with you,' she said, some time later. 'How did this happen?'

'I have no idea,' I said. 'Let's investigate.'

We investigated each other and things went further and further, until our clothes had disappeared and we were naked under the blanket. She was gawky, all elbows and kneecaps and as thin as a bundle of sticks, yet soft and giving at the same time – particularly at the very center of her, which when she directed me to touch her there was as hot and moist as a jungle flower. She liked giving orders. She wrapped her arms around my neck and whispered commands into my ear in a voice as soft as silk, her tongue flicking along my earlobe: touch here. Rub there. *Ay, Dios mio.*

'Maybe a real macho guy would have walked home in the snow,' I told her. 'Barefoot, even.'

'If you were macho, you wouldn't be here in the first place,' she said. 'I wouldn't have liked you. But I like who you are. You don't worry about stupid things.'

'Like what?'

'Like you don't ask if *this* is big enough to please me,' she said, grabbing my cock under the blanket. 'You don't worry about it. Now *that's* macho.'

'Do that again.'

'What?'

'That.'

She grabbed me again and squeezed. Pleasure flowed through me in both directions, all the way down to my toes and up to the top of my head. She straddled me and poised herself so I was just at the entrance to her. I could barely keep myself from thrusting, but she pressed down on my hips with her hands.

'I want to be in charge,' she said.

'Okay,' I said. 'Why?'

'Because I want to be the one doing it. Be still.'

'Why be still?'

'I have something to tell you,' she said. 'Don't move.'

I tried not to move. I could feel her trickling down along the length of my prick. It was maddening.

'Tell me,' I said.

'This,' she said. She lowered herself half an inch.

'Uh-huh.'

'Is.' She lowered herself a bit more.

'Oh, God.'

'My.'

She went down farther, and then I couldn't speak.

'First.' More.

'Time.'

She was halfway down now. She relaxed the pressure on my hips and sat up straight, whimpering as she sank the rest of the way onto me, letting her weight impale her completely. It seemed to take her forever to complete the journey. When she'd arrived she sat rigid on me, unmoving.

'Oh,' she said, her eyes shut.

'You all right?' I whispered.

'It hurts. A little.'

'Sorry.'

'It's okay,' she said. 'That's why I wanted to be up here. I knew it would.'

'I won't move,' I said, though it was killing me not to thrust.

'What do I do?' she asked.

'This is really your first time?'

'Beelee,' she said. 'I would not lie.'

'Just do whatever you feel like,' I said.

'Like this?' She moved her hips.

'Oh, yes,' I said. 'Just like that.'

'Or like this?'

'That's good, too,' I said.

I looked at her moving above me in the candle-light, and I thought that if she ever got any more beautiful than she was at that moment I was going to die of overappreciation. My entire body was singing in unison with hers, my muscles spasming, even my eyelids were trembling uncontrollably. She moved back and forth across me like a bow across a cello, and when her legs gave out and she couldn't take any more she laid down on my chest, with me still inside her.

'What do you think of me?' she whispered.

'I think you're just fine,' I said.

'You do not think I am easy?'

'No, no.'

'My mother would kill me.'

'Your mother's not here.'

She listened to my heartbeat for a while. I could feel the ring of her innermost muscles, contracting and relaxing around me as she worked them.

'Beelee. That night I first saw you? At the bar?'

'Yes?'

'I thought I knew you.'

'You did?'

'Yes.'

'Do you know me?'

She snuggled into my neck. 'Yes,' she said. 'I feel that I do. I feel I have always known you.'

'I feel I've always known you, too. Can I move now?'

'Yes. You can move.'

I put my hands on her hips and moved inside her, several short, sharp upward thrusts, each one eliciting a tiny gasp. She dug her nails into my shoulders until I yelped. I pulled out of her just before I came, and suddenly we were both soaked. The air under the blanket was filled with the rich smell of semen.

'My goodness,' she said. 'Such a lot of it!'

'You kept me waiting a long time,' I said. 'It was building up.'

'Is that how it works?'

'I don't know. I have no idea how it works. Should I get a towel?'

183

'No,' she said. 'I don't mind it. It came from you. Stay here.'

We fell asleep like that, our heartbeats merging into one continuous rhythm. When the night sky was beginning to lighten we were awakened by drunken giggling outside.

'Who's that?' I asked.

'Oh, no,' Consuelo said, stirring sleepily. 'My roommates.'

We could hear them fiddling with the doorknob outside, too drunk to fit the key in the lock. Someone began banging on the door. Consuelo pulled the blanket over our heads. I heard a woman call, 'Open up in there!'

'You want me to get it?' I asked.

'No. I do not want them to see you,' she whispered.

'Why not?'

'Because I hate them. They won't like to see you here.'

'Why not?'

'They don't like men.'

'Well, I don't care. I'm not scared of them.'

'I know you're not *scared*, idiot,' she said, biting me. 'I just don't want them to know about you. They're going to be rude.'

We lay still as the roommates figured out the lock. Then they stomped in, raucous and drunk, until they noticed the lump we made on the couch.

'Look,' one said. 'Who's that?'

'Consuelo?' said another.

'Go away,' said Consuelo.

'Ohh,' said one of them. 'She's got a *dick* under there.'

'I smell sex,' someone else said. 'Gross!'

'Consuelo got laid!'

'With a *guy*? Oh, honey. She's gone over to the dark side.'

'Go *away*,' Consuelo said. I was alarmed to see that she was near tears. The roommates lurched around giggling into their bedrooms, slamming the doors after them.

'What's the matter?' I asked.

She dried her cheeks on the blanket. 'I didn't want them to know,' she said. 'I *knew* they would try to ruin it for me.'

'They didn't ruin it,' I said.

'They tried to. They're always telling me I should try it with a woman.'

'So?'

'So maybe I'm scared of them, with their tattoos,' she said. 'You should hear the way they talk. I know what they're going to say later.'

'What are they going to say?'

'Bad things,' she said. 'Mean things.'

'We should have gone in your bedroom.'

'I share a room with Susie,' she said. 'Or I would have taken you in there.'

'Let's get out of here, then,' I suggested.

'Where can we go?'

I had a ready answer for that, of course. We put our clothes on and crept out of the house and into the snow, me carrying a bag with a few of her things in it. She cried a bit more as we walked. I put my arm around her shoulders and squeezed her tight.

'Does it still hurt?' I asked her.

She smiled weakly. 'No,' she said. 'I just cry for what they said.'

'Did it really bother you that much?'

'You don't understand,' she said. 'For a woman, you want everything to be perfect the first time. You don't want other people coming in after and making fun of you.'

We crunched along, me with my arm around her shoulders. The snow had stopped falling by now. It was early, with no cars or people about yet. This new blanket of white hid the town under its curves and hollows, softening the corners of everything and deadening all sound. I'd always enjoyed the feeling of being the first creature in the world to cross an unbroken snowfall, but now all I could think about was that the snow was like her, and it made me not want to step in it. But it was the fate of snow to get walked on, sooner or later. Things couldn't stay fresh and pure forever. I glanced at her trudging along, her tears already dry on her cheeks in the cold, still air.

'How old are you?' I asked.

'Twenty-one,' she said.

'Why did you wait so long?'

'You mean to make love?'

'Yes.'

'Because,' she said. She stopped, sniffling, and took my face in her hands. 'I was waiting.'

'For what?'

'For you.' She kissed me.

'You don't have to go back there,' I said.

'I don't want to,' she said. 'I am not happy there.'

That pretty much settled it. When we came to my house we got into bed and fell asleep again, and her moving in with me was as simple as that. She stayed all that day and the following night, and then the next night, and then the next, until it seemed perfectly ordinary that she should be there in my bed. I'd never lived with a woman before – not counting Mildred, of course – but I needed no convicing. I was already so in love with her it hurt; I was afraid of telling her just how *much* I loved her, for fear she would think I was exaggerating. And she seemed to take to being with me as naturally as if it had been planned that way all along. It was her belief that we'd been brought together by a higher power. When I asked *which* higher power, that was when I learned about her angels.

'You don't think I'm crazy, do you?' she asked.

'Not if you say they're real,' I said.

'Good. Because they are.'

'Will I see them?'

'I don't know. Perhaps.'

'When?'

She laughed at me. 'If you see them at all, it will

be at night,' she said. 'But nobody else has ever seen them.'

'Do *I* have angels?'

'Everyone has angels,' she said. 'Even bad people. It's just a question of knowing how to hear them.'

The snow had long melted, and we'd been together a week, when El Perrero came by.

'Yo, Jones,' he said. 'You still got that thing?'

I knew he meant the gun. 'Yeah, I got it,' I said.

'Get it and come on.'

I looked over my shoulder at my typewriter, with a sheet half in and half out of the roller. Consuelo was at the Cowgirl, cleaning the toilets. This, I'd learned, was how she supplemented her singing income. In fact, Franco had hired her first as a sort of maid, and only afterward did he give in to her request to sing one song for him, as a tryout – after which, of course, he had promptly made her the maid *and* the entertainment. Someday soon, she hoped, she would quit the toilet-cleaning part of it and devote herself fully to singing.

We had slipped into a comfortable domestic routine by then, as naturally as if we'd always been together: mornings were for work and afternoons for play. It had been a productive day so far and I was loath to stop. But El Perrero had already broken my concentration.

'Where we going now?' I asked, putting on my jacket. 'Not to the arroyo again.'

'No, no. Somewhere new,' he said impatiently. 'Come on. There's not much time.'

'What's the big rush?'

But he didn't answer; he just stood there, mirror eyed and waiting. To be honest, as much as he made me nervous, I'd enjoyed the feeling of the gun leaping in my hand. So I got the pistol from under the sink and stuffed it in my jacket, along with the box of ammunition.

'Are we driving?' I asked.

'I can't fucking drive, Jones,' he said.

'No license?'

'Pshh. What the fuck I care about a license? I got no car. We'll take your bike.'

'It's cold,' I said.

'Don't be a fucking pussy,' he said.

Another lesson in machismo: don't be a fucking pussy. So we got on my bike and rode shivering up to St James's, through the parking lot, and up a U.S. Forest Service fire trail until we were safely out of earshot of the buildings. There was still snow up in the mountains, but we parked when we hit the snow line and continued up the trail on foot, toward the crest of Atalaya. The world at this altitude was frozen and still, the air so clear you could see straight across the valley to Los Alamos as though it was right in front of your nose. The smell of piñon was sharp and fragrant, and the wind blew steadily. I was shivering, but I knew better than to complain. El Perrero had been silent the whole way, but now he said, 'Load 'er up.'

'Why'd we come all the way up here?' I asked him.

'To make it real,' he said. 'Today you're going to kill something.'

I stopped in my tracks.

'Kill *what*?' I asked.

'The first thing we see, Jones,' he said.

'Why do you keep calling me Jones?'

He just kept going, one foot in front of the other, Indian style. He was adept at walking silently through the trees.

'Perrero,' I said. 'Why do you keep calling me Jones?'

He stopped, turning, and looked at me.

'Why do I call you Jones, Jones?' he repeated.

'I just wondered,' I said. 'I mean, it's not my name.'

He stared at me for a while longer.

'Eight October, 1969. That's why,' he said finally.

Whoever this Jones person was that I looked like, it must have been someone he knew in the war. Suddenly my eagerness for more target practice was gone, and I was afraid of him again. El Perrero seemed too lucid to be having a flashback, but that didn't put me at ease – flashbacks were temporary, as far as I knew. Maybe he was permanently crazy.

'I don't want to kill anything,' I said. The weight

190

of the pistol tugged heavily on my arm. 'Besides, what if the first thing we see is a person?'

'Listen, Jones,' said El Perrero. 'One thing you got to understand. Nothing is as real as this right now. Got it?'

'No,' I said. 'I don't.'

He stared at me through those damn sunglasses. I had to fight the urge to rip them off.

'It's not about getting mad,' he said. 'Anybody can kill when they're mad. It's about doing it *cold*.'

'Cold?'

'Cold-*blooded*,' he said. 'I killed eight people, and I wasn't mad at any of them. I was a cold . . . blooded . . . killer. You understand?'

'Yes,' I said. I was seriously nervous now. He was still staring at me.

'You want to know what happened?' he asked.

'I guess,' I said.

'You guess. What the fuck does that mean? Do you or don't you?'

I knew I was going to find out one way or the other, so I said, 'Yes. I want to hear.'

'So listen,' he said. 'I'll tell you.'

He cleared his throat and thought a moment, as if trying to figure out the best way to explain it to someone like me. He seemed resigned. It was as if he believed somehow that I would never completely understand him, but that I had to be told, anyway. 'A sniper always goes out with a team, right?' he said. 'Sometimes it's just one

191

guy, sometimes it's a few. But you always had a spotter, even if you didn't have no one else. My spotter was Jones. One day we were out in the field, up in a couple of trees, waiting for a shot at the road. It was a busy road, *m'entiendes*? There was always somebody coming or going. So this Cong patrol comes along, but it was too big to take. Twelve men. We were just going to let them go by.' Perrero took a deep breath. 'Then they *left* the road,' he said. 'We weren't ready for that. I look at Jones, and he looks at me, and we're like, what the fuck do we do now? I motioned for him to be quiet. So those little fuckers sit down right underneath us and start eating. Then they finish eating and start taking a rest. We were just going to wait up there as long as it took, you know, as quiet as we could be, when my spotter slipped. He landed right on top of one of them.' El Perrero gave me another appraising look. 'You know what *that* means?' he asked.

'Jones was in trouble,' I said.

He nodded. 'They thought he was alone. They couldn't see me, because I hid myself too good. So they took their time with him.'

I gulped. 'Took their time?'

'It took him an hour to die,' he said. 'An hour is a very long time when you're being cut into little pieces. I could of got one or two of them but they would have got me for sure. So I just let them cut him up. He never called my name, not once. But he looked at me. He looked *right at me*.'

192

El Perrero fell silent, musing. He didn't seem upset. He seemed perfectly in control of himself. I began to wonder if he'd forgotten I was there. I hoped he'd gotten it out of his system now, whatever was bothering him, and that maybe we could go back to town now without having to kill anything. But then he said:

'A marine is not supposed to let that kind of thing happen to other marines, *m'entiendes*? A real marine would not have let that happen. So I decided right then and there that I was not a real marine. I should have opened fire on them, Jones. But I only had a single-shot weapon. There was no way I would have made it. I would have died. I should have died. I can still hear him screaming, right now.'

'I understand,' I said.

'Cowardice,' he said. 'That's what they call it. You know what the punishment for cowardice under fire is, Jones?'

I shook my head.

'Firing squad,' he said simply. He took a step closer. 'So what I want you to do, Jones, is point that pistol at me.'

'What?' I said, incredulous. 'No way!'

'Do it,' he said. He was about ten feet away from me. He took another step closer.

'I'm not pointing this gun at you,' I told him.

'What if I had a gun? Would you do it then?'

'No.'

'Yeah, you would. What if my gun was pointed

at you?' He came closer still, and I didn't say anything. 'Or what if I had that little girl you got living with you now down here on the ground, and I was carving her up nice and slow? Would you do it then? Huh?'

'But you don't,' I said, wondering how he knew about Consuelo. He must have been spying on us. He might even have been at the window, watching.

'What if I had your mama instead?'

'Fuck you,' I said. 'Don't talk about my mother.'

He was very close now. 'I'm gonna talk about her if I want to,' he said. 'And I might get her, someday,' he said. 'Or your little girl. When you're not home I might just sneak in there and do whatever I feel like doing to her. Then you're gonna wish you took me out now, when you had the chance. Right?'

Fine – I could point a gun. It was suddenly easy. I raised it and aimed at his head. He stopped.

'That's it,' he said. 'Now do it. Show me what you got.'

My hand was suddenly shaking so hard I couldn't hold the pistol straight. We stayed like that for what seemed a very long time, though it was probably only a few seconds. Then we were disturbed by a crashing in the trees.

We both looked at the same time. It was a rabbit, a long-legged jackrabbit. He was surprised at the sight of us, but he didn't run away. He just sat there with his nose twitched and his flanks heaving. His

194

fur was raggedy and patched, and he looked sick. I remembered reading in the paper that they were finding a lot of sick animals in the mountains these days – New Mexico was a bubonic plague area, and small animals got it first. I'd always thought the plague was a thing of the past, but cases of it cropped up once in a while here and there in the high desert, spread by animals such as this lone and defenseless rabbit.

Maybe this one had the plague virus, and maybe it didn't. I didn't care. I turned and fired without aiming, or maybe it was that my aim was so natural and unmarred by thought that there was no way I could miss. My first shot struck the rabbit square in the belly, knocking him backward and causing his legs to kick madly as he scrabbled for a hold on the empty air. The second shot hit him in his exposed chest, slightly above the first, and he stopped moving. His ribs heaved in and out once, then once more, and then he was still.

El Perrero looked from me to the rabbit and back to me. His lips curled into a smile. He was about to say something, but I didn't want to give him the chance. I turned and fled down the mountain, running as fast as I could without tripping head over heels. I heard him call something after me, but I didn't stop. I was still holding the gun, I realized, and I flung it far away into the trees. I kept running until I came to my bike. I kicked it into life and took off in a spray of mud.

I was shaking as I sped toward town. I hadn't

wanted to kill that rabbit. So why had I done it? I'd let him get to me, that's why. I'd let him force me into doing something I didn't want to do. I *liked* animals, even diseased ones. I had a sick feeling in the pit of my stomach now. *Screw that maniac*, I thought. *He can walk home. And if he ever knocks at my door again, I'll call the cops. Fucking psycho vet. Fucking murderer.*

CHAPTER 8

CONVERSATIONS WITH SKY

During the next several weeks I kept a very sharp eye out for El Perrero. I bought thick curtains for all the windows and kept them drawn tight, until Consuelo complained about living in perpetual darkness and forced me to leave them open. I froze at the slightest sound and took to sleeping lightly, lest he come for her in the night. Most of all, I never left her at home alone. I didn't know how much of his threat was serious and how much was calculated to provoke me, but I didn't want to find out the hard way that he'd meant it. I thought I understood now what he was after: absolution for the guilt he felt at letting the unfortunate Jones die. He was *still* a coward, I realized; by all rights he should have taken his own life a long time ago, as long as death was what he felt like he deserved. I wondered quite simply why he hadn't; but there was no figuring out the mental workings of a man that crazy.

I began to wish I hadn't thrown away the gun, because now I had no way to defend Consuelo. But after some time had passed the whole episode began to seem like a bad dream, and I wondered if it was really as serious as I remembered it. Gradually I relaxed, and though I still checked carefully before leaving the house to see if El Perrero was watching from his yard, I eased up on my constant vigilance.

I didn't tell Consuelo about any of this, of course. I didn't want to worry her because things were starting to go well for her. Her shows were getting more and more popular these days, drawing in a mixed group of people whom Ralph referred to as 'townies,' as well as the usual Jimmies who hung out there for the cheap beer. It was getting to where one had to arrive early just to get a good seat. The guy who'd brought the roses that first night didn't come around anymore, but there was no shortage of other dreamy-eyed losers to take his place. Despite my supposed lack of machismo, I couldn't help getting a little touchy at the way they mobbed her. There weren't exactly hundreds of them, but it usually took her half an hour to disentangle herself from them afterward. I didn't miss a single performance, and I always waited, still a little edgy, to walk her home afterward – under no conditions, I told her, was she ever to walk home alone.

'I don't understand this,' she said. 'I can take care of myself, *tu sabes*.'

'It's just to make me feel better,' I told her. 'I worry about you.' I'd stopped worrying about El Perrero in particular, but now I worried about everyone else, too; I began to see danger in every man in the bar.

'You are getting more macho every day,' she said, teasingly.

'It's not that,' I mumbled, embarrassed. 'Just promise me. Even if I'm not here, get someone else to walk you. Like Franco. Or Ralph.'

'Oh yes, Ralph,' she said. 'Everyone quakes in their shoes when they see *him*.'

'Promise,' I said. 'Please?'

'All right,' she said. 'You're being silly, but I promise.'

Our financial situation, meanwhile, hadn't improved much. Franco was delighted with the boom in business that resulted from Consuelo's growing reputation, but he was still only paying the band a flat rate: fifty dollars per member per show, which at three shows a week came to a hundred and fifty bucks for each. When Consuelo complained, he said he wasn't getting rich off selling cheap beer; he wanted to start charging at the door, but he was afraid it would drive away business.

'Franco *is* a cheapskate,' Sophia told me one night. 'I've been working here for two years, and I've never gotten a raise.'

'Why don't you get another job?' I asked her.

'What else can I do?' she said. 'If I wasn't waiting tables here, I'd just be doing it somewhere else.'

'You ever think about going to college?'

'Sure, I think about it,' she said. 'I *dream* about

it. You happen to have several thousand extra dollars handy?'

'There's scholarships,' I said. 'There's financial aid. You could do a lot better than this if you had a degree.'

'Listen to the dropout extol the virtues of higher education!' said Ralph, who was sitting with me.

'Blow it out your hole,' I told him.

'Maybe someday,' said Sophia wistfully. 'I'd still have to take out loans, though.'

'Marry me, Sophia,' said Ralph, leering. 'You'll never have to worry about money again. My daddy is a dentist.'

'You're gonna get cut off, Ralph,' she threatened. But she smiled when she said it, a very little bit; lately I'd detected a slight improvement in her overall mood. I began pulling the same trick Mildred had used on me, slipping her brochures from the University of New Mexico whenever she had a spare moment. I read up on the process of applying for loans and explained it to her carefully. It wasn't all that daunting, I told her. She could do it, if she really wanted to.

'What do *you* care if I ever get out of here?' she said one day, when we were alone for a moment. Ralph hadn't shown up yet, and Consuelo was hiding behind the curtain at the back of the stage, where she was sipping warm lemon water. 'Come to think of it, why are you so nice to me?'

'Is it so unusual that someone would want to do something for you?' I asked.

She looked at me solemnly, her eyes wide. 'Yes, it is,' she said. 'It's a first. Usually guys are only nice when they want a certain something from you. But *you* don't want anything from me. You have someone.'

'Nothing improper,' I assured her, and because I still didn't want to tell her who I was, I changed the subject. 'Don't you have a boyfriend or anything?'

'No.'

'You want one? What about Ralph?'

'Oh, *Jesus*,' she said. 'He's too *short*.'

'Yeah, but he's got a motorcycle now. Isn't that kind of sexy?'

'His *nose* is too big,' she said. 'It takes more than a bike.'

'You're very picky.'

'Listen, Billy. If you were a cocktail waitress, you'd tend to be kind of critical of men in general. No offense.'

'On behalf of men everywhere, we are all deeply offended.'

'I'm serious,' she said. 'I'm starting to think nice guys don't go to bars.'

'*I* go to bars,' I said.

'You go to *this* bar. You don't go to other ones. Do you?'

'No. Just this one.'

'Besides, you're taken.'

'Yeah, but Ralph's not.'

She rolled her eyes. 'No Ralph,' she said. 'No

way. No *nobody*. Sophia is alone because Sophia likes it that way.'

Ralph came in at that moment, carrying his helmet under his arm. His new bike was a Suzuki, with a 550-cc engine. I'd helped him pick it out. Even before he knew how to ride it, it sent him into seventh heaven. He polished it lovingly – he *crooned* to it as though it were a child, and he made me repeat the names of every single part of it until he knew them too. But before he could launch himself onto the highways of the world I'd had to teach him how to ride a bicycle, because to my disbelief he told me he'd never been allowed to have one.

'Why the hell not?' I asked.

'Too dangerous,' he said. 'People die on bicycles.'

'People die in bathtubs,' I said. 'They die in bed, even.'

'You're preaching to the choir, Mann,' he said. 'It was my mother's doing.'

'What kind of mother doesn't even let her son have a bicycle?'

'A paranoid personality with a strong need for control,' he said. 'That's what the shrinks tell her, every time. But she always quits going to them as soon as they figure her out.'

I made Ralph borrow a bike from the Student Activities Office, and I drilled him until he could ride no-handed without falling. He was uncoordinated at first, and soon he was sporting the scabbed elbows more typical of seven-year-olds, but he mastered it within a few days, and then he practiced putting around campus on the Suzuki. When he had taken his first obligatory spill – you never really know how *not* to fall until you do it once, Grandpa always told me – but only a very minor one, I graduated him to the back roads near the college and then to traffic. After a few weeks of that he went and took the test for his license, passing it on the first try; he looked as proud as if he'd just been awarded an honorary doctorate. Then he was ready for two-lane highways, which meant we could go on our next mission: White Sands National Monument.

There was no mystery about how White Sands got its name. It was a vast area of pure white gypsum, partly used as a secret missile-testing range and partly open to the public for camping. The three of us, Ralph, Consuelo, and I, planned our trip so that it would coincide with the full moon. We rode down together, bundled against the cold, and spent the day hiking around, listening to the jets flying overhead, and the occasional shudder of the earth as test bombs were set off underground – 'a very American experience,' as Consuelo described it.

'What do you mean by that?' I asked.

'Only Americans would go camping on a military base,' she said. 'Think about it! It's – *como se dice*? It's weird.'

'It's *cool*!' said Ralph, watching a jet streak across the horizon. 'God bless America!' he said. 'Loudest country on earth!'

And I thought of my father, who'd flown an F-4 in the war – there was a picture of him in his uniform hanging on a wall back in Mannville, with an American flag stretching out behind him. I wondered if he would be blessing America now, if he was still alive – I wondered what kind of person he'd have been when he came home, if he would have ended up like El Perrero, bitter and guilty, or whether he would have had the same broad grin I knew from photographs, that he'd had on his face when he left.

That night we lay huddled in a great depression in the sand, wrapped in blankets. The moon hung over us and reflected off the dunes until the night was nearly as bright as daylight. Consuelo sang softly as Ralph and I fell asleep on either side of her. It was the first time she'd ever been camping, she said; and except for Ralph's farting and the odd explosion, it was one of the best things she'd ever done. So now we were three, and despite it being really far too cold to go riding anywhere, we went everywhere we could think of: El Paso, Juarez, the Gila wilderness, Carlsbad Caverns; always south, where the warmth was.

I went on trips of my own, too. During the first few months of the new year, I went to see my mother as many times as I could, without arousing undue suspicion. I tried to keep my visits spaced out, to make them seem casual and unintended.

I was just in the neighborhood, I'd say. *Just down to see that knee doctor again, thought I would bring you a couple things.* Sky was grateful for my visits, and though she still had no idea who I was, she accepted my sudden presence in her life with the childlike unquestioning of someone who was beyond caring. Her eyes were listless and dull, her expression blank, as though she'd already made up her mind to surrender her hold on life. Generally, she lay on the couch with her eyes closed. I sensed that time was running short, so I did my best to get her talking.

'Why do you want to know so much about me?' she asked.

'I'm a writer. I like to know about everyone,' I said. 'Plus, I liked your stories about the waterfront. I was hoping you'd tell me more.'

'I've never done anything important,' she told me. 'You should spend your time talking to more interesting people.'

'Believe me,' I said 'You're plenty interesting as far as I'm concerned.'

'I'm glad *someone* is here to talk to me,' she said. 'It gets lonely, being sick.'

I made her tea, and gradually she started to talk again. She'd been born in San Francisco, she told me, when her parents were already in their forties; they'd died when she was twenty-one – her father of a heart attack, and her mother of the same disease that was killing her now: ovarian cancer. 'Must be genetic,' she said. Both her parents had

205

been professors of mathematics at Berkeley. Her mother had written a book on complex variables: 'Don't ask me what *that* is,' said Sky, 'because I never figured it out.' But her father's work she understood much better; he'd been instrumental in making the calculations that ensured that the Apollo spacecraft would land on the moon, where and when it was supposed to, and then make its way safely home again. My grandparents, as it turned out, were mathematical geniuses.

'You've probably never heard of the McMeel Derivative,' she said.

'No,' I said. 'What's that?'

'It's some kind of equation that helps you figure out when to launch a rocket ship. They have to do it at just the right time, when everything is lined up a certain way, or they miss their chance. That's all I know about it. It was my father's greatest accomplishment in life. If it hadn't been for him, we might never have made it to the moon at all.'

'Did you get along with your parents?' I asked.

'I suppose,' she said, 'but it wasn't easy. They communicated in numbers, even to each other. I never had a head for that kind of stuff. I was more of a touchy-feely kind of person. I think they were frustrated that I didn't like math as much as they did. Really, they couldn't under-stand why *everyone* wasn't infatuated with numbers. Everything in the world could be described in numbers just as easily as in words, they told me. There was an equation for everything, even the little things about life that you would think didn't have anything to do with math. Like falling down the stairs.'

'How would you do that?' I asked.

She had just finished a course of chemotherapy, which made her feel sick, but her voice regained a touch of animation as she talked about my genius grandparents.

'Well, you have gravity, first of all,' she said. 'And the weight of the person, and how tall they are, and how far they have to fall. And the force of the impact they make when they hit the ground. All these things have values, and there's an equation to go along with every one of them, and then you can combine those equations into one formula somehow. Don't ask me how – I never learned any of that stuff. But my father claimed it could be done. He said there was no story in the world that couldn't be expressed mathematically.'

'It seems kind of pointless,' I said.

'That's exactly what I used to think, but never say out loud – not around *my* parents,' she told me. 'To me, numbers were cold. They didn't mean anything. Numbers don't arouse emotions in people. They don't paint pictures, like words do.'

But her parents were otherwise unconventional people, she said. They chose to live in the houseboats of Sausalito because they liked the gentle motion of the water, the steady flux of the tides

– it was like living on a waterbed, and it helped them think. And despite their seemingly staid positions in society, and their dry habit of immersing themselves for hours on end in textbooks, they were completely swept up in the revolutionary fervor of those times.

'There was no place on Earth like the waterfront in Sausalito in those days,' she said. 'And there never will be again. It was the best place to grow up there was.'

'What was so great about it?'

'It was a lawless society – but lawless in a *good* way,' she said. 'We weren't under the jurisdiction of the city, but we weren't covered by marine laws, either. It was all private property, really. So the cops couldn't touch us. It was owned by one man – Don Arques. That whole area used to be part of his shipyards during the war, and afterward he let anyone who wanted to come live there. He liked having us there.

'I was born in the city, but we moved to the waterfront when I was six or seven. We were one of the first. Everyone had a little dinghy, and we used to row from boat to boat, visiting whoever we felt like. There were fascinating people living there then. Artists, and poets, and painters, and later all kinds of hippies.'

Her father had volunteered for government experiments with LSD years before anyone else knew about it – the government had unintentionally started the whole LSD craze, in fact, which was something everybody these days seemed to have forgotten.

'It was part of their whole mind control thing,' she said.

'*Mind control?*'

'They wanted to see if it made you telepathic. They took volunteers in the late fifties and dosed them to the gills. Have you ever taken acid?'

'No,' I said.

'The weird thing is, it works.'

'It does?'

'Well, I don't know if it exactly makes you *telepathic*,' she said. 'But it makes it really easy to read people.'

'How?'

'I don't know,' she said. 'It just does. You might be tripping with a bunch of people, and someone gets an idea, and within seconds everyone has the same idea, without anyone ever saying anything about it. Or you start humming a song, and every-one says, Wow! I just had that song in my head!'

'That happens anyway, though,' I said.

'I know. But something about acid makes it even more so. My father believed people were naturally able to read other people's minds.'

'But what about this mind-control business?'

'Oh, that. Well, that was just what my father told me. He was always telling me strange things about the government. Either he knew a lot more than he let on, or he liked making up stories to scare me. But he wasn't interested in mind control himself. He was more interested in finding out what sorts of equations he could think up while he was tripping.'

'Did he come up with any good ones?' I asked.

'Certainly,' she said. 'He came up with the McMeel Derivative.'

She managed a wan smile. In better times, I thought, it must have been a great smile.

'You want to know a government secret?' she whispered.

'Okay.'

'If it wasn't for LSD,' she said, 'America would never have made it to the moon.'

There were more stories: she had almost as many stories as Grandpa, once I got her going. Her parents, Helen and Richard – whom everyone called Hellion and Rocko – had encouraged her to see as much of the world as she could. In those days you could still hitch-hike around the country because, as she explained it to me, people then weren't as suspicious of everyone as they are now. When she was sixteen she'd taken off for the first time, heading up to Humboldt County for a week or so. She didn't get in trouble for this with her parents, who in fact had greeted her upon her return as though she'd just stepped out for a breath of fresh air. They were interested in her experiences, and in the people she'd met, but, as she said, 'They understood that my experiences were my own, and they didn't grill me like most parents would. They wanted me to be a whole person, and they knew the only way to do that was let me go when I wanted.'

'What about school?' I asked.

'I went sometimes,' she said, 'when it suited me. I did a lot of reading on my own. But my parents taught me as much math as I needed, and there were others on the waterfront to teach me the other subjects. I used to go listen to people talk – just sit in a corner and listen to them rap on and on, about art or music or society or whatever. I picked up a lot from listening. And from traveling. The thing is, Billy, you never know who you're going to run into when you uprot yourself for a while. You meet people who change your life forever. You have a conversation with someone, and some little thing they say sticks in your mind for months afterward, until it turns into something all its own. You have to let people influence you. We're a tribal kind of creature. We learn from stories. And from quests. You have to go on lots of quests.'

'Quests for what?'

She waved one thin hand in the air. 'It doesn't matter,' she said. 'You just go on them. You find out what you were looking for when you get there.'

'Where else did you go?'

'Everywhere,' she said. 'All over the U.S., into Canada, Mexico – anywhere you could hitch to. Once Rocko sent me out for some groceries and I met up with a couple of guys in a bus who were going to San Diego. We hung out there for a couple of days and then we just kept on going. A month later we were in Guatemala. I was gone for nine weeks altogether. When I walked in the door again Hellion said, "Did you have a nice time, dear?"' And Rocko said, 'You forgot to get the milk, didn't you?' I think I was eighteen or nineteen.'

'What did you do for money, though?' I asked.

'You didn't worry about something like that,' she said. 'If people let a lack of money keep them from living, they might as well just drop dead. You can't let bullshit values like that determine the course of your life. You need money, you work for it. Or you trade something. Or you meet people who take you in for the night and give you something to eat. You'll always get by *somehow*.'

'I don't know why you don't just tell her who you are,' said Ralph.

We were sitting at the table in my kitchen – *our* kitchen now, mine and Consuelo's. She stood at the counter, working a bowl of dough. I could see the cords in her neck stand out as she kneaded. In the months she'd been living with me I'd gained nine pounds. She'd cautioned me not to get used to it, but I ate with such enthusiasm that she kept trying to outdo herself. She cooked things I'd never heard of: *posole, tamales, enchiladas, menudo, rellenos, quesadillas*. I could neither identify nor

212

pronounce most of what I ate, but I didn't care. It was all delicious. Ralph thought so, too. He'd become a frequent dinner guest, because according to him Consuelo's cooking beat the cafeteria on campus by a mile.

'I don't know why he doesn't tell her, either,' Consuelo told Ralph now.

'It's hard to explain,' I said.

'But you spent all this time looking for her,' Ralph said. 'It doesn't make any sense.'

Consuelo said nothing, but in the way her shoulders tensed I could see she agreed with him. By now she knew the whole story, and it was her opinion that I was going about everything backward. I didn't even try to make her see things my way; there was no point. She disagreed with everything I said. A son had a duty to his mother, she told me. And what about a mother's duty to her son? I countered. She was the one who gave me up, not the other way around. Could I not be forgiven for being cautious?

'I can't explain it,' I said again. 'I don't know why I can't tell her. The words just stick in my throat.'

But there was more to it. I had come West to find the tattered pieces of my family, and found them instead where I least expected to: right here in my own kitchen. That was the real reason I didn't identify myself to my mother. Somehow, it had ceased to matter quite as much as it used to. I couldn't explain it to them because I didn't

213

understand it myself. I needed something new now, and Consuelo was it. Suddenly I didn't feel like looking for anything anymore. For the first time in my life, I had it all in front of me.

Later, after dinner was eaten and Ralph had gone home, we lay in bed.

'What do you think about?' she asked.

'Nothing. What are *you* thinking about?'

'I am thinking about *los angeles*,' she said.

I knew enough Spanish by now to know that *los angeles* meant 'the angels.' 'Are they talking to you again?' I asked her.

But she said, 'Not the *angels*. The *city*.'

'Why are you thinking about Los Angeles?'

She snuggled under my arm. 'If I had to move there, would you come?' she asked.

'Why would you want to move there?'

'For my singing,' she said drowsily. 'It's just an idea. Nothing more. Never mind.'

'Are you seriously thinking about moving there?' I asked. 'I was just getting comfortable. I like it here.'

But she was already asleep.

On my next visit, Sky's voice had been reduced to a croak, a further sign of her dwindling state. In the time I'd known her, her skin had gone from yellow to translucent and was now bordering on transparent. Soon, I imagined, I'd be able to see her weakened organs pulsing feebly inside her, see the cancerous mass on her ovaries that had for years been sitting as benignly as a house cat and then without warning turned ravenous, all-consuming, a jungle lion. I was hit with a memory of the aquarium in my second-grade classroom, the little fish with their glass bodies darting here and there, living their tiny piscine lives under the watchful gaze of twenty eight-year-olds. My mother had become one of these fish. Everything about her was visible.

'I can't take much more of this,' she said. 'I can't even take care of myself. If it wasn't for you . . .'

She didn't finish.

'I, uh – I know you and Sophia have had some problems,' I said. 'But you know, she's sorry about everything. She wishes none of it had ever happened.'

Sky nodded. Her lower lip began to tremble. 'It's my fault. I was so irresponsible,' she said. Her croak weakened to a whisper. 'How could I have done that to them?'

I perked up.

'To who?' I asked. 'Who do you mean?'

She gasped for air. Even crying wore her out.

'My kids,' she said.

'You . . . you have more than one?'

She began to choke on her own saliva. I got up and held a glass of water to her lips. She managed a tiny sip. I could smell her breath – fetid, rotten, as though cancer had an odor. I sat down again.

'I was not the best mother in the world,' she said.

215

'Everyone always thought I was so wonderful when I was young. Strong, and carefree, and spirited. But I wasn't. I wasn't what I acted like. I got scared of things, too, sometimes. I made mistakes.'

I felt a terrible pain in my hands suddenly, and I looked down to see that I was gripping the arms of my chair so hard my nails were digging into the wood. I tried to relax them, but I had the feeling I was no longer in control of myself.

'Like what?' I said.

'I can't talk about this,' she said, almost as though I wasn't there. 'But what's the point of keeping secrets now? I had another baby,' she said, as though talking to herself. 'Once I had a son.'

Her eyelids were fluttering like they always did when the pain medication began to overwhelm her. Unmooring, she called it – as though the ropes that kept her tethered to Earth had been cast loose. She felt herself floating out of her body and up through the roof, and sometimes, she told me, it was an effort to come back. It hurt.

'What happened to him?' I asked. Her eyes were shut, but she was still awake.

'I gave him up,' she said. 'Right after he was born. I couldn't take care of him.'

'Why not?'

'I was always broke,' she said. 'And his father was dead. Eddie was a pilot in Vietnam. I barely knew the guy. I left the baby with his father – Eddie's dad, I mean. They had a lot of money, so I figured he'd be better off there. And a big extended family, like Eddie told me about. I thought . . .' Her lip trembled again. I moved to sit on the coffee table and took her hand. She squeezed, but she had no more strength in her grip than I did on the morning she was talking about now, no more strength in her than a baby.

'Go on,' I said, trying not to squeeze back too hard, not to hurt her fragile bones. *Eddie didn't tell her they were all gone*, I thought. *He didn't tell her we lost all the money, either. She thought we were still at full strength. That was why she left me there.*

'I hope you don't mind me telling you this,' she said. 'I never talk about it with anyone. It's been sitting on me ever since. God, I felt like such an evil person. If I was religious I would want to confess this to a priest. It's the only thing I've done that really seems like a sin.'

'You did the best you could,' I said. I did not add, *probably*.

'I wanted to go back for him. I wanted to *so much*. Just to watch him from a distance, even, to see what kind of kid he turned out to be. But I didn't think I could see him and not say anything. And I didn't think it would be fair to confuse him. His grandfather would probably think I was terrible, and then I started getting sick on top of everything . . .'

'You've been sick that long?' I asked, shocked.

She nodded. 'On and off, pretty much since Sophia was born. For a while I didn't know what it was. I just ignored it. I found out I had cancer almost nine years ago. It's been in remission, but it's . . . it's awake now, I guess. Sometimes I think it's punishment.'

'Punishment for leaving the baby?'

'No,' she said. 'Not just that.'

She fell silent for a while. I didn't want her to fall asleep then. I considered poking her in the ribs – anything to keep her talking.

'You awake?' I said.

She nodded, eyes still shut. 'Uh-huh.'

'What happened next?'

'I went back to where Eddie was from, to find a friend of his,' she said. 'Freddy Simpson. Eddie told me about him. He said if there were any problems . . . if I got pregnant, I mean . . . and if anything happened to him over there, I should go look up Freddy. He would help me. They were best friends, him and Eddie. Their fathers hated each other but they were friends, anyway.'

'Why did he think something was going to happen?'

'Well,' she said, 'we weren't exactly *careful*.'

'Did you go look for Freddy?'

'Yeah. I did.'

I waited, breathless.

'I found his house, but Freddy . . . he was hurt. In the war. His father wouldn't let me see him. He thought I was one of Freddy's old girlfriends, coming around to make trouble. He said he couldn't see anybody. He wouldn't even say why.'

'But what was it you felt like you were being punished for?' I asked her. 'Giving him up?'

'There was that,' she said. 'But there was also the note.'

I knew what note she was talking about, too. I could see it clearly if I closed my eyes. I reread it about thirty thousand times a year, puzzling over it. It was the note she left on the basket with me, the note which contained what I'd always thought of as my real name: not William Amos Mann IV, but *Eddie's Bastard*.

But I said, 'What note?'

'I said something not very nice in it,' she said. Tears came again, leaking sideways out from under her eyelids and trailing her cheeks. I wiped them away with a tissue. 'I don't know why I said it. I was angry, I was scared, I was trying to make myself get mad at the baby so I would have the courage to give him up. You know how when you can't have something you want, you make it look like it's not worth wanting . . .'

'Yeah,' I say. *But that's something you do with things. Not people. Not babies.*

'He was so darling. He had these big blue eyes, just like his father's. Little lips like a cupid's bow, his tiny ears, his fingernails. He used to smile a lot. He was a happy kid.'

I was?

'I called him a bastard,' she said. 'God damn it. I called him that. Billy,' she says. 'If ever there was one thing I've done I wished I could take back, it's that. That word.'

Her bony chest was heaving. I put a hand on her

219

forehead. Her eyes were still shut against the light leaking in from around the curtains.

'Why are you so good to me?' she whispered.

I said nothing. She took my hand again. Her voice was barely audible. 'If he's got half as much as you . . .,' she whispered.

But she never finished that thought. Suddenly, she was asleep again.

I thought back once more to my visit to Henry Hutchins in Buffalo. Hutchins had told me there'd been something electric about that moment when my parents first met, and also something electric about Sky herself. She had poise, he said, and grace, and beauty – every guy in the bar had had his eyes on her that night, but she'd only had eyes for Eddie.

In the relic of the woman sleeping before me on the couch I could almost see what he was talking about. Her smile was faded, and her eyes had lost a great deal of their spark, but there was still something there worth noticing, something within her that called attention to itself.

I took advantage of her slumber to leaf through a few old photo albums I found in the living room, hoping to see more of that spark. I wanted some image of her restored to life. There were her parents – both of them smiling, with snapping eyes and rosy cheeks. Hellion had been taller than Rocko by a good two inches. In one memorable photo, they stood on the prow of their houseboat, both of them in traditional academic clothing: he in a jacket and tie, with a pipe in his mouth, and she in a long dress, with spectacles perched on the end of her nose. My mother stood in front of them, aged perhaps four or five, completely naked and with finger paint smeared all over her body.

There were others: my mother in early girlhood, as a teenager, as a young woman. The settings began to change as time progressed. First she was in the desert; then in some unknown city; then with mountains in the background; then in the embraces of various men, all of them bearded, beaded, longhaired. Then I found a blurry photo with a familiar background. After studying it I realized I was looking at the first picture of my parents together I'd ever seen.

The background was Lake Erie. I even recognized the broken concrete pier that jutted out behind them into the water. It was part of an abandoned boathouse, unknown to most people because you had to walk through half a mile or so of woods to reach that part of the shore – only a small boy could possibly be interested in braving the scratches and sprains and mosquito bites and soaked shoes that were necessary to get there, but somehow Eddie had persuaded her to go out there with him. It had been one of my favorite haunts as a child; I'd always thought I was the only person who knew about it. But I could see here that my father knew about it, too.

He was holding out the camera and pointing it back at them, so their faces were too bright and the lake too dark. But they had pressed their cheeks close together and were both grinning madly, ear to ear. With a sidelong glance at Sky, asleep on the couch, I lifted the plastic sheet of the album and slipped the picture into my pocket.

'You haven't forgiven her yet,' said Consuelo.

'I'm not mad at her, if that's what you mean.'

'Are you sure of that?'

'Sure, I'm sure.'

'Then why haven't you told her you forgive her?'

'It's not that easy,' I said.

'Why not? What's so hard about it?'

'You wouldn't understand,' I told her. 'Your mother didn't give *you* up.'

'You have to stop feeling sorry for yourself,' she said. 'If you're going to forgive her, then forgive her. If you just going to keep torturing yourself, then stop going down there. You starting to drive me *loca*.'

'I will when I'm ready,' I said.

'Fine,' she said. 'Can I ask you something else?'

'What?'

'Have you thought more about moving to Los Angeles?'

'No,' I said. 'I thought you said it was only an idea.'

'Well, maybe it's more than an idea. Can you think about it?'

'I can think about it,' I said. 'It would make it a lot easier if you'd tell me why, though.'

'Maybe something is going to happen that will take me out there,' she said.

'Like what?'

'Something big,' she said. 'Something important.'

'Like what?' I repeated.

But Consuelo shook her head. 'Not yet,' she said. 'Just think. Imagine yourself standing in the ocean, and palm trees all around. Seafood. Big waves. Wouldn't that be nice?'

It sounded nice, sort of, though I had never seen the ocean before. At best I could imagine it only as a larger version of Lake Erie, which was the biggest body of water I'd ever seen. It was hard to think of anything bigger. And I was only half listening to Consuelo, anyway. I had other things on my mind, and I was too busy thinking about them to waste time imagining myself in the ocean. I was thinking about my mother.

The second weekend in March I rode down to visit Sky again. We had a system by then; the key was kept in the mailbox, and after knocking I simply let myself in. She would know it was either me or Sophia. But this time, the house was empty. She was not on the couch, not in her bedroom, not in the bathroom. I even checked the closets, on the slim chance that somehow she'd gotten trapped in one of them. But there was nobody home.

I went outside again and sat on the porch to think. She couldn't have gone anywhere by herself. She had no car, and even if she did she was far too sick to drive it. Dread overwhelmed me. I was afraid I'd waited too long; maybe I was too late.

An old woman had been watching me from across the street. She came out now into her yard, clutching her pink chenille bathrobe to her throat.

'You looking for the girl who lives there?' she called.

'Yes,' I said. 'Do you know where she is?'

'They took her back in to the hospital this morning,' she said. 'The one at the university.'

'What time?' I asked her.

'Early,' she said. 'The lights woke me up.'

'What lights?'

'From the ambulance. You her son?'

The question caught me off guard.

'I . . . yeah,' I said. 'I am.'

'You're a good boy, to come see her so much,' she said. 'I watch out my window all the time. It's nice you take care of her.'

She went back in the house, her slippers rustling over the gravel of her yard.

I rode in the elevator with a kid in a wheelchair, both his legs encased in plaster. The door dinged open and let me out on the third floor.

Nurses padded by me in their thick white shoes. I checked the numbers on the doors until I found the right one.

She was unconscious, or maybe just asleep. The shades were drawn, and the room was as murky as the bottom of a pond. I pulled one blind to the side a bit so I could see. Light flooded the room and illuminated her face, her veined eyelids. She didn't even blink. I sat down next to her.

'Sky? It's Billy. You awake?' I said.

There was no answer.

'If you can hear me, wiggle your left finger.'

I watched her hand closely. One finger twitched, but I was almost certain it was nothing more than a dream movement, an electrical impulse – the motion was too jerky to be intentional. She wasn't even there. I decided to tell her, anyway.

'I'm him,' I said. 'I'm that baby you gave up. It's me.'

Her only response was the same light, fitful breathing.

I sat there all through the morning and into the afternoon; she never stirred, never made a sound. After a while I went out again and rode back up to Santa Fe.

CHAPTER 9

GETTING WARM

Consuelo was in a high state of excitement when I walked in the door. Whenever she was in a good mood she dressed up in her finest clothing, as though she was Cinderella going to the ball – now she was wearing a low-cut shimmering dress and stiletto heels, and uncharacteristically she had made up her face with lipstick and mascara, so that her eyes seemed even bigger and wider than usual.

'President coming to dinner?' I asked her. I sat down on the couch and began to remove my boots with numb fingers.

'What? *Who* is coming to dinner?'

'Never mind. It was a joke.'

She didn't get it. 'What did you do today?' she asked. 'You look tired.'

I *was* tired, but it was the kind of tired that sleeping wouldn't fix. And I was about to tell her that I'd just been to the hospital when she interrupted me.

'*Yo tengo algo a decir,*' she said – *I have something to say.*

My mother could wait until later, I decided. 'What?'

226

'There was a message for me at work.'

I let one boot drop and then the other. 'From who?'

'From a friend of Franco's. A promoter.'

I pushed the back cushions off the couch and sank deeper into it. There was a wool blanket on the backrest, an old handwoven serape that I'd picked up at the flea market out by the Opera. I pulled this over me and tucked it under my chin. 'What promoter is that?' I asked sleepily.

She straightened her spine and folded her hands in front of her, as if about to recite a poem.

'You remember me asking you about if you would maybe move to Los Angeles?'

'Yes.'

'Good. Now, you have heard, no doubt, of the magnificent Cha-Cha Mendoza,' she said. 'Well, the other day—'

'I've never heard of Cha-Cha Mendoza,' I interrupted her.

'You *haven't*?'

'No.'

'Maybe you know of Boom Chica Boom?'

'What the hell kind of name is *that*?' I said.

Consuelo flung her hands into the air. 'Boom Chica Boom is only the most famous girl singing group in all the world,' she said. 'I cannot believe you have never heard of them. They played in Mexico City three times last year and there were more than fifty thousands of people there every time!'

'I must have missed them,' I said.

'*Ay, mi vida.* Listen. The man who promotes them,' she said, 'is a friend of Franco. They grew up together. His name is Jaime.'

'And?'

'And Franco told him about me. And sent him a tape.'

'You mean your demo tape? With Esteban and the Wisniewskis?'

'Yes. That is the only demo tape I have.'

'That could be good,' I said.

'It *is* good. He came to see me sing.'

Instantly I was wide awake.

'What? Here, to Santa Fe?'

She nodded.

'To the *Cowgirl*?'

'To the Cowgirl!' she said, her voice suddenly full of fiestas and parades.

'That's something,' I said.

'Beelee, it is more than something. It is *every-thing*. It is what I have been praying for.'

'When was he here? Why didn't you know anything about this before?'

'I *did* know. But Franco told me not to say anything. He said I shouldn't even think about it. That was why I couldn't tell you right away.' She sat on my legs and pulled the blanket from under my chin. 'But Beelee,' she said. 'I met him this morning. He has offered me a contract.'

'Come on,' I said. 'Are you serious?'

'Yes!'

228

'What kind of a contract?'

'To make a record,' she said. 'And to do shows. *In Los Angeles*. This,' she said, 'is exactly the thing I have been praying for. It's what *mis angelitos* have been telling me all this time! It's coming true!'

'What are you going to do, fly out there for a couple of weeks?'

'No. You are not understanding,' she said. 'This is why I have been asking you about moving. He wants me to go there.'

My excitement left me and I began to grow tired again. 'Move to Los Angeles?' I said. 'Are you crazy?'

'I am not,' she said. 'Why would you say such a thing?'

Suddenly I knew there would be no time for me to get warm that day, or to rest. I pulled my legs out from under her and got up. Then I went over to the cast-iron stove and opened the door. I built a fire, leaving the door open so the heat would spread through the room. I was feeling oddly discombobulated.

'Billy?' said Consuelo. 'This is for jumping around and singing. Not making a fire.'

'I'm not moving to Los Angeles,' I said.

She said nothing. It was rare that I could shock her into speechlessness – it was the first time I'd done it, in fact.

'Not now,' I said. 'Maybe not ever.'

'But you—'

'Why do you have to *move* there? Why can't

229

you just go out there for a while and then come back?'

'Come back to *what*?' she said. 'To cleaning the toilets?'

'Of course not to cleaning the toilets,' I said. 'To me. I'll be here.'

She clacked into the kitchen and came back with her purse. She took out her wallet and produced a check.

'*Mira*,' she said.

'What is it?' I'd found some sticks and I threw them into the stove now. The fire was crackling merrily.

'*Mira!*'

I had to look twice at the sum before I was sure I was seeing it right. It was for five thousand dollars.

'I am done cleaning toilets,' she said. 'You understand?'

I gave it back to her. 'It's made out to you,' I said. 'Congratulations.'

I went into the kitchen and washed my hands in the sink. She clicked in after me and stood behind me.

'I do not understand why you're not happy,' she said. I could tell by her voice that tears weren't far off.

'I *am* happy,' I said – but I didn't feel happy. I didn't understand it myself. I was just tired. I was beyond tired – I was half dead. I had the feeling I'd left most of myself in that hospital room in Albuquerque.

'Then why do you not act happy?'

'I just don't want,' I said, 'to move to Los Angeles. That's all.'

'Why not? What is keeping you here?'

I turned off the water and dried my hands on a dishrag. Then I turned to face her. She held her chin high, her nostrils were flaring. Her eyes snapped with fury. I hadn't realized how mad she was.

'My mother,' I said. 'That's what.'

'You are a coward,' she said.

It was my turn to be shocked. The words came out of her as though she'd been storing them up, just waiting for the right time to use them, and the idea of that hurt. Nobody had ever called me a coward before.

'Stop it. I'm not. You don't—'

'You are a *coward*,' she said again. 'If you were even a little bit of an *hombre* you would take control of your life.'

'I thought you liked it that I wasn't a *macho hombre*.' I was feeling nasty now.

'*Macho* has nothing to do with it. You don't tell her because you are afraid.'

'You better just shut up,' I said.

'You can't tell me to shut up.'

'Move to Los Angeles. I'm not going.'

'Coward!'

I stepped forward fast. I had my hand raised when something in her face changed and she put one hand out to block me. I stopped. We stood

231

looking at each other for a very long time, me with my arm out and her hand on my wrist.

'Oh,' she said. 'Maybe you are full of *machismo*, after all.'

I couldn't say anything. Feeling suddenly ridiculous, I dropped my arm.

'You were going to—'

'No, I wasn't,' I said.

She went into the bedroom and grabbed her suitcase from the closet. It was all she'd carried with her when she moved in with me. Consuelo owned even less than I did. She threw the suitcase onto the bed and came back into the kitchen.

'*Bueno*,' she said. 'I was wrong. I apologize. Only a big strong *hombre* would hit me, not a coward.'

'I didn't hit you.'

'You were going to.'

'If I was really going to hit you there wouldn't be anything you could do about it,' I said.

That made her even madder. She went back into the bedroom and pulled her clothes out of the closet. She threw them onto the bed and then came back out again.

'All right,' she said. 'So you didn't hit me.'

I sat down at the kitchen table.

'Why did you not?' she asked.

I folded my arms on the table and rested my head on them. I closed my eyes and sat there like that, not moving or speaking.

'I asked you something,' she said.

'Just leave me alone,' I said. 'Just go.'

232

She went back into the bedroom and finished packing. Then she clacked her way to the front door. I heard her pause for a moment before she opened it, as if she was waiting for me to say something, but I was too tired even to lift my head. Then I heard the door open and slam shut, and I could hear the echoes of her footsteps die away as she picked her careful way through the gravel of the driveway and then down the sidewalk.

CHAPTER 10

CONSUELO

There were only two people in town who knew about my angels. Billy was not the first. He was the second, and until that moment when he raised his hand as if to strike me I had thought he understood all about them. But I could see then that I was wrong.

The first person I told about them was Esteban, the guitar player from Spain.

Sometimes I think Esteban is even older than he lets on – older, perhaps, than it is possible for a person to be. His fingers are still nimble and untouched by arthritis; he attributes this to the copious amounts of marijuana he has smoked every day for countless decades. But they are the only part of him that still works as though he was young. The rest of him is decrepit, dilapidated. Esteban is a house on the verge of collapse.

I have known Esteban almost since my first moment in this town. Musicians are a tight-knit society, and they have a way of passing each other around from group to group, especially in a town where there is a lack of other skilled players to perform with. That was how we met. What I liked best about Esteban was that I never actually had to tell him about the angels, because he saw them for himself. When we first met, he looked not at me but around me; his face wrinkled with confusion at first, and then smoothed as he understood. He was following something with his eyes, something that moved around me quickly, over and over in an infinite and unpredictable pattern. Later, when we had gotten to know each other a bit, he asked me in an almost matter-of-fact way what were those little lights that danced around me all the time. Angels, I told him. He nodded.

'I knew you were lucky,' he said. 'I could see it in your face.'

That is how it is when you're old, I think. You've seen almost everything, and such things are no longer surprising.

Now Billy does not want to come to Los Angeles; he wants to stay here in his state of perpetual limbo, neither committing to anything nor pulling back from anything completely. Fine. You cannot force someone to do something they don't want to do. I do not need him. I don't need anyone. But if there was someone for whom I would confess some sort of attachment, someone who I thought would help me get where I was going just a bit faster in Los Angeles, it would not be Billy, anyway. It would be Esteban. So it's to his house I go, and within half an hour he has packed his meager possessions and is ready to get on the road. He has traveled so much in his life that such a small journey means nothing to him. It's just another leg on his interminable voyage around the world.

In public, Esteban speaks to no one but me, and then only rarely. In private, we converse without reservation, but with some difficulty. Esteban speaks an ancient version of Spanish that is nearly impossible to comprehend. Imagine the playwright William Shakespeare coming back to life and having a conversation with a speaker of modern English, and you'll have some idea of what it is like for me to talk to Esteban. He comes from a tiny village somewhere in Andalusia, a village that he claims has not changed for more than five hundred years, because no one knows it is there. There is no electricity, for example; there is running water, however, provided by a network of Roman aqueducts built in a style so flawless that two thousand years later they're still in perfect working order. There are schools, but no books – the children are educated orally and must commit everything to memory. It sounds impossible, but is true that Esteban can recite by rote much or all of the following works: the Book of Genesis, the Code of Hammurabi, *La Chanson de Roland*, and *Poema del Cid*. Yet the spoken language of his village has remained unmodified by the passage of time, because modern travelers almost never stop there, and few people ever leave.

And, of course, in his village there are guitars.

Esteban learned to play when he was five years old, under the tutelage of his uncle, whose mother

236

was a *gitana* – a gypsy. The guitar itself is the one concession his people have made to modern influences, for the guitar is not an ancient instrument. It has roots in other, older instruments, of course; people have been constructing boxes with strings stretched over them since time out of mind. The people of Esteban's village saw no need for electricity; similarly with automobiles. And their language had already attained such a peak of mellifluous perfection that there was no reason to change it. But the guitar was something exciting for them, an innovation that none of them had thought of, and they adopted it as their own. According to Esteban, his childhood was full of music – it was not so much a pastime as a second language, and now that he has been largely deprived of the power to communicate vocally, it is his first.

Esteban does not speak because there are so few people who can understand him. But he is full of words, and it is he who writes the words to my songs for me now. I never had any great talent for lyrics; I admit that freely. My talent lies in the singing of the words, not the words themselves. That is why many of the songs I sing are unintelligible to the people of Santa Fe, most of whom learned Spanish first and English later, as a concession to the Anglo presence in this land – but a different Spanish from the language I spoke as a child in Mexico, different from that spoken in Spain, in Cuba, in Central and South America, Portugal, Puerto Rico. Every version, in fact, varies slightly from the others. But I have never heard Spanish spoken like Esteban speaks it. Neither, for that matter, has anyone else.

I am learning slowly to speak in the old Spanish as Esteban speaks, so that he and I may understand each other better.

'Wherefore didst thou leave your village?' I asked him once. 'If all was as you say, quiet and peaceful and serene, what reason had you to go?'

He grunted, looking at me through his clouded reddish-blue eyes. He greets each morning by puffing on a large marijuana cigarette, which causes the veins to stand out in his eyeballs.

'I wanted to see if the world had an edge, as I was taught,' he said, 'or if it was true, as others said, that it was round.'

'And hast thou been around the world?'

'Many times since then,' he said. 'Times without number. It is round,' he added, as though this might be news to me.

'Dost thou not wish to return home, to thy village?'

He grunted again and looked sad. He caressed his guitar, laid his wrinkled cheek briefly on its curved side.

'I cannot find it,' he said. 'It has vanished.'

'Surely you must be mistaken,' I said. 'How can a whole village disappear?'

He shook his head, plucked the strings of his guitar to hear them vibrate.

'I left home still a young man,' he said. 'I was

gone a long time. I knew that my children would be grown, and my wife, if by Divine Grace she was still alive, would have another husband. Twenty years I traveled – it took me that long to make my journey. I went back to the very spot, to the same valley between the two great peaks that I had known every day of my childhood. But . . . I found nothing. Only ancient ruins.'

'But how is this possible?'

He did not answer right away. He strummed an agile melody as old as he, and ten times older; the music of a forgotten place, a folk song from a vanished country. I understood then that he had already answered me, and his answer was this: *I gave up my place in time, and now I am lost forever.*

Poor Esteban: I am the only one who knows the source of his heartache. He never speaks of it to others because no one else would believe him. These are the ravings of an addict, they would say. Villages do not disappear; there is nowhere in Europe where modern technology has not yet arrived. But the people who would say this are the same people who don't believe in angels.

Poor Esteban, old and lonely. He has a little room in the house he shares with the family, who treat him like a grandfather, and there he is as happy as it's possible for him to be – smoking his marijuana, playing his guitar, and setting on paper the songs he remembers from his childhood, so that he can pass them on to me. I am the sole heir to the musical legacy of his village. Everyone else is gone, and when he finally dies, I'll be the only one who knows them. Only when he's written all the songs he remembers, he says, will it be time for him to die. But his memory, stretched and fluid and limber from memorizing all those old stories, seems inexhaustible, and the supply of songs shows no signs of slowing: twenty so far, and every other day or so he begins to transcribe a new one.

'This is the first time these songs have ever been set on paper,' Esteban tells me. 'Sometimes I fear I am committing a sin by doing so.'

'Why a sin, Grandfather?'

'Because then they become fixed and are prone to decay,' he says. 'Time is a disease, Granddaughter. Only in my village was it possible to hide from it. But it's like a plague – once exposed to it, one is polluted forever.'

'Is the passage of time truly such a tragedy?'

He blinks, his face long and lugubrious.

'Only for those who never knew of it before,' he says. 'Only for those who believed differently.'

Now we walk toward the Cowgirl, he carrying his guitar in its case, me carrying his suitcase and mine. Both are light; between the two of us, we own almost nothing. He walks in silence, ignoring everything, looking down at his feet. His pace is shuffling and slow. Out of respect I do not rush him, but inside I am dying to run. I always thought Billy would be coming with me when this moment came; but now, I realize, it doesn't matter if he comes or not.

'The young man?' Esteban asks, at that moment. 'Whither the young man?'

'At home,' I say.

'He comes?'

'No.'

He says nothing. We draw nearer the bar, where I will ask Franco to drive us to the airport. Esteban pauses at the steps to catch his breath, and he looks up at me anxiously.

'This is a large city, this City of Angels?' he asks.

'Yes,' I say. 'Very large.'

'Will there be a place for us there?'

I put a hand on his shoulder.

'You do not have to come,' I tell him. 'You have earned a rest.'

He shakes his head. 'I am not afraid,' he says. 'I have faced greater dangers than what a large city can offer. I only ask.'

'There will be a place for us there,' I say. 'We will play.'

'If thou sayest it, it will be so, Granddaughter,' he tells me. He looks around him, down Guadalupe Street with its trendy shops, at the low-riders, the youths with their tattoos and piercings. I wonder how much of what he sees he understands. I am one of the few windows into this modern world that he can glimpse through to make sense of things. I take his hand and help him up the steps. Together

241

we go in. Soon Esteban's songs will be sung in the largest clubs of Los Angeles, and people will love them, because it will be my voice they hear: my voice, his words. He was the only one I needed, after all.

CHAPTER 11

THE SECOND LONG, BAD DAY

Consuelo left on a Friday, which was when she and the band usually played. Franco hadn't had time to schedule another act, so the Wisniewskis were forced to play by themselves. Old Esteban had gone with her, too, Franco said. He'd driven them to the airport himself, just an hour after Consuelo stormed out of the house.

'I'm not sure it was such a good idea for the old man to go along,' he told me that night, as I was finishing my fourth beer. 'You should have seen his face when we got to the airport. Terrified. I don't think he'd ever been on a plane before.'

I didn't want to hear about it. 'Gimme another beer,' I said.

'You oughta take it easy,' he said. 'I've never seen you drink this much before.'

'I can handle it.'

'Sure, I know you can handle it. Just watch yourself is all. I don't wanna see you getting sick.'

'Nobody's getting sick.'

Franco slid the beer to me. 'On the house,' he said. 'If you want to get good and loaded tonight, go ahead. It's on me. I understand.'

He puttered around the bar, dusting off bottles and filling the occasional drink order. The place was starting to fill up. I looked around, but I didn't see Ralph anywhere. He'd be showing up later, I figured. Sophia wasn't around, either. Meanwhile, I could tell by the way Franco was lingering near me that he had something else on his mind.

'Just say it,' I told him.

'Say what?'

'Whatever it is you're not saying.'

He sighed. 'All right. This is none of my business, but how come you didn't go with her?'

'You really wanna know?'

'Sure.'

'Because I'm a coward.'

He stopped puttering and looked at me. 'What's *that* supposed to mean?'

'I don't know. It's what she says.'

'She couldn't have meant that.'

'She sure sounded like she meant it.'

'She was mad,' he reminded me. 'People say things they don't mean when they're mad.'

'She just wants to be famous,' I said. 'That's all *she* cares about.' I was really starting to feel those beers, and the self-pity flowed over me in a comforting ooze. I reveled in it. 'She was just using me!' I said, a little too loudly.

'That's not true. She cares about you, too.'

'Funny way of showing it,' I said.

'People fight, Billy,' said Franco. 'Lovers quarrel. It's not the end of the world.'

I drained my beer and pushed the mug over for him to fill it again. 'Where's Sophia?' I asked.

'Down in Albuquerque,' he said. 'Why?'

'I got something to tell her.'

'What?'

'I should tell her myself.'

Franco shrugged. 'Suit yourself,' he said. 'She said she'd be back in time to help me close.'

'I'll be here,' I told him. 'You'll have to sweep me off the floor to get rid of me.'

The two burly Poles played a few songs, but their hearts weren't in it. Nobody had told them Consuelo was leaving, either, and that she'd gone without them and had taken Esteban with her to boot was a devastating blow. Janusz was high on vodka, and after the first song he put down his maracas and his tambourine and sat with his face in his hands, weeping quietly.

'Goddamn it,' said Franco to me. 'If there's anything more depressing than seeing a man that big cry, I don't know what it is.'

'What are *they* so upset about?' I asked.

'They wanted to go, too,' he said. 'But Jaime didn't want them. He only wanted Consuelo and the old man.'

The beginning of Consuelo's dream was the end of the line for those twin Polish lummoxes. Wieslaw tried to sing some sort of Polish ballad on the accordion, but his voice was more suited

245

to drinking songs, and he received only scattered applause when he was done. Instead of beginning another song he sat looking numbly at the audience, half of whom had already left. The sound of his brother's stifled sobbing was picked up by the microphone. The whole bar had the air of a funeral. After a moment Wieslaw took off his accordion, picked up the mike, and took a deep breath. I could see the struggle on his face as he looked for the right words. I sensed he was trying to eulogize the whole thing, the end of the era of Consuelo – but his limited vocabulary prevented him from attaining any level of eloquence, and finally, his voice sad and heavy, he said the only thing there was for him to say, 'We finish now.'

He looked at Franco and drew a finger across his neck, telling him to kill the spotlight. Franco hit the switch behind the sink, and the little stage was suddenly dark.

'Thank God for that,' Franco said under his breath. 'I was about ready to shoot myself.'

The two brokenhearted brothers left their equipment lying on the stage and came over to the bar. Janusz grabbed a stack of napkins and wiped his red-rimmed eyes.

'You boys doing all right?' Franco asked them.

'We shoot be heppy,' said Wieslaw.

'*Tak*,' agreed Janusz, still blubbering. 'We shoot be heppy for her.'

They lifted their glasses and clinked them together.

Then they raised them to me. I toasted them with my beer.

'To America,' said Wieslaw.

'To rockanroll,' said Janusz.

The three of us drank together. They clapped me on the back with their massive hands.

'You like *wotka*?' Wieslaw asked me.

'I don't know,' I said. 'I've never tried it.'

'He is not Polak,' Janusz told him.

'*Tak*. He is not Polak. But mebbe he can like it.'

'Give him *wotka*,' said Wieslaw to Franco.

Franco looked grim, but he poured me a shot and gave them two more.

'You hev onion?' said Janusz. 'You have bret?'

Franco was by now used to the drinking habits of the Slavic giants; he took out an onion and cut it into thick slices. Then he found a loaf of dark bread and cut that up, to. He set it all on a cutting board in front of us.

'To Elvis,' said Wieslaw.

'To rockanroll and also Hollyvoot, home of Chimmy Dean,' said Janusz.

'To Consuelo,' added Wieslaw.

We drank again, and again and again, toasting some things in Polish, some in Spanish, some in English. The brothers showed me how to chase the vodka with a big bite of bread and a piece of onion.

Franco leaned over and said in a warning tone, 'Watch out for these guys. They're professionals.

There's no way in hell you can keep up with them.'

'When is Sophia coming?' I whispered.

He shrugged. 'You going home soon? Whatever it is, I can tell her.'

'I'm staying right here until she shows up.'

'All right. But you better take it easy.'

'You like rockanroll?' Janusz asked me.

'Sure,' I said. 'Who doesn't?'

'We come to Amerika for rockanroll,' said Wieslaw. 'We want to be rockanroll stars.'

'Just gimme det rockanroll moozik,' sang Janusz. 'Any olt way you choose it.' His voice was surprisingly high, for someone so large.

'Hey, Pilly,' said Janusz, smacking my shoulder again. 'You going okay?'

'I guess,' I said.

'Don't you cry,' said Wieslaw.

'I'm not crying,' I said.

'Well, *I* cry,' said Janusz, unabashed. 'We come to Amerika for dat rockanroll.'

'Rockanroll does not make accordion,' Wieslaw explained to me sadly. 'It makes electric guitar.'

'I hef idea,' said Janusz, suddenly excited. 'Mebbe so, we can go to New Orleans. Dere dey make accordion *and* shaka-shaka-shaka.'

'Dat is *goot* idea!' said Wieslaw. He brightened considerably. 'To New Orleans!' he said, hoisting a fresh glass of vodka.

'To New Orleans!' said Janusz.

We drank.

★　　★　　★

The next thing I was aware of was Sophia's face swimming in and out of my field of vision. I had a dim memory of several more glasses of vodka, and later of being led to the bathroom, where I'd spent a very long time sitting on the floor; but I couldn't remember if I'd been sick or not. I couldn't remember much of anything.

'You all right?' Sophia was saying.

I groaned and tried to get up. Nausea and dizziness overwhelmed me.

'Oh, my *God*,' I said. 'What happened?'

'You got drunk,' she said. 'You've been sleeping there for hours.'

'What time is it?'

'Three-thirty.'

'In the *morning*?'

'That's right,' Sophia said.

She brought me a glass of water. I drank it greedily, and she brought me another. After I drank that I sat up straight and looked around the bar. Everyone had gone home, and the lights were off.

'Where's Franco?' I asked. My tongue felt thick.

'He's putting stuff away in the kitchen,' she said. 'He told me you were waiting for me.'

'Yeah,' I said. 'I was.'

'You want me to walk you home?'

'Okay. If you feel like it.'

'Sure.'

She got my jacket for me and helped me into it. Then she slipped her arm through mine and led me out the door. After the fug of the bar the clear air helped my head; I looked up and saw stars and a sliver of eggshell moon.

'You go see your mom?' I asked.

'Yeah.'

'You guys talk?'

'Yeah. She woke up for a few minutes. At least I think she did.'

She didn't seem to want to say anything more, but the tension she'd had about her before seemed to have eased. I wondered what she'd said. I hoped they'd made up. But I didn't ask, and she didn't volunteer anything further, so we walked the rest of the way in silence.

We came to my house. As I was fumbling for my keys I heard muffled shouting from across the street, coming from El Perrero's house.

'I haven't been in the old neighborhood for a while,' said Sophia. 'Sounds like not much has changed.'

'He's nuts,' I said.

'You should stay away from him, Billy,' she said. 'He really *is* nuts. I should know – I grew up next door to him.'

'You don't have to tell me twice,' I said.

I turned and looked at her old house across the street. The way the starlight and the bit of moonlight was hitting it, the walls were glowing in a weird, spooky way.

'Look at your old house,' I said.

'I don't want to,' she said quietly. 'Just let me in, please.'

I unlocked the door and we went inside. I headed straight for the bathroom and brushed my teeth, which felt like they were covered with pond scum. I gargled twice and then stumbled out onto the couch. My head was beginning to clear.

'Thanks for walking me home,' I said.

'Sure.' She sat at the end of the couch, her knees drawn up close to her chest and her arms wrapped around them. She was watching me with a mixture of concern and curiosity. I sat down at the other end of the couch. I'd had a whole speech planned, but now that it was time to give it I hadn't the slightest idea what to say. But she said, 'There is something with us, isn't there?'

I nodded, relieved she was going to start.

'I felt it,' she told me.

'When?'

'Right away. But I didn't know what it was. I *thought* I knew, but I was wrong,' she blushed, remembering.

'Don't be embarrassed,' I said. 'It was a perfectly natural assumption.'

'But it was *wrong*,' she said. 'Right? I don't know why, but it was.'

'Yes, it was wrong.'

'Do you know why?'

'Yes. I do.'

She cocked her head to one side and waited.

My speech had completely deserted me now, but I thought of an easier way to tell her. I got up and went into my bedroom, where I retrieved the picture of my mother and father I'd taken from Sky's photo album. I handed it to her and sat down again.

It was almost amusing to watch her as she looked at it: she would open her mouth to ask a question, and then it would answer itself in her mind before she could get it out. She sat there with her mouth opening and closing like a fish.

'That's my dad, there,' I said, as tears began spilling down her face. 'And the other person in the picture is my mother.'

Later, after she'd calmed down, we stood side by side in front of the bathroom mirror, looking at our noses. She said, 'Who was he, exactly?'

'His name was Eddie,' I said. 'He was a pilot. Who was yours?'

Sophia snorted. She had one hand on her nose and the other on mine; she gave my nose a gentle squeeze, as if to see whether she could feel that, too. 'A casual,' she said.

'A casual?'

'A sperm donor. I don't think she even knew him very well.'

'Did *you* know him?'

She shook her head. 'I've met him once or twice. He lives in a commune up in Idaho. A real weirdo.'

'But you met him, right?'

'Well, sure.'

'Isn't that worth something? That you at least got to meet him?'

'I guess,' she said. 'It wasn't exactly a pivotal moment in my life, though. Was your dad a casual, too?'

'No way,' I said, offended. 'They were in love.'

She snorted. 'How long did they know each other?'

'I don't know for sure. A few days, I think.'

'A few days, and they were in love?' There was a note of scorn in her voice. 'Come on,' she said. 'I hate to break this to you, but Eddie was a casual, too. We're both accidents, Billy. Like it or not.'

I pushed her hand away from my nose. 'No, he wasn't a casual,' I said.

'Sorry,' she said. 'But the sooner you know the truth about her the better. She got around, Billy. Our mom is not the most farsighted person in the world. Or the most careful.'

I closed my eyes and rubbed my forehead. What she was saying went against the legend I'd built up in my mind ever since I was a little kid. The only thing that had kept me going through countless empty days and nights was the thought that my parents were lovers, ripped apart tragically by the war. It was the only thing that gave the rest of it meaning, the only thing that could explain my having been left alone to be raised by a drunken old man. I'd never wanted to believe that I was simply a mistake. But Sophia knew her better than I did, and I knew she must be right.

'Don't look that way,' Sophia said. 'It's not the end of the world.'

'Just give me a minute,' I said.

She rubbed the back of my neck. 'Nobody should ever know the whole truth about their parents,' she told me. 'At least not with a mother like ours. It's not healthy. Believe me, I know more about her than you do, and a lot of it I'd rather not know at all.'

'Did you know about *me*?' I asked. 'Did she ever hint that I might be out there?'

'Once or twice, I think she did,' Sophia said. 'She might have mentioned it.'

Might have mentioned it. That hurt worse than if she'd told me she'd never spoken of me at all.

'Did she ever say anything about why she gave me up?'

'Can't help you there,' she said. 'She must have just decided she couldn't deal with you. That's all.' She put her arm around me and dug her chin into my shoulder. 'Don't look that way,' she whispered. 'It's not like she was any more responsible with *me*. I know you know the whole story about how we lost the house, and everything.'

'Yeah,' I said.

'That's the kind of mother she was,' Sophia said, her lips against my ear. 'Everyone always thought she was wonderful, but nobody knew what I knew

– that she was really not very good at mothering. You might have been better off where you were,' she said. 'Did you ever think of *that*?' She gave me a big wet smooch on the cheek.

'No,' I said, blowing my nose.

'Well, it's true. It was always, Sky is so strong! Sky is so liberated! Sky is so free and easygoing! Everyone thought she was so *great*. Meanwhile, I had to learn how to make my own meals by the time I was eight years old because I couldn't count on her to be home in time to feed me. *That's* how liberated she was.'

'I had to cook for myself, too,' I said. Maybe Sophia was right; maybe I was better off. At least Grandpa had always been *physically* home.

'Where were you, anyway?' she asked. Where did you grow up?'

'New York State,' I said. 'Next to Lake Erie.'

'What made you come all the way out here?'

'Her,' I said.

Our eyes met in the mirror. Hers grew large.

'You mean you came all the way to New Mexico just to find her?'

I nodded.

'How did you know where to look?' she asked.

I put the lid down on the toilet and sat on it. 'I've been looking for her my whole life,' I said. 'I've been wanting to find her ever since I was old enough to look.'

'You mean . . . you tracked her *down*?'

'Yeah.'

She sat down on the edge of the bathtub and took my hands.

'Jesus, Billy,' she said. 'I had no idea.'

'I kept it a secret,' I said.

'Why didn't you just tell me who you were right away? Why haven't you told *her*?'

'If you were the one she'd given up,' I said, 'you wouldn't be asking me that.'

'You want to sleep here?' I asked her. 'It's going to be morning in a couple of hours.'

'I guess so,' she said. 'You want to come down to the hospital with me after? I told Franco I was taking the day off. In fact, now that she's in the hospital again I'm not going back to work until . . .'

Until she dies, is what she meant.

'That sounds good,' I said. 'Maybe she'll wake up a little bit. Enough for us to talk to her.'

'Maybe she will,' said Sophia, with that same false, hearty brand of optimism that must have carried her through a thousand lonely childhood moments, the feeling that told her everything was going to be all right when she had no reason to believe that it would.

We fell asleep in my bed, curled around each other – not like lovers do, but like people who have just found each other and who are hanging on for dear life. It would be easy for me to love her, I thought as I drifted off. She was just like me after all, dark skin notwithstanding. When she'd said *maybe she will* like that I'd realized that we were the same kind of person, not just blood relatives but somehow even closer than regular brothers and sisters. Once you have come through a childhood without much in the way of comfort or nourishment – either nutritional or spiritual – and have gotten used to making your own lunch and tucking yourself in at night, you're never the same as other children. And the only people who really understand you are other children who grew up the same way. Everyone else is only pretending to understand you; either that, or they're just guessing. Or, what is more likely, they don't even try.

I was awakened the next morning by pounding. It took me a while to figure out where it was coming from. The clock said 10:00 A.M., which meant we'd only slept for a few hours. I struggled out from Sophia's grasp and went to the front door. When I opened it, a blast of chilly wind hit me, and there was El Perrero.

From the waist up he looked normal. He wore the same camouflage jacket and sunglasses, and in his lenses I could see my hair, wild and tangled. From the waist down, however, he was nude. I caught a brief glimpse of his penis poking out from underneath his jacket, shriveled and forlorn in the cold. He was holding something wrapped in a towel. He held it out to me.

'You shouldn't of thrown this away, Jones,' he snarled.

I pushed the door shut fast. He tried to stick his foot in the jamb, but I pushed him back with one arm and got it closed. Then I locked it and went to wake Sophia up.

'Mmf,' she mumbled as I shook her. ''Sa matter?'

'Get up,' I said, shaking her harder. 'Get away from the window.'

My bedroom window was next to the front door, and I could tell without looking that he was standing there, looking in. I didn't even wait to see for sure if he was there or not. I grabbed Sophia by the feet and dragged her into the living room.

'What the *fuck*?' she protested, twisting out of my grasp. 'What are you doing?'

'Stay away from the window,' I said. 'El Perrero's out there.'

There were windows in the living room, too, and it was only a matter of time before he remembered that. I grabbed her under the arms and hoisted her to her feet. Then I pulled her into the bathroom with me. I closed the door after us and turned on the light. She sat on the floor, rubbing the sleep out of her eyes.

'What do you mean, he's out there?'

'He was knocking on the door,' I said. 'Didn't you hear him?'

'I was *sleeping*,' she complained. 'So what if he was knocking?'

'You don't understand. He's naked,' I said. 'He's pantsless. I think he's finally snapped.'

That woke her up completely. 'Jesus,' she said.

'He thinks I'm some guy named Jones,' I said. 'From the war.'

'He's having a flashback?'

'I think so,' I said. 'Listen.'

We both sat quietly and listened, but we couldn't hear anything. Sophia said she had to pee and couldn't hold it any more, so I turned my back and listened to the hiss of her urinating in the bowl. 'I'm glad we're related,' she said, and I heard her rip off a couple pieces of toilet paper and wipe herself. 'This is embarrassing.'

'Shh,' I said. 'Do you hear anything?'

'No.'

'Don't flush.'

'Why not?'

'I want to hear.'

'Do you think he's—'

'He's *lurking*,' I said.

'You should definitely call the cops,' she said.

'Can't. I don't have a phone.'

We stayed deathly quiet, but I didn't hear anything – no jimmying of the door, no breaking of window glass. I turned off the bathroom light and opened the door a crack. He wasn't outside the living room window. I crept out on my belly and went to the doorway of my bedroom, sticking my head cautiously around the corner. I could just see out the window from there; no El Perrero.

259

'Is he out there?' called Sophia from the bath-room.

'Shh!' I whispered.

I crept onto my bed and poked my head up just above the level of the windowsill. I didn't see anything unusual. He wasn't in the driveway, or in the street, or in his yard. Then I caught a flash of movement in the old cottonwood across the street. Branches parted, and I saw his lenses staring back at me, like the eyes of a giant chromed lizard. The morning sun flashed off his pale thighs. He would have to be on some serious drugs to be climbing a tree with no pants on in this weather. I didn't think he saw me. I watched as he raised something to his shoulder in a gesture that was suspiciously familiar.

'Where is he?' Sophia said. She was in the door-way of the bedroom.

'Jesus, Sophia!' I said. 'Get down!'

I dove across the room and tackled her just as the first shot came through the window. Sophia lay on her stomach and I lay on top of her, burying my face in her hair. She screamed, her face pushed into the floor. I heard the round thunk into the adobe opposite the window. With the glass gone I could hear sounds from outside more clearly; I heard him muttering, and the click of metal on metal as he worked another round into the chamber. I crawled back over to the window, keeping well out of sight. Sophia stayed right where she was, whimpering.

'Hey! Perrero!' I yelled. 'Cut it out!'

'Why don't you shoot back, Jones?' he hollered.

'I don't have a gun!' I said. I wasn't sure if he could hear me, but I was too afraid to lift my head over the windowsill. 'I got rid of it, remember?'

'Yeah, well, I gave it to you for a reason, you dumbass!' he shouted.

'I'll buy you another one, if that's what you're upset about!' I called. But he only laughed. Another shot came, hitting the far wall just below the first one. Without the window to muffle it, this one was deafeningly loud. Sophia screamed again.

'Is he going to kill us?' she wailed into the floor.

'Come here,' I said. 'Get under the bed.'

She snaked along the floor with amazing speed and disappeared under the bed frame. 'Is he going to kill us?' she asked again. She was crying.

'No,' I said. 'I don't think that's what he wants.'

'Then why is he *shooting* at us?'

El Perrero shouted something unintelligible. There was a third shot. I heard this one spang off the pavement of the street and ricochet into a parked car. Then there was a fourth. It whizzed away with a long, trailing whine without hitting anything.

'You wish you had that gun now, don't you, Jones!' he yelled. 'Hey! Jones!'

'I'm not Jones, you fuck!' I screamed. 'I'm Billy Mann!'

'Go open your door,' he said. 'I won't shoot.'

'Why?'

'There's something there for you,' he said. 'I promise I won't shoot till you get it.'

I knew what it was, of course, but just to be sure I crawled to the door and opened it a crack. There it was, the pistol I'd gotten rid of. It must have been what he'd wrapped up in that towel he was holding earlier. I was starting to get the whole picture now. El Perrero wanted me to shoot him. No – he wanted me to kill him. He wanted to be rid of the terrible guilt he felt over watching poor Jones get hacked to death by the Vietcong while he himself did nothing to prevent it.

I saw everything then, but I wanted nothing to do with it. It was too sick.

'I don't want to do this!' I yelled. 'Please, Perrero! Find someone else!'

'It's gotta be you, Jones,' he said. 'Nobody else can do it.' He started to sing then: 'It had to be yoooouuuuuu,' he crooned, his voice creaky and demonic.

I closed the door again and crawled back into my bedroom.

'I fucking well hope someone called the police by now,' said Sophia. She had calmed down now. She was lying on her stomach with her chin resting on her arms, looking almost relaxed. 'Why don't you have a phone?'

'Couldn't afford the deposit,' I said.

'Yeah,' she agreed, 'the phone company can be a real bitch about that.'

It occurred to me that perhaps I was dreaming.

Here we were being fired on by a raging lunatic with a sniper rifle, and yet we were having a conversation about the phone company. And to top it off, El Perrero was still singing.

Then, off in the distance, over the ratcheting of his voice, I heard a lovely sound: sirens. 'Thank God,' said Sophia, who'd heard them at the same moment.

Then I heard something else. It was the sound of a motorcycle engine coming down South Blossom Street, from the direction of Agua Fria. It was much closer than the sirens. What was worse, I recognized the sound of the engine.

'Oh, no,' I said, horrified.

'What is it?'

'It's Ralph!' I said.

I had to do something. I raised my head over the windowsill for a split second to shout Ralph's name, but he couldn't hear me as he pulled into the driveway, although he saw me – there was a look of puzzlement on his face as he spied my head sticking up over the sill, and noticed the window with the large hole in it. I motioned crazily for him to get out of there, but it was already too late. I saw El Perrero raise his rifle and I ducked again.

The fifth shot came just as a police car screeched to a halt in the street outside. I heard Ralph roar in pain and surprise as the bullet slammed into him. I didn't know where it hit him, but I heard his bike fall over, and he roared again.

'Billy!' he shouted. 'Don't shoot!'

'It's not *me*!' I yelled. 'It's the guy across the street!'

'Drop your weapon!' said someone. I heard another set of tires squeal on the pavement outside.

'*Que chinga todo!*' yelled El Perrero – *fuck everything*!

'Ralph! Are you okay?' I called.

'No,' he wheezed.

'Where did he get you?'

'Ohh,' he moaned. 'My leg. He shot my leg off.'

'Drop your weapon now or we'll open fire!' said the police.

I dared to peek over the windowsill again. Ralph was lying in the driveway just outside my window. His bike had fallen to one side and he'd fallen to the other; he was clutching his leg, which was covered with blood. Blood had also leaked out in astonishing quantities onto the gravel. A small lake of it had already formed around him, but his leg hadn't been shot off – it was still attached to him, as far as I could tell.

'Your leg isn't shot off,' I told Ralph.

'Ohh, God!' he screamed. 'It feels like it!'

There were four cops in the street now. They were hiding behind their cars, guns drawn and pointed up at the tree. I could hear more sirens coming. They shouted at El Perrero to drop his gun.

'Jones!' he yelled. 'Tell these fuckers to get out of here! You have to do it! Not them!'

Which, as it turned out, would be the last words El Perrero would ever speak.

Without warning, the cops opened fire. It sounded like a string of firecrackers going off in my ear. I was still watching over the windowsill, and I was a witness to the end of the tragedy that had begun twenty years earlier, half a world away. They kept firing until El Perrero had fallen out of the tree like a great, flapping bird, crashing through the branches and falling with a thick, wet sound to the earth.

CHAPTER 12

THE BEGINNING OF THE END

At Sophia's urging I took the back road down to Albuquerque, the same road Ralph and I had traveled the previous August. There was always less traffic on the Turquoise Trail, so there was less risk, she said, of me slamming distractedly into the back of a semi; I told her I didn't think I would ever do anything so stupid, but she said she had death and disaster on the brain now, and nothing would get rid of it. She was gripping me so tightly around the waist that I had to tell her to ease off, unless she wanted me to black out.

'I'm sorry,' she said in my ear. 'I'm just scared.'

'Don't be,' I told her over my shoulder. 'I know what I'm doing.'

'I know,' she said. 'I'm not scared of *you*. I'm just *scared*.'

I myself felt calm, considering what we had just seen. I should have taken some time to pull myself together, but we had to get down to the hospital – we had no choice because we didn't know how much time Sky had left. Hours had been wasted already. First Ralph had been taken away in an ambulance, his bleeding temporarily halted with a tourniquet; I promised I would come see him as soon as I could.

'This is all my fault,' I told him. 'It should have been me that got shot, not you.'

Ralph was woozy from loss of blood, and he didn't quite hear me. 'Probably next Tuesday,' he said, lifting one hand in a weak farewell. 'See you at the Cowgirl, Billy.'

He was gone in a blaze of flashing lights. Sophia cried on my shoulder as they pulled away.

'He looked so *little*,' she said.

'He'll be okay,' I said. 'Ralph is tough.'

'I need to sit down,' Sophia said. She wandered off dazedly to my porch and put her head between her knees.

Then the cops had wanted to question me about how much I knew of El Perrero. It turned out *they* knew quite a bit about him; they'd known him by name, and one of the younger officers had cried unashamedly over his body as it was covered with a sheet and then carried away by another pair of ambulance attendants. El Perrero was a repeat customer, an older cop told me – they arrested him once or twice a year, usually for public drunknness. But nobody knew he still had his old Remington stashed inside his house.

'Your name is Jones?' the older cop said, writing it down in his notebook. 'You a friend of his?'

'My name is *not* Jones,' I said. 'It's Mann. M-A-N-N.'

The cop looked puzzled. 'But he *called* you Jones, right?' he asked. 'I heard him.'

'Yes, he called me Jones. He always called me Jones.'

'So Jones is your alias?'

'I don't have an alias,' I told him. 'It was his idea to call me Jones, not mine.'

The cop snapped his notebook shut and stuck it in his pocket. 'Right. Forget it,' he said. 'Whatever your name is, do you know why he was shooting at you?'

'Because he wanted me to shoot back,' I said.

'Shoot back with what? Are you armed? Put your hands on top of your head!'

I did as he told me. 'I'm not armed,' I said. 'There's a pistol sitting on my front porch. It's *his* pistol,' I added.

'Don't move,' he said, grabbing my thumbs. To another cop he said, 'Go over there and see if there's a gun on that porch.'

'It's not my gun,' I said. 'He gave it to me this morning, right before he started shooting.'

The cop patted me down. 'Okay, Jones, you can put your arms down,' he said. 'Why did he do that?'

'He wanted me to shoot him,' I said.

Yet another cop came back with the pistol. 'This the one?' he said.

'Yes, that's it,' I said.

'Jones here says Perrero wanted him to shoot him,' said the cop who had patted me down. 'Says he gave him this gun before he started shooting, so's he would shoot back.'

'That right, Jones?' said the other cop – I was fast losing track of which cop was which. They all looked alike. 'Sounds kinda crazy to me.'

'It *is* crazy, my name is *Mann*, and I'm telling you this has been coming for a long time,' I said to both of them – to *all* of them, for there were now several cops gathered around me, listening. I had to tell them the whole story from the very beginning, which took a lot longer than I wanted it to; for all I knew my mother was dying at that very moment, and I wanted to be in Albuquerque with her, not here with a bunch of note-taking policemen. But they listened carefully, and they seemed to believe me. At least they let me and Sophia go. I had to promise to be available to come tell the story again at the official inquest. There was always an inquest after a shooting, they said.

'I promise I'll be there. But can I go now?' I asked. 'We have to be in Albuquerque.'

'Sir,' said yet another cop, 'you have suffered a trauma, and you're in shock. I have to tell you it is not wise for you to drive right now.'

'I have to drive,' I said. 'I have no choice.'

'Well, you be careful,' he told me. 'I don't want to have to come scrape your brains off the tarmac later.'

So I took it slow – for Sophia's sake and mine, and for the sake of my brains. I was oblivious to the scenery this time. Sandia Crest loomed huge and close as we approached the city. It was just past noon. El Perrero had been dead for two hours, and Ralph would soon be on his way to the same hospital our mother was in – the attendants told us they would send him down to Albuquerque after a preliminary patching-up at the smaller hospital in Santa Fe. We skirted the crest and drove past Tijeras, and then I took I-40 into town. I had only one helmet, which I'd insisted Sophia wear, and I could hear her crying steadily inside it. It was like listening to a small child trapped inside a refrigerator. I got off the interstate as soon as I could and took back roads the rest of the way to the university hospital. When we pulled into the parking lot I had to help her off the bike and steady her as she worked the kinks out of her legs. Then I undid the chin straps for her and lifted the helmet off. Her face was swollen and puffy, her eyes red with fear and grief. I prayed Sky hadn't gotten any worse, because if she had, it might send Sophia over the edge. But she saw the concern in my face.

'Don't worry about me,' she said, wiping her nose with the back of her hand. It was running freely and she did nothing more than smear snot all over her upper lip. She hawked and spit. 'I'm tough,' she said. 'I can take it.'

'Here,' I said, untucking my shirt from my jeans. 'Blow.'

She bent over and blew her nose on the tail of my T-shirt. 'Sorry,' she said, straightening up.

'Don't worry about it,' I said.

We held hands as we were crossing the parking lot. There was no need to ask directions of the nurses at reception – we both knew the way. We crossed the lobby to the elevators and rode up to the third floor to Sky's room.

She was still out cold, and a nurse told us she hadn't woken up at all. They'd been turning her every few hours, changing her sheets, giving her sponge baths, but she gave no sign that she was aware of any of it. Food came in through one tube and out through other tubes; they were keeping her alive.

'It's not down to making a decision yet,' she said. 'There's still some brain activity. You can see it on that monitor there.'

There was a green screen with erratic patterns on it, lines dipping and rising in jagged peaks and valleys, the electronic translation of my mother's thoughts. I wished I knew how to read them. There were more stories encoded in that mysterious geography, stories I felt with rising dread that I would never get to hear. We were too late.

Sophia was watching them, too. 'What if they stop?' she asked.

'I'll have a doctor come in and talk to you about that,' she said. 'But it might be time to start thinking about what you want to do when that happens.'

When, she'd said. Not *if*.

'I know what she would want to do,' said Sophia. 'She would want us to let her go.'

Her tone was suddenly matter-of-fact and practical, and all traces of her earlier hysteria were gone. I looked at her with new eyes. She was calm and composed, and she stood looking down at our mother with no more expression showing than if she was watching a television program. *My sister has guts*, I thought. When it came down to the wire, she was ready to deliver. I was glad. It wasn't a decision I could have made myself, not after having spent all this time looking for her. Someone else would have to take her away from me – or, rather, someone else would have to let her go.

'Is that your decision?' asked the nurse.

We nodded.

'I'll tell the doctor, then,' she said.

Sophia and I made ourselves comfortable in a couple of chairs and prepared to wait. We didn't talk much at first. We even napped, on and off, as the bright sheet of sunlight emerging from under the blinds traced a receding path along the sheet-metal windowsill and then disappeared. Later we talked a little, not about anything important – our jitters had turned into exhaustion, and it was all we could do to keep our eyes open. The various machines in the room kept up a steady backbeat of pings and rattles and whirrs. My hands had begun to sting from several tiny cuts, though I hadn't noticed them until now, and Sophia kept finding more shards of glass in her hair – my bedroom window, I guessed. Finally she borrowed a brush from the nurse's station and went into the bathroom. I heard the brush rasping and the tinkling sound of the glass as it fell into the sink.

'Listen,' I said through the door, 'I better go see about Ralph.'

'Go ahead,' she said. 'I'll be here.'

I went back down to the lobby and found the reception desk. They told me that Ralph would be out of surgery sometime that night, but I wouldn't be able to see him until the next morning.

'Are they going to be able to save his leg?' I asked.

'We can't tell you anything about that,' one of them said. 'You'll have to wait and talk to his doctor.'

I went back upstairs. Sophia had resettled herself by the bedside.

'How's Ralph?' she asked.

'They won't say. She do anything?' I asked.

At that moment there was a ping from one of the machines – a different ping, I mean. We looked at Sky. Then we looked at the readout of her brain waves. Their outline had changed. They were growing less defined, rounder, almost, as though they were leveling out.

'What does *that* mean?' Sophia asked.

'I don't know,' I said nervously. 'Maybe I better go get a nurse.'

But the nurses already knew. A hefty blond woman came in and made a check of the various devices in the room, interpreting their various signs and auguries with a practiced eye. Then she disappeared and came back with a doctor, who performed the same check all over again. He shone a small flashlight in her eyes and tickled the bottoms of her feet. Then he shook his head.

'It's not going to be long now,' he said. 'If you have any family members you need to call, this would be the time to do it.'

I sat dumbly in my chair.

'We're it,' Sophia told him. 'She doesn't have anyone else. How long?'

'It's hard to say,' he told us. 'But it's probably down to hours now. She might hang on as long as a day, but no more than that.'

Then he was gone. The nurse lingered a moment longer, looking at us sympathetically; but then she was gone, too.

Sophia sat at one side of the bed and I sat at the other. We each took one of Sky's hands in ours, and we clasped our other hands together over her midriff. Sophia bent her head down out of sight. I did likewise.

I thought of the picture I'd taken from the photo album, the one of Sky and Eddie together at the broken pier. I fixed that image in my mind and tried to imagine what the weather must have been like that day. It would have been cold – I was conceived in October, when the winds would have already begun to bluster down from the north. There would have been whitecaps on the lake, most likely. The water was steely gray that day. I could imagine Eddie's arm around her waist, her leaning

274

into him and smiling, telling him through the side of her mouth to hurry up and take it already, she was freezing. I might already have existed by then, perhaps nothing more than a microscopic zygote floating in her uterus. His hand over her belly would have sent gentle waves through the warm, salty sea inside her. Those waves would have rocked me, no bigger than a pinpoint, nothing more than a cluster of cells. Maybe life was sparked into me in that moment, with the flash of the camera, the touch of his hand on her belly. That weekend would have been the first and last time she would have seen him.

We watched as the lines on the screen slowly flattened until they were nothing more than a single horizon. Her chest was still moving up and down with a mechanical gasp from the machine that did her breathing for her. When some more time had passed – how much, I don't know, but I think it was hours – I was aware again of the doctor standing behind me. He put his hand on my shoulder.

'Brain death at 7:04 P.M.,' said the doctor. 'Do you still want to stick with your decision?'

I looked at Sophia.

'Yes,' she said.

We got up and moved to the foot of the bed. The same nurse was with him, the hefty woman with blond hair tied up at the back of her head in two thick ropes. They flicked a switch, pressed a button here and there. The room began to grow quieter. He bent down and did something to the machine that controlled the tubes going into her throat. I put my arm around Sophia and she buried her face in my neck. Then the whirr and click and ping of the machines grew silent as they shut our mother down.

CHAPTER 13

ANOTHER LETTER FROM MILDRED

Dear Billy,

I have not heard much from you recently, so I guess you must be busy. I just wanted to drop you a quick note and ask if you would be coming home soon. I didn't get to see you at Christmas, and I have not had any phone calls from you yet, though it is nice to get your letters.

The reason I wonder if you're coming home, even if only for a brief visit, is that there is something going on here I could use your help with. The mothers and I could all use your help, actually. We have been facing a little bit of trouble from certain people in town, and there is going to be a meeting to straighten everything out. It might be a good idea if you could come home for a couple of weeks. I will explain everything when I hear from you, but please, think it over.

Love,
Mildred

CHAPTER 14

PASSING ON THE MEDICINE

Two days later, I was sitting at another bedside – Ralph's.

'The hell of it is,' he told me, 'this rod they implanted is going to be in there forever. I'm doomed to set off metal detectors for the rest of my life.'

'At least they saved the leg,' I said.

'Oh, I don't mean to complain.' He settled himself deeper into his mattress, wincing in pain. 'Although, to make an egregious understatement, I do have to admit this was completely unexpected. I was really only looking for something to do when I showed up at your place. Talk about bad timing. I had to pick the very moment when you were being besieged.' He reached out and put a hand on my shoulder. 'I feel lucky to be alive,' he said, his voice resonant with significance.

'If he'd wanted to kill you, he would have,' I said. 'He was a trained marksman. He couldn't have missed at that range.'

'That doesn't make me feel any better,' he said, dropping his hand. 'I mean, I was in his *sights*.'

'I'm sorry, Ralph. Very, very sorry.'

'It's not your fault, Mann,' he said. 'I don't blame you. What were you supposed to do about it, anyway?'

I should have done *something*, I thought. I should have told somebody. I'd had every indication that El Perrero wasn't in his right mind. I should have had a damned telephone. Now poor Ralph was laid up for months, all because of my own negligence. I was a fool, I realized, to think I could have protected anybody against that kind of craziness. I had to make it up to him somehow.

'You want me to call your parents for you?' I said. 'To tell them it was my fault?' I didn't know what good that would do, but it was all I could think of – a pathetic gesture, at a time when gestures were useless.

'Ha,' he said. 'You don't want a piece of *that* action. No offense, Mann, but you couldn't handle it. She's already hysterical – my mother, I mean. As soon as I'm well enough to move they're flying me home, and I don't know if I'll ever escape again.'

'Ralph, you're twenty years old,' I said.

'And helpless.' He pointed to his leg. 'For now.'

'*I* know,' I said. 'You should come out to Mannville with me. You could convalesce there. There'd be people to take care of you – me, and Mildred, and whoever she's got staying with her now. You could get better in peace and quiet.'

Ralph folded his hands into a steeple and thought. '*She's* not going to like it,' he said, meaning, I presumed, his mother.

279

'Who cares?' I said. 'You're a free man, my friend. You've got to stand up to her sometime.'

'Well, it's an idea,' he said. 'I appreciate the offer, and I just might take you up on it. It will require some consideration. So you're going home for real?'

I nodded.

'You sure about that? I mean, you're sure it's the right thing for you to do?'

'I don't know,' I said, because for the last couple of days I'd had no idea what was the right thing and what wasn't. Since Saturday, the day Sky died, I'd been in a kind of fog. Consuelo was gone, and so was the only reason I'd stayed behind. Sophia had told me she might be moving on soon herself. There were too many memories in this town, she said, and my talk about improving her future had been having some kind of effect on her, though not quite the effect I'd intended. She thought she might like to see a bit of the world and then reassess her options. She felt the need to travel, to move. I understood that completely. I needed to move myself. But I was running out of money again, and most of all I was still tired – deeply tired, the kind of tired that turns the bones to rubber, that saps the will. Home was the only place I could think about going that didn't make me even *more* tired. I couldn't bear the thought of starting over somewhere else, and I couldn't bear to stay in Santa Fe without Consuelo there. Los Angeles was out of the question. She didn't need me anymore, anyhow. She'd never needed me at all. She hadn't even called. It was I who needed her; but it was too late to fix that, too. She was gone. *Everyone* was gone, or going.

'You okay?' Ralph asked. 'You look spaced out.'

'Sorry,' I said, coming out of my reverie. 'Yeah, I'm all right.'

'Did you get the chance to tell her who you were?'

I shook my head. 'I was too late,' I said. 'I waited longer than I should have.'

'You did the best you could, Mann,' Ralph told me. 'You were someone for her to talk to, at least.'

I hadn't allowed myself much time to think about everything, to let it sink in – I'd kept myself busy with packing, with minor details. But Ralph's words budged the floodgates a little. I grabbed some tissues from a box on Ralph's nightstand and stepped out into the hallway while I honked and blew. The noises I made sounded strange, echoing in the hallway. An old man leaning on a walker stared at me curiously. When I had let out as much as was coming I came back into the room. Ralph looked embarrassed. But he said: 'You're all right, old sock. You'll be fine.'

'Sure,' I said. 'I know it.'

'I'll think about your offer. I kind of like the idea of seeing your town.'

'Just let me know,' I said. 'You have my number out there, and everything.'

'Yup.'

'All right, then.'

'You're going right now?'

'Just gotta run by Sophia's. I'll leave early tomorrow morning.'

He stuck out a hand. I took it, and we shook warmly.

'Don't take any wooden nickels,' he said.

'Catch you on the flip side,' I said.

'God bless America.'

'God bless the president and the New York Yankees.'

'You're a complete son of a bitch, leaving me in a fix like this.'

'You're a big-nosed pain in the ass,' I said. 'And I love you for it.'

He beamed, his buck teeth displaying themselves prominently in the false, antiseptic glare of the hospital's artificial lights.

'I'll remember you said that,' he said.

Sophia lived in a run-down apartment complex about a mile from the Plaza, the kind of place that was thrown up in a hurry overnight about ten years ago, and then left to decompose peacefully, with no interference from maintenance workers. I parked my bike in the lot and grabbed my saddlebags and backpack from the frame. She opened the door wearing an apron, and the smell of something delicious wafted out and tickled my nose.

'I quit the Cowgirl,' she said.

'Good on you,' I said. I stepped in and threw my bags on the floor. 'Franco take it all right?'

'No, but who cares? I told him I was tired of being taken advantage of. He finally offered me a raise, though. I should have threatened to quit months ago.'

'What are you cooking?'

'I'm being domestic,' she said. 'It's a roast.'

'No green chile?'

'You sound disappointed,' she said.

'No, no,' I assured her. 'I love roasts. I just don't know when I'll be tasting green chile again.'

'I'll send you some frozen. Here, sit down. It's almost ready.'

We took two hours over dinner. Neither of us had really recovered our appetites yet; there was something about death that made eating seem futile, almost obscene. I pushed my food around on my plate and managed several bites, but I was full quickly, and so was she. Later, we flopped down on the couch, me with my head in her lap. We just sat quietly. She turned the television on, but muted the volume, and I watched the silent two-dimensional figures move about on the screen, oblivious to everything that was really happening in the world.

'I never had a television when I was a kid,' I said.

'Me neither. Sky claimed it was bad for the brain.'

'What'd you do instead?'

'I read,' she said.

'Me, too.'

She toyed with my hair, winding it around my ear. 'We're a lot alike,' she said. 'It's fun having a brother. I wish you weren't leaving.'

'*You're* leaving, too,' I reminded her.

'Yeah, but I don't know when. Or where. Or even why.'

I was beginning to drop off to sleep, her fingers in my hair sending pleasant chills down my spine.

'You should come out and see me,' I said. 'Come stay with me for a while. Bring old Ralph with you.'

She made some reply, but I didn't hear it. Finally, with my head in her warm lap, I was able to relax more fully than I had in weeks. It was all over, I told myself. Everything had happened that was going to happen. I'd thought once that I could control things, but now I knew that I could only ever hope to participate in the events of my life, not direct them. Once upon a time that thought would have scared me to death, but now it felt good to admit it, as though I'd dropped a heavy load I didn't even know I'd been carrying. Her legs under my head were soft and pillowy, and even though it couldn't have been later than eight o'clock I fell asleep.

I slept like a log for twelve hours. I didn't even notice when she wiggled out from underneath my head and lay down next to me on the couch, her plump body pressed against mine, keeping me warm.

284

In the morning she made coffee, and we drank a cup together without saying much. Then she walked me down to the parking lot and watched me tie everything back down: saddlebags just so, with my typewriter in one side and my still-unfinished manuscript in the other, and my backpack full of clothes tied against the sissy bar so I could lean back into it if I wanted to. Then I took off the eagle medallion I'd bought months earlier, on my first day in town. The keen eyes of the eagle had helped me find what I was looking for, just as the Indian man had told me it would. Now she was the one who needed the gift of strong sight, so she would know what she was looking for when she saw it. I tied it around her neck. She bowed her head graciously, as though an honor was being bestowed upon her; and when she lifted her face again, her eyes were moist and shining.

'I *will* see you again,' she said. 'I want to know you more. You're my very own *brother*.'

'I hope so,' I said.

She brought a hand to her mouth. 'Oh no,' she said. 'I almost forgot. Wait here.' She ran upstairs and came back down a moment later with a Tupperware container, the lid secured further with duct tape.

'It's your half of the ashes,' she said. 'I hope you don't mind I put them in there. I thought the urn might be too bulky for you to carry.'

I put it in the side of the saddlebags that contained my manuscript. Then we hugged. I turned

285

the engine over on my bike, kissed her one last time, and pulled out of the parking lot, waving over my shoulder, with one half of the remains of Eliza McMeel, otherwise known to the world as Sky, pressed against my right calf. Once on the highway, I settled back against the backpack so that my arms just reached the handlebar. It was going to be another long five days, headed east, and I thought I might just as well take it easy on myself.

CHAPTER 15

THE REVENGE OF THE ILLEGITIMATE

I put the Tupperware container high up on a shelf in the closet of my old bedroom, far from where inquisitive little hands could reach it. I set my manuscript on my desk, and the typewriter next to it – the pages of my so-called book looked almost like medieval relics by now, wrinkled and torn and stained with various beverages, and some of the earliest pages already yellow, though they were not more than a year old. But I didn't dwell on the implications of that because I intended to get back to work on it soon. As I dumped my clothes into a hamper and prepared to carry it down to the basement, where the washing machine was, I heard a tapping on my window. I pulled up the shade to see Ellen, strapped into a rappeling harness, hanging twenty feet in the air. She was clutching what looked like a bunch of Frisbees to her chest.

'These yours?' she said, when I opened the window. 'I found 'em while I was working on the roof.'

'Must be,' I said, taking them from her. 'I haven't seen them in a while.'

'You probably lost them up there when you were a kid.'

'I remember now,' I said. 'We never had a way to get them down before.'

'You never had a mountain climber living with you before,' Ellen said. She took a pack of unfiltered cigarettes from inside her surplus flight jacket and lit one up.

Ellen was a wiry, bronzed little woman in her mid-thirties; she was one of what Mildred referred to as her 'girls,' though she was anything but a girl and was the only woman in the house, besides Mildred, without a child of her own. Mildred had told me that Ellen was her surrogate man-of-the-house in my absence – there was nothing she couldn't do with a set of tools. Ellen had regarded me with some suspicion at first. It seemed she'd grown quite happy in her role and wasn't looking forward to being supplanted. But in the day I'd been home she'd already warmed up to me considerably, once she found out I wasn't particularly interested in taking over her job; she didn't know it, but I was too brokenhearted to care. Now she looked up reflectively toward the roof and then spat downward.

'It looks pretty bad up there,' she said. 'Whoever built this place wasn't thinking about water collection. There's about a million places where the rain doesn't get carried away, and it just sits up there and eats away at everything. We're gonna need a whole new roof put on, I think.'

'Well . . . shit.'

'Yeah. Shit is right.'

We both thought for a while, her swaying gently at the end of her rope, me leaning on the windowsill. I picked idly at the peeling paint. The whole damn place was falling apart; Mildred had kept the inside of the house in perfect condition, better than it ever had been before, but the outside was in bad shape.

'Well,' said Ellen finally. 'We'll figure something out, I guess. Maybe we can take up a collection from everybody.'

'Let me tell Mildred myself,' I said. 'She's got enough on her mind already.'

'Suit yourself,' Ellen said. 'I'm gonna look around some more up there.' She pulled on a rope, and with the creaking sound of metal pulleys she was gone.

Though Mildred had started out modestly, there were nine mothers now, and ten babies, too; the total number of people in the house, not including myself and Mildred, was twenty-two. The place had been built with that many people in mind, and in the old days it had accommodated them easily; but it was the first time in my life there'd been more than three people knocking around the hallways, which were no longer gloomy, and the various bedrooms, which were no longer empty and covered in dust, and the parlors, which were no longer the residence of furniture shrouded like ghosts in sheets, but which served as hiding places

289

for children's games and as trampolines for those who were short and light enough to bounce on the old springy couches. The children were allowed to play in all rooms except the main parlor next to the foyer: that was the Conflict Resolution Room, and you were supposed to stay out of it unless you had 'an issue' with someone that needed discussing.

Most of the rooms had names now, in fact. There was also the Common Room, the Birthing Room, and the Diaper Room; and in the second- and third-floor hallways, I'd noticed that there were numbers affixed to all the bedroom doors now, just like in a hotel. That had been Mildred's idea. It made it easier, she said, to keep track of who was where, in case someone needed to be found in a hurry.

I went downstairs, past the Play Room, which at this time of day was filled with a herd of infants and toddlers, as well as those mothers whose turn it was to be on duty – they went in shifts. Some of them had gotten jobs in town or were looking. The number of moms changed as some left and others came in to take their places, but Mildred required all who were able, to work at least part-time. That was how she kept the operation afloat, though she was barely making it. And this roof business was going to put a damper on things. Already, after being home only twenty-four hours, I knew that money was going to have to come from somewhere else.

I stuck my head in the Play Room and waved

at the three on-duty mothers, who smiled back somewhat warily. They were still adjusting to the fact that I was the actual owner of the house, and not Mildred, though I'd promised I wasn't throwing anybody out. A few kids came at me, grabbing at my pant legs. None were old enough to talk yet, but they cooed invitingly at me in their own languages. I played with them for a few minutes and then went and found Mildred. She was sitting at the kitchen table, a ledger spread out before her. I poured myself a glass of milk and sat down.

'How's it look?' she asked.

'Bad,' I said. 'Ellen's saying the whole thing needs to be replaced.'

Mildred took off her bifocals and sighed. 'Shit,' she said.

I was surprised, but only mildly; a lot of things had changed around here.

'I'll go take a look at it myself,' I said. 'Maybe we can get by with some patching here and there. But Ellen sounds like she knows what she's talking about.'

'She sure does,' Mildred said. 'You should have seen how fast she got your grandfather's old Galaxie running.'

I was surprised again, this time at the sudden pang I felt. 'Do me a favor,' I said. 'Let her know that's my baby. I don't want anyone else working on it.'

'Oh, she was just being helpful,' Mildred told

me. 'We needed another car at the time, Billy. And that one was just sitting there.'

I felt ashamed of myself. 'Sorry,' I said. 'It's just—'

'I know. It was Grandpa's.'

'Yeah.'

Mildred laid a hand on mine. 'I *do* hope you're really okay with all this,' she said. 'It's a lot to come home to, I know. And by all rights I should have asked your permission.'

'It's fine, Mildred. Really.'

'You're sure?'

'I kind of like having all these people around,' I said. 'It's different, that's for sure.'

Mildred got up and set a kettle to boil on the stove. 'I'll make some tea,' she said. 'We haven't had much of a chance to talk yet, you and I.' She glanced at the clock. 'Though I have to start dinner soon,' she added.

'What gave you the idea for this, anyway?' I asked. She set a tray of milk and sugar on the table.

'I'm not sure I can explain it,' she said. 'You remember those books I was reading when you left?'

'Yeah.'

'I guess you could say they sort of inspired me,' she said.

'Inspired you how?'

'To *do* something. I didn't know what, at first, but it just sort of happened this way. First there

292

was Abby, and then there were more, and then more, and then more. They just started coming out of the woodwork after a while. I never knew there were so many girls in trouble, Billy. A place like this was *needed*.'

'I guess so,' I said.

The kettle whistled and she poured out the water. Then she sat down again.

'Now tell me, young man,' she said. 'When did you drop out of St James's?'

I gaped at her. 'How did you know?'

'I figured it out pretty quickly,' she said. 'You never mentioned anything about it in your letters, you know.'

'I never really went,' I said. 'I just—'

She held up a hand. 'You don't have to explain,' she said. 'Not unless you want to.'

'It's a long story,' I said. 'A very long one.'

'When you have time, dear,' she said, sipping her tea. 'I'm ready to listen, whenever you have time.'

But there was very little time in that house for anything any more. Everyone was always busy, especially Mildred; I scarcely saw her. It was Letta, another of the 'girls,' who explained to me a few days after my return more about what Mildred was doing, and why. In her blunt, plainspoken way, Letta had a perfect understanding of the satisfaction Mildred gained from all her hard work and from laboring constantly in the service of motherhood.

'It's helpin' her get better,' she told me. 'Y'know,

it's a damn shame – she had all them kids of her own, and ever' one of um took off on her. She don't even hear from um at Christmas. Ain't that wrong?'

'It's horrible,' I agreed.

'An' her husband used to whomp on her sump'n *awful*,' Letta went on. 'It just about breaks my heart, to hear about that. I know all 'bout it. My daddy used ta whomp on my mama, when he was drinkin' – and she used to act like there was nothin' wrong with it, like it was normal. Ain't *that* wrong, too?'

'It sure is,' I said.

'Well,' Letta said – she had her baby on her lap, and she'd already lost her modesty in front of me – the infant began to squall, and Letta hoisted out one massive breast from under her milkstained T-shirt. She offered it to the baby, who was silenced immediately. I didn't know whether I was supposed to look away or act like everything was normal. I looked away, but then I snuck a glance. Either Letta didn't notice me looking, or she didn't care.

'Well,' she said, 'ever' one of us had some kinda problem or other. Used ta be, you didn't have no choice but to stick around, if folks was treatin' you bad. But Mama Millie knows how it is, and she says you don't have to put up with it, not if you don't want to. You can make a choice. If *my* mama coulda come here, I think she woulda.'

'Choices are important,' I said.

'And Mama Millie,' Letta went on, 'never got to make a choice. So it makes her happy to see us have a choice – to see us on our own, which sad as it is better than stickin' around someplace that ain't good for you. Ain't that right?'

'Right,' I said.

'Well, there ya go,' said Letta.

I settled into a routine that seemed to come as naturally as if I'd never been gone. I'd had a vision on my ride back East – not a religious vision, but a literary one, a vision of a multitude of imaginary people suddenly ordering themselves, simplifying their numbers, until they were reduced to only a handful. These were the characters that had been shouting for my attention all this time. Seemingly out of nowhere, I'd realized how things were meant to be with them, what their story was. I spent the better part of a day reordering the skewed pages of my manuscript, and then I realized things were not as bad as they had seemed. There had been an order to those pages, but it took everything getting knocked out of whack to see it. A story couldn't be about everything all at once; it had to be about one thing, and you had to let it come out naturally, without getting in the way of it.

Once again I confined myself to my bedroom, writing all the bits that still needed to be filled out, coming down only for meals or to stretch out on the living room floor to ease my aching back. Instantly

I was smothered with children – they crawled over me like puppies, trailing long silver threads of drool after them and chortling wetly in my ear. I grew accustomed to damp shirt fronts – mine, I mean – and the constant, lingering odor of Desitin, and having to watch where I stepped at every moment, lest I crush someone's fragile fingers.

The work kept me from thinking about Consuelo. In the onrush of events that had followed her departure, there'd been no time for regrets or recriminations on my part, and my mother's death had left me too empty to feel upset about her leaving. But now, as soon as I stopped work for the day, she would creep back into my mind on tiptoe and stand there, waiting for me to notice her. It wasn't the real Consuelo I was thinking of – already she'd transformed herself into something else in my thoughts, a figment, a dream. This was the Consuelo I'd left behind in Santa Fe; but that Consuelo didn't really exist, because I *hadn't* left her. She'd left me. And yet in the eyes of this Consuelo was a look of longing, of sadness. I was consumed with guilt that I'd entertained the thought, however briefly, of hurting her. I guessed it made a difference that I hadn't actually done it, but she knew I'd thought of it – she'd put out her hand to stop me. All it had taken was the slightest pressure of her hand on my arm to make me come to my senses. I wouldn't have hurt her for anything. Maybe I was only guilty of wanting to scare her. But I'd felt sadness when she said she was leaving, and rage when she called me a coward. Maybe she was sorry about that now, and maybe she wasn't. But I found myself wanting to know for sure one way or the other. We'd never gotten the chance to finish the argument we'd started in the kitchen the day she left, and now I felt it hanging over my head, suspended like an anvil – just waiting to drop.

The days ended early in the farmhouse – everyone was exhausted by dinnertime, and by ten they were all asleep, except for the very littlest ones who still woke up every two hours to be fed. One night around midnight, I went downstairs to the kitchen telephone and dialed New Mexico.

'Cowgirl,' said a terse voice.

'Franco?'

'Who's this?'

'Billy Mann.'

'Well! How's it going?'

'Okay,' I said. 'How's it with you?'

'Quiet,' he said. 'Nobody comes in here anymore, now Consuelo's gone. And I have a new waitress who doesn't know what she's doing.'

'Sorry to hear it,' I said.

'Yeah, well, that's life. What's going on?'

'I wanted to ask you something,' I said. 'It's kind of a weird question.'

'I hear everything in this job,' Franco said. 'Lay it on me.'

'You remember the day Consuelo left? When you drove her and Esteban to the airport?'

'Sure.'

'How – how'd she seem?'

'What do you mean?'

'I mean . . . was she crying? Was she upset?'

There was a long pause on the other end. I could hear a couple of voices in the background, voices that I remembered as belonging to some regulars.

'No,' he said finally. 'She seemed pretty happy.'

I didn't say anything.

'You still there?'

'Yeah, I'm here,' I said.

'What'd you wanna know for?'

'I was just wondering, that's all,' I said. 'Just trying to figure something out. Thanks, Franco.'

'Where are you, anyway?'

'I'm in New York,' I said.

'New York! When you coming home again?'

'I am home,' I said. 'Take it easy, Franco.'

I hung up and went back to bed. That answered that. I would forget about her.

Mildred let me alone most of the time. She was busy; besides, she knew something had happened to me out there, and she was letting me get ready to tell her about it. She knew that I needed to be quiet for a while – or that I needed to write it all down first before I could tell anybody what went on out there in the desert. But sometimes we talked during a few stolen moments in the kitchen, when she wasn't organizing, or feeding, or cleaning something or someone. That was how I first

298

learned about the threat of the Ladies' Benevolent Circle. This was the 'trouble' she had alluded to in her last letter, in which she had asked me to come home – not knowing, of course, that I would be coming home anyway, for other reasons.

'Witches,' Mildred said. 'That's all they are. Meddling, superior old witches.'

'They really want to shut you down?'

'As if I was running a business!' Mildred said botly. 'As if I was doing this for *money*!'

I remembered the Ladies' Benevolent Circle. They were a group of elderly women with high morals and long-standing family trees, though none of them were as deeply entrenched in the history of Mannville as us Manns had been. They'd plagued Grandpa for years, pestering him to come to church, to send me to Sunday school, to stop drinking and become a responsible member of society once more. He'd called them the Lady Malevolent Screwballs – but never to their faces. Nobody ever insulted the Ladies to their faces.

'What on earth would the LBC have against you?' I asked. 'You'd think they'd be sympathetic. I mean, *they* were all mothers, too, once. Most of them, anyway.'

'Yes, you would expect a little more in the way of understanding from them,' said Mildred. 'They must find us threatening, or they wouldn't bother. Church ladies, my goodness me – what about Christian charity? My girls aren't *bad* girls, Billy. They're just unlucky.'

'I know,' I said. I knew all about running out of luck – and some of these girls had bad luck written all over their faces.

'We have a hearing next month, actually. I made a request for funding from the town council, and you should have *heard* the stink those ladies raised. I've been worried sick about it. Now I have to speak in public, and I've never done that before in my life. But *you* could help,' said Mildred, brightening.

'I've never spoken in public, either,' I said.

'They'd listen to you, Billy.'

'You think so?'

'Heavens, yes. This town is named after you!'

'Not after *me*,' I said. 'After my great-great—'

'I know the story,' Mildred interrupted. 'What I mean is, this is Mannville, and your name is Mann. They'd have to *listen* to you, at least.'

'Maybe,' I said. 'I don't know.'

'Think about it,' she urged me. 'Otherwise everyone will have to leave. And *that*,' she added unnecessarily, 'would be a disaster.'

I thought about it. I was getting attached to some of the kids, and I'd gotten to be friends with Ellen, who knew as much about engines as I did, and Letta, whose laugh was like the constant twanging of a rubber band. I didn't want them to have to leave – I knew that most of them would have nowhere to go, at least nowhere as good as this.

Another few weeks went by. One of the mothers

left and was replaced by a new one, who was not properly a mother yet but about to become one very soon; she gave birth in May, with the encouragement of Mildred, a professional midwife, and several sidelines coaches. I was not even allowed in the hall while she was in labor, but I got to see the baby the next day. He was a wrinkled gnome of a thing, with a pinched and reddened face. His mother was fifteen years old and looked about twelve – she had come all the way from Ohio, she told me, because word was spreading about a lady in New York who would take you in for a while if you had nowhere else to go.

'Mama Millie is famous,' she said to me. 'And I *didn't* have anywhere else to go. Do you know how long I'll be allowed to stay?'

'You can stay as long as you want,' I said, wiggling one finger at the baby's nose. His eyelids flickered open briefly and focused on nothing; then they closed again. He yawned.

'Who are *you*, anyway?' she asked me. 'Were you born here?'

'No – I was born in town,' I told her. 'But I grew up here.'

'She's been around a while, I guess,' said the girl – speaking of Mildred. She must have thought I was just another of the babies and that I'd simply stayed on. I let her think that. That was what I was, in a way; I was just the first of these babies, even though I had twenty years' seniority over them. I'd been left here so I could have a choice, too.

Who knew how things would have been for me otherwise? I wouldn't have this house, if Sky had kept me – I wouldn't have the lake, or Mildred, or Mannville. I wouldn't have my room to write in, either. I wouldn't have had any of the things that made me me – I would be someone else.

And I wouldn't have the book.

I finished it seven weeks after coming home. Once I'd decided to simplify the story, it had turned out all right; maybe there was a chance I could get it published. I went to the library and perused a copy of the *Guide to Literary Agents*. I didn't know much about publishing, but I did know I was going to need representation. I mailed off letters to a few agencies in New York City.

I didn't say anything about this to anyone, especially Mildred – she had enough to worry about. While I'd been busy up in my room, Mildred been growing more and more worried as the day of the council hearing drew nearer. She refused to speak of it, but I could see the signs; she muttered to herself, dropped things, forgot where she had put other things.

'Look,' I said finally. 'I'll do it – I'll talk to them.'

Mildred threw her arms around me and squeezed until my neck bones cracked.

'I knew you would,' she whispered. 'I feel better already.'

I persuaded one of the mothers to cut my hair the day of the meeting; she was a Chinese girl from

Buffalo, and she'd gone to hair-dressing school, although she was frank with me about the fact that she'd never actually been *employed* as a hairdresser. Afterward I put on one of Grandpa's old suits. The sleeves were too short and I tried to stretch them out by pulling on them while I waited for Mildred to get ready. She came down in her church clothes, wearing a touch of makeup. The Chinese hairdresser had done her hair, too.

'How do I look?' she asked.

'Hot,' I said. She smacked me on the shoulder.

'I'm serious,' she said. 'I'm too old to look "hot." I want to look *respectable*.'

'You do,' I assured her.

'I don't look like a madame?'

'A *madame*?'

'I don't want to leave any room for misunderstanding,' she said primly.

'They don't think you're running a—'

'I know what people are saying, and I want there to be *no room*,' she repeated, 'for misunderstanding.'

'You don't look like a madame,' I said. 'Not even close.'

'Good,' she said. 'Now let's get moving.'

We pulled up in front of town hall at exactly one o'clock. I spent several minutes saying hello to people I hadn't seen since leaving for Santa Fe – I'd delivered groceries to a lot of them. At five after one a man came out of the meeting room and announced that we were running late, and if we were going to get started, it might as well be now. He stopped short on seeing me; it was George Lemmon, owner of Lemmon's Autobody.

'Well, whaddaya know,' he said. 'How de do, young Billy.'

'Hi, Mr Lemmon,' I said.

His greeting was somewhat restrained; I'd last seen him years earlier in the living room of Elsie Orfenbacher, the woman who'd taught me the art of carnal love in the days when I was a delivery boy. Elsie had gotten around some, I knew; I hadn't been the only recipient of her attention. George Lemmon and I had Elsie in common, and I could tell he was remembering that now as he looked at me.

'You the sergeant-at-arms?' I asked him.

He grinned, all teeth. 'Naw,' he said. 'I got voted in as town manager last year.'

'Is that right,' I said. 'Congratulations, then.'

'Thanks. You here to speak about the . . . the house?'

'Yup.'

'Thought so. Didn't know you were home again. Well, come on in,' he said.

Mildred and I and the others waiting in the hallway entered the meeting room, which was in pretty much the original condition it had been in since my great-great-grandfather had built town hall. Old Willie had built the place, and it was set up like a miniature version of what he must have imagined a courtroom was supposed to look like. It had been intended to double as exactly that; there hadn't been then, and weren't now, enough crimes committed in Mannville to warrant an entirely separate courthouse. Where the judge's bench would have been was a long table, which was where the members of the council sat. To either side were what were supposed to be jury boxes. They looked more like church pews, with ornate wooden carvings on the ends. On the wall behind the council table, facing the doorway, was an elaborate mural of Blind Justice holding her scales. On one tray of the scales was a scroll of paper, presumably meant to represent the law; on the other sat an old man with a flowing white beard, his legs dangling off the scale like a child seated high up in a tree. With a start, I realized the old man was Willie himself. He leaned forward, his elbows resting on his knees. He appeared to be listening and watching intently.

There were a number of items of business to be attended to before we got to the part that concerned me. We sat through a desperate plea for more shelves from Miss Willoway, the librarian. We just did not have enough shelves, she said, and people were tripping over books that were stacked on the floor. It was only a matter of time before someone broke their neck and we had a lawsuit on our hands. George Lemmon said let's take a vote on it, then, all in favor of new shelves for the library, say aye. There were two men and one woman on the council, including George himself, and they all said aye.

Next on the agenda was a new drinking fountain for the high school. At this juncture the other man on the council was moved to passionate speech; the old fountain had been vandalized so many times that he was just plain sick and tired of it, he said, and if these damn kids, excuse me, these *darn* kids today didn't realize the value of a brand-new drinking fountain, why then they didn't deserve one, and that was that, as he saw it. He sat down and crossed his arms. Another thought occurred to him, and he stood up once more: he just wanted to add that if *he* had ever been caught vandalizing *anything* when *he* was a boy, why, his old man would have taken a switch to his bee-hind, and no mistake, and there was just not enough discipline in schools these days. He sat down again. There was a murmur of assent from the onlookers, but then the lone woman on the council, a plump lady in a pants suit, stood up and said: 'For heaven's sake, Tom. You can't just let them go thirsty. Why doesn't the principal put the hall monitor near the fountain, instead of all the way down to the gym, where he can't see what's going on?'

I stared in disbelief at the woman. I hadn't recognized her now-rotund face, but I recognized her voice immediately. It was none other than Elsie Orfenbacher herself.

Principal Meyer stood up from his seat in the audience.

'George, lemme get a word in here,' he said.

'All righty,' said George.

'I just wanted to say that Mrs Lemmon has a point.'

I began to choke. Mrs Lemmon? *Mrs Lemmon?*

Principal Meyer turned to look at me. 'You okay, son?' he said. I waved one hand. He faced the council again.

'I have an idea,' he announced.

There was a respectful silence.

'I'll appoint *two* hall monitors,' he said, a note of triumph in his voice. 'We have to have one by the gym because that's where the kids sneak out to smoke. But I'll put the other one by the new fountain, if the council agrees to buy us one, that is, and then that hall monitor can watch it, and that way we'll . . . why, by golly, we'll have two hall monitors.'

Principal Meyer had grown flustered at the last minute, being unused to attention from so many adults, but his wisdom carried the day, and there was a smattering of applause. George went through the vote again, and Tom, the other man on the council, said nay, but George and Elsie said aye and that was it. Apparently a majority was all that was needed.

More items: people just had to quit throwing their lawn clippings in the street, that was that, no discussion, they had to be bagged up, where did they think they lived, anyway, Cambodia? Next guy who didn't bag up his lawn clippings was gonna get fined twenty dollars. Applause. Next: Officer Madison wanted a raise. Oh, crap, said a man from the audience, again? He doesn't do nothing but sleep in that car, which I would like to remind the council is brand-new, anyway. Officer Madison stood up, unperturbed; he knew they probably wouldn't give him a raise, heck, that was all right, he had to ask, but in that case could he please have the money to order a new case of pepper spray? George fumbled through some papers. What on earth, he wanted to know, had happened to the *old* case of pepper spray? Madison hemmed and hawed and finally said he had used it all up. In training, he said.

'Well, I thought your deodorant smelled different!' called some wiseacre.

General laughter, verging on hysteria. George hammered and hammered until everyone calmed down, and then he gave the gavel a couple more bangs; I could tell he didn't get the chance to use it much and was enjoying himself.

'All right, all right,' he said. 'We're almost done. One last thing, though. This is kind of a big deal. This is about—' he consulted the papers in front of him again – 'the case of the Thomas Mann Junior Memorial Haven for Single Mothers versus the Town of Mannville. Now, I know some folks are likely to get kind of het up over this one, so I want to remind you of the rules: no talking out of turn. You want to say something, you raise your hand and wait till I say it's okay. We got two people speaking today, and then we'll open it up for general discussion. Everybody got it?'

Nods, more murmurs. George banged his gavel again.

'Right,' he said. 'First up is Henrietta Blankenship, representing the Ladies' Benevolent Circle. You ready, Hen?'

'Yes, George,' said a buxom elderly woman. She stood up and produced a sheaf of papers from her purse. There was an audible groan from everyone; this was going to be a long one.

'"It has come to our attention,"' she read from the papers, '"that a request for funding from the town council has been received by one Mildred Mahoney, who is operating a sort of—"' here she grew flustered, and put the papers down. 'Well, I don't know *what* to call it,' she said. 'All I know is, there's some questionable characters up there, and we oughtn't to give them any money. We can't even afford a snowplow for our own people, and a lot of those girls up in that house are from out of town – they're not Mannvillians at all. Now we have *morals* in this town. We're not New York City. There are certain kinds of things that people will do no matter what. You can't change human nature. The Ladies' Benevolent Circle recognizes that. But that doesn't mean you have to flat out say it's okay for folks to just do whatever they want, and then give them money to *do* it.'

'What kinds of things are you talking about, exactly?' said George. 'I mean, what do you think they're doing up there?'

Henrietta Blankenship drew herself up and pointed

309

her nose at the council. 'I'm not talking about what they're *doing*,' she said. 'I'm talking about what they *did*.'

Some in the audience found that funny. George got to use his gavel again. 'Order,' he said. 'Let's just get this straight, Hen. You object to the town funding the Mann House because they're not good people, or because they're from out of town, or what?'

'Well, Mannville never had a problem with illegitimate children before,' said Henrietta Blankenship heatedly, 'and all I know is all of a sudden we seem to have a whole bunch of them. That kind of thing doesn't sit well, George, and you know it. It makes the town look bad.'

'You don't want to give them any money, then,' said George. 'Is that it?'

'Not just that,' said Henrietta. 'We . . . well, we want them to go.'

'Go where?'

'Oh, George, I don't know. Back where they came from, for heaven's sake. Why did they have to come here, of all places? This was a nice, happy little town. Nothing bad ever happened here. Is that why they came? So they could feel clean again?'

Everyone grew silent and reflective for a moment. Even Henrietta Blankenship appeared to consider the weight of her own words. I knew them to be complete lies, of course – many bad things had happened in Mannville. Take the infamous case of Annie Simpson versus her father, for example, which had never been tried in front of the council; if Henrietta Blankenship had known about it, she might not say these things never happened. But I was the only one who knew about that. I shifted in my seat and did my best to hold my tongue.

'You got any more to add?' George asked her.

'I guess not,' she said. She sat down.

'Right,' said George. 'Thank you. The council has heard everything you said, and we're going to think about it carefully. Okay. Next up we had Mildred Mahoney, who is in charge of the house in question, but there's gonna be a little change, because we got someone else instead.'

'Now just hold on a minute,' said Henrietta, standing up again. 'That's not according to procedure. If Mildred doesn't want to talk, that doesn't mean—'

'Okay, Hen,' said George. 'Your objection is duly noted. No more interrupting, please. We have Mr William A. Mann the Fourth with us here today, so I guess you have the floor now, Billy, if you're ready.'

Everyone turned to look at me when I stood up. I felt myself growing red all over as two hundred pairs of eyes fixed on my face.

'You mind if I come up in front, George?' I asked. 'I want to be able to look at everyone when I talk.'

'Sure,' said George. 'Come on up.'

I went to the front of the hall and stood there, unable to decide what to do with my hands. I

311

settled on putting one in my pocket and leaving the other at my side. My fingers encountered something strange in there; after a moment, I identified it as a pacifier. The discovery of it discombobulated me – someone small had been playing in my pants before I put them on. I wrapped my hand around it and squeezed it as I talked.

'Well,' I said. 'I wish I'd made some notes, because Mrs Blankenship said a lot of things I'd like to respond to. But I guess I'll just have to try and remember them as best I can.'

I cleared my throat, looked at my toes for a moment, then looked up again. There was dead silence. Their faces were neither hostile nor defensive; a lot of folks were actually smiling at me. Mildred's eyes were shut. I began to loosen up a little.

'Most of you know me,' I said. 'I delivered groceries for Harold and Emily Gruber for a long time, and I bet I've probably knocked on every door in town at one time or another. You all had me come inside and wait in your kitchen while you paid the bill. Sometimes you left me alone in there while you went and found the right change, and there was never any question that you couldn't trust me, because that's the kind of town this is. We may not always get along with each other, but if there's one thing about Mannville, it's that we trust each other. Right?'

I was laying it on a little thick, but they liked it. There were nods of assent, more smiles.

'So you know I wouldn't want to do anything that I thought would be bad for the town. I've been gone the last couple of years, but my family has been here since Mannville was founded. In fact, I don't have to remind you that Mannville was renamed after my great-great-grandfather Willie, who I think is in that painting right up there.' I turned and gestured to the outlandish piece of art behind me. I had never been inside town hall before, and I wondered who on Earth had commissioned that monstrosity; from what I knew of Papa Willie, he would never have allowed such a thing.

'I don't say that to brag,' I continued, facing them again. 'We had a lot of money once, which is all gone now, thanks to an idea my grandfather had which didn't quite work out.' I permitted myself a small smile here, to show them it was okay to laugh if they wanted to. 'I guess ostriches just aren't suited to the climate in Mannville,' I said. George had to bang his gavel again while everyone laughed at that one, but I was glad they laughed. The tension in the room was now broken completely.

'But even though the money is gone, we're still here,' I went on. 'We never thought we were any better than anyone else. Grandpa took it pretty hard when his plan failed, and he kind of pulled back from everyone. But it wasn't because he was stuck up. It was because he was . . . well, he was brokenhearted.'

313

I had to clear my throat a couple of times before I could go on. 'Brokenhearted' really didn't begin to cover it. I thought of my old Grandpa asleep in his rocking chair in the living room, an empty bottle of whiskey lying on its side on the floor. I remembered being small enough that my head only just came over his knees, pulling on his pant leg, trying to get him to wake up.

'Anyway,' I said, 'Mrs Blankenship pointed out that this town has never had a problem with illegitimate children before. Well, Mrs Blankenship, there's an illegitimate child standing up here right now in front of you, in case you'd forgotten. There was never any secret about that. Nobody ever treated me any differently because of who I was. Well, not too many people did, anyway. You all knew it wasn't my fault, the way I was born. It wasn't anyone's fault. It just happened that way. You can't blame babies for the way they come into the world. And you can't blame their mothers for getting pregnant. Women get pregnant. That's how it works. Sometimes it happens by accident, but as far as I'm concerned that doesn't make them bad people.

'Now look. Mildred came to live with us after my grandfather quit drinking because they loved each other. When Grandpa died, I told her my house was her house, for as long as she cared to stay. Most of you know her by now. You know she's just like the rest of us, even if she isn't from here. She's a good person who wants to help other people. So if there's any question about her having the right to do whatever she wants in that house, I want to lay that to rest right now. That house is as much hers as it is mine, and that's that.

'And as far as these single moms go,' I said, 'I've met them, and they're not bad people. They haven't committed any crime. They're no worse than the rest of us. Mildred's not running a bordello, for heaven's sake. She's trying to give some people a break because no one else will. A lot of these girls were too young to know any better. That kind of thing happens in towns all across America. The only difference is, in most cases, if a girl gets pregnant she has people to help her out. She has parents, a boyfriend, maybe she gets married. These girls don't have anyone except Mildred to help them. Some of them,' I said, thinking of Abby, 'didn't get pregnant through any fault of their own. They got pregnant because – well, because there are bad people in the world, people who will take advantage of someone weaker than them. People they thought they could trust, but it turned out they couldn't.'

I stopped to collect my thoughts. Everyone was silent. They were hanging on my every word. I had been speaking without a thought as to where it would come from – and they were paying attention.

'There's a whole bunch of little babies up there in my place right now, with their mothers to take care of them,' I said. 'When I showed up a couple of months back, those mothers got scared because they thought I was going to throw them out. Even Mildred told them that if I said they had to go, then they would have to go, because it's my place and I make the rules. But there was no way I could look those women in the eye and tell them they had to leave, and I think every single one of you would feel the same—' here I looked directly at Henrietta Blankenship, who bristled – 'if you were to meet them yourselves.'

'Now let me tell you a story. When I was born, my mother didn't have any place to take me. She couldn't take care of me herself – I can't explain why, but that was just the way things were. What she did was the next best thing. She took me somewhere where she knew I would be taken care of. She left me at the very house we're talking about today, and that was where I grew up. People might have thought it was a little strange, but nobody questioned my right to be there, because I was one of the Manns.'

You can always tell a Mann by his eyes, Grandpa used to say. *All babies have blue eyes when they're born, but Mann eyes are always blue, come hell or high water.*

'It's the biggest house around,' I said. 'There are tons of rooms in that place that have been sitting empty for decades. Houses are for people to live in. And that house in particular, for all the time I've known it, has been the kind of place you could go when you didn't belong anywhere else. That was what it was for me. I know there isn't much money to give, but the fact is we don't need the town's money. Some of those women have jobs, and they'll get by just fine. But I have to ask you, please. You didn't throw me out when I came to live there. Don't throw them out, either.'

I was finished. It was a lame ending, and everyone seemed to think there was more to say. They waited, but I couldn't think of anything else that wouldn't sound redundant. I turned to George. Elsie Orfenbacher was staring at me hard. I met her gaze unflinchingly. If there was anyone in the world who could sympathize with those mothers, it was her, and I begged her with my eyes to say aye when it came to the vote. She might be respectable now that she was married, but I knew she hadn't forgotten those afternoons we spent together when I was a delivery boy, when she taught me those things I was so desperate to learn. She winked at me; just the barest hint of a wink, a sign of complicity. Suddenly I was very glad to see Elsie up there on the council.

'I guess that's it,' I said.

'All right, then,' said George.

'Wait a moment, please,' said Mildred.

'Yes, ma'am,' said George. 'You have something to add?'

'Yes,' said Mildred, standing up. 'You forgot to tell them about the open house, Billy.'

'Which open house is that, now?' said George.

Yes, I thought – *which open house is that?*

317

'The open house for everyone to come up and see for themselves,' said Mildred. 'I guess it slipped Billy's mind. But everyone is invited to come up to the Mann House this weekend so they can meet the babies and their mothers for themselves. Saturday afternoon. Four o'clock. Hope you all can make it.'

She sat down again, as cool as a cucumber.

'That right, Billy?' said George.

'Oh,' I said. 'Yes. I completely forgot. George – I mean, Mr Lemmon – I mean, I would like to request that the Council hold off on taking a vote until they have a chance to come on up and see with their own eyes what's going on. Would that be okay?'

The council members looked at each other. More specifically, George looked at Elsie, who arched her eyebrows and set her lips in a firm line. I had seen that look from her more than once myself, and I knew full well what it meant. George was receiving silent instruction from his wife.

'I think that's a good idea,' he said. 'Tom?'

'Oh, sure, what the heck,' said Tom.

'Right,' said George. 'This meeting is adjourned until two weeks from today, same day, same time, at which time we will have visited the house and will be better prepared to make a decision.'

'I object,' said Henrietta Blankenship, but nobody paid any attention to her. George picked up his gavel and banged it once. I noticed for the first

318

time that it was not a proper gavel at all. It was a Black and Decker hammer.

Mildred waited until we were back in the car and heading for home. Then she said, 'I was all right, wasn't I?'

'You were great,' I said. 'You surprised me.'

'I didn't even know I was going to say that until I said it,' she told me. She fluffed her hair with one hand. 'I've never spoken to a crowd before,' she said. 'I wasn't nervous at all. I kind of liked it.'

We drove along in silence for a while. Then she said, 'You didn't just come home because I asked you to, did you?'

'No,' I said.

'You never meant to go to school at all.'

'No,' I said.

'You were out there looking for your mother.'

It wasn't a question; it was a statement. I reached into my breast pocket and pulled out the snapshot of my parents I'd taken from Sky's photo album. I'd stuck it in my pocket as a new sort of talisman, to replace the eagle medallion. Sophia had told me I could have all the pictures I wanted, but this was the only one of my mother that seemed to have anything to do with me. The rest of them were of someone I didn't know.

I handed the picture to Mildred and let her look at it for a while. She'd known as much of the story as I did before I left, and it didn't take her long to put the rest of it together now that she had the evidence in front of her. She just looked at it and looked at it, and after a while she reached over and put her hand on top of mine as it gripped the steering wheel.

CHAPTER 16

THE EAGLE DREAM REVISITED

People would talk about that open house for years – as far as spontaneous parties go, it was only *fairly* good, but it was probably the most exciting thing that had happened involving us Manns since the great Ostrich Fiasco, when we had first attained local notoriety. It seemed like the whole town came, though of course they hadn't; word of the invitation had spread rapidly from those at the meeting, and by the end of the day perhaps two hundred people had trooped through the farmhouse to peer at the babies, and also to see for themselves just what kind of women unwed mothers really were. It was the first time in at least fifty years that so many Mannvillians had been invited inside. Legends had sprung up around us, and around Grandpa, and now around Mildred and her mothering project. Some folks came out of a sense of moral duty, but most were there out of curiosity; also, I had let it be known that there would be free beer.

The LBC was there in force, of course, and then I saw the wisdom of Mildred's plan – the babies had all been dolled up as cute as they could be made, and even Henrietta Blankenship, who was both mother and grandmother, couldn't resist them. The house was filled with admiring women, and the noise level soon reached cacophonous proportions. Their husbands took refuge with me outside by the beer cooler, where we stood around sipping Labatt's in the shade of an old sycamore.

George Lemmon and I were cautious around each other at first, but it turned out he'd been stationed at Kirtland Air Force Base when he was in the service, so he and I fell into conversation about Albuquerque – it was yet another thing he and I had in common. I was relieved to find that he didn't seem to bear me any ill will about Elsie; *he* seemed relieved that I didn't bring her up.

Someone had a guitar in his trunk, and he broke it out and played a couple of rollicking country tunes. Another man went into the house and came out with a pair of spoons. Andy Andersen asked me if Grandpa's banjo was still playable, so I went to see if I could find it. The strings were old and out of tune, but Andy worked on it until it made a passable sound, and within moments the three men were playing a country breakdown. There was nothing Mannvillians liked more than live country music – I'd forgotten how much I liked it myself. Inevitably, as the music picked up the beer disappeared, and I was sent out for more.

By the time I got back it had turned into a real party, and at dark the musicians moved inside. There was some dancing, and a small amount of beer-induced silliness; a very short man named Hans had had far more to drink than was good for him, and after falling asleep in the bathtub he awoke to find his pants full of shaving cream. His forty-year-old brother was accused and gleefully confessed. There followed a wrestling match, during which the shaving cream was liberally squirted out of Hans's pants all over the living room, until I made them take it outside.

Other than that, however, the event was a success. The LBC seemed to part with Mildred on considerably better terms, though this was not purely due to a change of heart. George whispered to me that *their* annual request for funding was up for renewal, and that Elsie had let it be known she was on the fence about which way to cast her vote – she didn't see why the town should keep funding the LBC's social events, but if they were to ease up on poor Mildred, and therefore on me, she might be disposed to make the vote unanimous.

'God bless 'er,' I said.

'Here's to Elsie,' George said. We clinked bottles.

The next morning I got out of bed late and was scraping shaving cream out of the living room rug when a familiar car rolled into the driveway and came to a halt in front of the carriage house. It was a little Japanese job, a green one. As I watched out the window, Sophia got out of the driver's side and stretched. Then she went around to the passenger door and opened it. A pair of crutches emerged, followed by a head, followed by the rest of him. I let out a whoop of joy. She'd brought Ralph along with her.

I went out onto the porch as they were coming up the steps. Sophia grabbed me around the middle and hung on as if for dear life. Ralph waved a crutch at me and nearly toppled over, his bad leg sticking out in front of him. He caught himself on his other crutch and pivoted around wildly before regaining control.

'Surprise!' he said.

'It's us!' said Sophia.

'What the hell took you guys so long?' I asked. 'I've been expecting you for weeks!'

'I had to wait until I could bend my leg,' Ralph said. 'I had a big old cast on there for a while. Plus, we went to Vegas.'

'I won four hundred dollars,' said Sophia, kissing me.

'And I spent five hundred,' said Ralph. 'Nice haircut, by the way. You working for the government now?'

I ignored that. 'Looks like you brought a lot of stuff with you,' I said. The roof of the car was loaded down with luggage. 'You planning on being gone a while?'

'A *long* while,' said Sophia. 'Actually, forever. I've left Santa Fe for good.'

'Me, too,' said Ralph. 'Or at least I'm taking a break.'

'You want help unloading the car?' I headed for the driveway, but Ralph put his hand on my chest.

'Hold up there, sport,' he said. 'Not just yet.'

'Why not?'

'We need to talk for a minute.'

There was a bench on the porch, and Ralph levered himself over to it and sat down. Sophia sat next to him and patted an empty spot. I sat down, too.

'Two things to tell you,' said Ralph.

'I'm listening,' I said.

'Okay. First . . .' He looked at Sophia. 'I don't know how to tell him,' he said.

'Let's show him,' she suggested.

'Good idea.' Ralph leaned over and kissed Sophia hungrily on the lips. She threw her arms around him and kissed him back passionately. After several moments Ralph leaned back, out of breath. Sophia smiled at me in triumph.

'What do you think of *that*?' said Ralph.

I could have gone my whole life without ever seeing Ralph kissing someone, but instead of saying so I pumped his hand and slapped him on the back. Sophia was blushing. I kissed her on the cheek. 'Lovely,' I said. 'Perfect.'

'I *knew* you'd be happy for us,' said Ralph. 'Thing is, Mann, you can't spend all that time in a car with someone without wondering what they look like naked.'

'Tell him the truth,' Sophia said, hitting him on the leg – his good one.

'Right,' said Ralph. 'The truth is that I've always sort of had the hots for your sister here.'

'What are you talking about? You two hated each other!'

'No, we didn't,' said Sophia. 'We just *thought* we did.'

'Right,' I said. 'I won't even ask you to explain that one.'

'And I *am* pretty cute, as it turns out,' Ralph told me. 'There's something kind of sexy about a guy with a bullet wound.'

'You're really happy for us?' said Sophia.

'Of course I am,' I said.

'So it puts you in a good mood?'

'A good mood?'

'I mean, you're feeling pretty happy right now?'

'I'm happy to see you guys, if that's what you mean,' I said, puzzled.

'All right,' said Sophia. 'So now we'll tell you the second thing.'

They looked at each other again.

'You tell him,' said Ralph. But she shook her head.

'We should show him this one, too,' she said. 'It's easiest.'

'Yeah,' said Ralph, 'but what if—'

'Oh, for Chrissake,' I said. 'One of you tell me.'

'All right. Wait here,' said Sophia. She got up from the bench and went over to the car.

'Maybe you should close your eyes,' said Ralph.

So I shut my eyes. I heard the car door slam and two sets of footsteps walking over the gravel. I think I smelled her before I saw her, so I knew who it was even before I looked. But I was afraid I might be wrong, so I sat there in darkness, waiting.

'Open them,' said Sophia.

I opened them to see her, standing with Sophia.

'Hello, Beelee,' said Consuelo.

Later, when everyone had been introduced to everyone, Consuelo and I went to the only place in the house where there was any privacy: my bedroom. We hadn't said much to each other, yet. She seemed nervous, hesitating to meet my eyes, and I was too shocked at seeing her to do much more than mumble a few vague words. I closed the door to my room, and we were alone.

She was sitting on my bed, looking out the window at the lawn below, where a few of the mothers were sunning their babies. I stood there, wondering what to do with myself. Consuelo wore a bemused half smile, as if she couldn't quite believe where she was. I couldn't believe it, either. I had given up hope of even a phone call, and now here she was in Mannville, in my very own house.

'Long time no see,' I said finally.

'Yes,' she said. 'I know.'

I sat down on my desk, facing her. She sat with her hands in her lap.

'Things going okay for you out there in Los

Angeles?' I asked her, wondering meanwhile that if they *were* going okay, it was strange that she'd come all the way out here. Something must be up, I thought. She wouldn't come to Mannville just to say hello.

She nodded. 'Things are okay,' she said.

'You getting much work?'

'A little,' she said. 'Some clubs, here and there. Things are pretty good.'

'Uh-huh,' I said.

She looked at me now, her eyes wide. I moved to the bed and sat down next to her, not touching her. We looked out the window together.

'It's weird to have you here,' I said. 'This is where I grew up.'

'I know,' she said. 'I wanted to see it. You told me so much about the house, and the town, and Mildred. I like her,' she said. 'She seems like a very good woman.'

'Mildred's all right,' I said. 'When they made her they broke the mold.'

'They broke what?'

'It's a saying,' I said. 'It means there aren't many people like her in the world.'

'I see,' she said.

After a few more moments of pensive silence, she said, 'I guess you are wondering why I came here.'

'Yeah,' I said. 'It's crossed my mind.'

'Are you glad to see me?'

We looked at each other again. 'You never called,' I said.

'Beelee, I didn't know where you were,' she said. 'We had no phone, first of all. I called Franco to ask if he'd seen you, but he said you were gone. I went back to Santa Fe to see if you had moved or something, and that was when I ran into Ralph and Sophia. They said you were back in New York, and they were going to see you. So I asked if I could come.'

'You wanted to see me that badly?'

She nodded. 'Yes.'

'Is there anything wrong?' I asked.

'No,' she said slowly. 'Not exactly wrong, no.'

We sat facing each other now. When we looked at each other it seemed like talking was the least important thing; I just wanted to look at her. After a few moments I realized we were holding hands, our fingers interlacing. Still we didn't say anything. She leaned forward, and I put my arms around her, smelling her hair.

'I'm sorry,' I said, into her neck.

She nodded.

'Me, too,' she said.

'I missed you,' I said. 'I *more* than missed you. It hurt to think about you.'

She nodded again. 'It hurt me, too,' she said. 'I wanted you to come with me more than anything.'

'Did you come all the way out here just to tell me that?'

Instead of answering, she lay down on the mattress. She pulled me toward her and wiggled up close to me, so that we were like spoons. That had always been my favorite way to be with her. I put my hand on her shoulder and squeezed it; I ran it up and down her side, spitting her hair out of my mouth. Then she took my hand and placed it on her stomach.

'You see?' she said. 'This is why I came.'

I froze. I hadn't noticed anything different about her before, because her dress was loose and covered the stark lines of her body. But now that I was touching her I could feel the difference in her shape. Her belly was lightly rounded, convex, hot and hard.

'Oh,' I said.

'Yes,' she said. 'I thought you might say something like that.'

I touched her gingerly. 'Wow,' I said.

'You want to see it?' she said.

She rolled onto her back and pulled her dress up over her stomach. I could see the gentle protrusion now, a soft hill in the landscape of her where none had been before.

'How far along?' I asked.

'Three months,' she said.

'Wow,' I said.

'This is why I couldn't just call you,' she said. 'I had to tell you myself.'

'I see,' I said.

'I am not here to force you into saying anything, one way or the other,' she told me. 'But I had to come and tell you to your face.'

'Yeah,' I said. 'I understand.'

'You're not mad that I came?'

'No.' I stroked her belly.

'Are you still glad to see me?'

'Yes,' I said. 'Yes, I am.'

She lay on her back now and looked up at the ceiling.

'Good,' she said. 'Right now, that's all I want to know. We can talk about the rest of it later. I'm very tired, Beelee. It was a hard trip for me.'

'Do Ralph and Sophia know?'

She nodded. 'I told them right away,' she said. 'They said it would be the right thing, for me to come here. They said they were happy to bring me. They were very nice to me, too. Ralph was so sweet. And Sophia and I seem to like each other, now that things are so different.'

'Things are *very* different,' I said.

She closed her eyes and rolled onto her side again. I put my arms around her tightly and held her. I couldn't stop touching her stomach.

'Don't poke him,' she said. 'He's very young.'

'Sorry,' I said. 'You think it's a boy?'

'I don't know. I just say "him." It sounds better than "it."'

'Maybe it's a girl, though,' I said.

'Do you care what it is?'

'No.' I ran my fingers along her arms, her neck. 'I've missed you,' I said.

'I missed you, too.'

'You mean in Los Angeles?' She sighed. 'We

331

have much to talk about, Beelee. I told Jaime I was leaving, and he got upset. Things were starting to go very well for me. But when I told him why I had to see you, he understood.'

'Good,' I said. 'You hear all kinds of stories about sleazeball agents.'

'What do *you* know about agents?'

'Nothing,' I said. 'Yet. But I'm looking for one.'

'For your book?'

'Yes. It's finished.'

She squealed delightedly. 'It *is*?' she said. 'Can I read it?'

'If you want to,' I said. 'But there's no need. You lived it.'

She sat up on the bed. 'What do you mean?' she asked. 'You mean – is it about *me*?'

'Among other people.'

'Who else?'

'All of us,' I said. 'It's all in there, the whole story.'

'Ralph, too? And Sophia?'

'Yes. With different names, of course.'

'And you?'

'A little,' I said.

She lay down again. 'I knew you would finish it someday,' she said. 'I am very proud of you.'

'Thank you.'

'But listen. I have to go back.'

'To L.A.? When?'

'Whenever *this* is finished,' she said, patting her belly. 'When the baby is born, and you and I have talked about things. I wanted to come see you first. But I left Esteban out there all by himself, and I am worried about him. But Beelee.'

'Yes.'

'I came to you first, because I wanted you to come to me.'

'What do you mean?'

'If you want to be with me,' she said, 'and with this baby, you're going to have to come to *me*.'

'To Los Angeles?'

'Yes. To Los Angeles.'

'We'll talk about it,' I said.

'No. There is nothing to talk about. You *think* about it,' she said. 'I have nothing more to say than that. I am still going to be a singer, and for that I have to be there. Nothing is going to stop me, even if I have to be alone with the baby.'

I didn't say anything. I kept my hand on her stomach, feeling it rise and fall as she breathed.

'Do you understand?' she said.

'Yes,' I said.

'Good. Now, there is one more thing.'

'What?'

'When I left, that day?'

I knew what was coming. I didn't want her to say it; I tried to speak, but she interrupted me.

'I know you would not want to hurt me,' she said. 'But sometimes we hurt people without wanting to. But I tell you this right now. If you ever hit me, you will never see me again. Do you understand?'

'Yes,' I said.

'I mean it,' she said.

'I know,' I said. 'I'm sorry. I apologize.' I lay quietly for a while; I'd had the law laid down for me, and I was feeling chastised. But still I touched her stomach. Consuelo snuggled into me, and we lay like spoons.

'It was very inconvenient that we didn't have a phone in that house,' she said.

'Yes, it was.'

'Is there a phone in *this* house?'

'Yes.'

'Good. From now on, I never want to live without a phone.'

'Okay,' I said.

'You promise?'

'I promise.'

'Beelee,' she said. 'I am very tired.'

We lay there as she began to drift off. I wondered if she'd slept at all on the way out here, thinking about what I would say to her. I wasn't exactly the hardest-nosed guy in the world, but it still would have taken some courage on her part. I still wasn't thinking about what any of it meant for me. There would be time for that later. Right then I thought only about her, sitting cramped up in that car for the three days or so it must have taken, to what would be to her a totally strange and foreign country.

I let her sleep for a while, and then I slipped out of the room, closing the door after me carefully. I felt curiously light-headed. I'd never imagined myself as a father. That is, I'd always thought that someday I would become one, but it was an abstract feeling, a version of me that existed so far in the future it was useless to think about it. But now here it was – and the guy in that far-off abstract future was me. It was too much to take in.

There was one thing I knew for sure, though. If she was going to have a baby, I thought, she'd certainly come to the right place.

Later that afternoon, Sophia and I took a walk together. I carried the Tupperware container with half of my mother's ashes in it; she carried the urn with the other half. We walked down to the woods and cut through the trees until we came to the lake, where the broken concrete pier jutted out like a tooth into the water. There we sat with our feet dangling, and at the same moment we opened our containers and poured the contents into the water. Then we watched the ashes fall slowly to the bottom. It was only a few inches deep here, with the sandy lake floor rippled by the constant rolling of the waves. There were a couple of chunks of bone that hadn't been burned completely. I dug a hole in the sand with my toe and prodded them into it, covering them up again.

'This is probably illegal as hell,' I said.

Sophia smiled, sniffling. 'That's perfect,' she said. 'She wouldn't have it any other way.'

'Hardly anybody knows about this place, anyway,' I said. 'It's more private than a cemetery. Just us and the fishes.'

'And now her.'

'Yeah. Now her.'

We sat there for a few minutes, just thinking.

'What changed your mind about Ralph?' I asked.

'Ralph did,' she said. 'I decided to be nice and go visit him in the hospital after you left.'

'And?'

'And . . . well, he just looked so helpless, lying there in his gown, and with his poor leg in this huge cast. I kept going back to see him, bringing him things. He seemed so *grateful*. He kept calling me his little Florence Nightingale.'

'And he won you over?'

'He didn't really try,' she said. 'It just happened. We got to talking about how we both wanted to leave town, and it just made sense we should go together. I had a car, and he couldn't ride his bike anymore. So we went together. It was spontaneous.'

'So when did it happen?'

'When did what happen?'

'You know,' I said, poking her. '*It*.'

She blushed again. 'Las Vegas,' she said. 'If you really want to know everything, we almost got married. We even found a Jewish Elvis to perform the ceremony. But we both got cold feet at the last minute.'

'Probably better that way,' I said. 'That's not something you want to rush into.'

'I know,' she said. 'Sometimes you can be *too* spontaneous.'

Boy, I thought. You got *that* right.

'You want to go back up to the house now?' I asked.

'In a minute,' she said. 'I like it here. I've never seen the ocean before.'

'This isn't an ocean,' I said. 'It's only a lake.'

'It is? Jeez, it's *huge*.'

'Canada's over there,' I said, pointing to the horizon. 'You can't really see it, though. It's just out of sight.'

'I've never seen this much water, anyway. I love it,' she said. She looked down at the ashes, which by now had all but dissipated. '*She* liked water, too,' she said. 'This was a good place to put her.'

'She told me about growing up on the houseboats,' I said.

'I'm glad you at least got the chance to know her a little.'

'So am I. And I'm glad you made up with her.'

'Are you sorry you never told her who you were?'

'I've decided,' I said, 'that I'm not going to be sorry about anything anymore. But I *did* tell her. I just don't think she heard me.'

'When was that?'

'In the hospital, before you and I went there together. When they first took her.'

337

'You think she heard you?'

'I don't know,' I said. 'She moved her finger. But maybe she was only dreaming. Some part of her heard me, anyway. I'm pretty sure.'

'I told her I was sorry,' she said. 'For calling her a bad mother – for everything. I think she heard me, too.'

We sat and watched the sun swing slowly toward the western horizon. After a while we got up and walked back through the woods to the house.

Consuelo was awake by then, chatting with Mildred and a few of the mothers. I kissed her when we came in, and rubbed the back of her neck. Walking in the door and seeing her sitting there in my house had made me feel good – I'd forgotten, or had not allowed myself to remember, that she had a baby in her now. But when I saw her I remembered, and I was suffused with that strange light-headedness again. It was not entirely unpleasant. Maybe in a few months I would have gotten used to the whole idea, but it was still so new it seemed like a dream. And I would have to tell Mildred soon – though I suspected that she would know before I told her. She might even know already.

When dinner had been eaten and wine drunk, when Ralph and Sophia had been given a room to themselves and Consuelo and I were alone again in mine, we got back into bed. She yawned. She was often tired these days, she'd told me. She had a lot of sleep to catch up on.

'Do you *want* to be a father?' she asked, as we lay there. 'I mean, do you want to have a baby with me?'

'Why?' I asked.

'Sometimes people don't want babies. You have to tell me, Beelee.'

'Sure,' I said. 'I already have babies, in case you hadn't noticed.'

'Those are not *your* babies.'

'I know. But they're kind of everybody's babies. You get attached to them pretty quick.'

'Are you ready for one of your own?'

I got up and turned off the lamp on my dresser. Then I slipped out of my clothes and helped her out of hers, and we got under the sheets together.

'If there's one thing I've learned about babies,' I said, 'it's that sometimes they just come.'

'Yes.'

'They come before you're ready, sometimes.'

'I know. But what about you? Are you ready?'

'You have to *get* ready, is all,' I said.

'This is not an answer,' she said.

'All right. No, I'm not ready. Not today. But by the time it gets here I'll be ready.'

'You will?'

'Yes.'

'I love you, Beelee.'

'I love you, too,' I said.

'I know that,' she said.

★   ★   ★

That night, I dreamed.

I was riding my bike along a desert highway, the wind blowing my hair out behind me – it had never been cut at all. The sun loomed before me on the horizon, as huge as though it was only a few miles away, but its heat didn't burn. As I sped along the road I felt the wheels lift gently from the cement of the highway, and the ground slowly *dropped* away; then I was free of the bike, and it was just me moving forward, going faster and faster now, stretching my arms out to my sides, my legs straight out behind me. I looked at myself as though I were an observer, as though I had left my body, and I saw my clothes ripped away in the teeth of the wind. I was naked. As I watched myself soar through the air, feathers began to grow out of my arms, my body, my legs, and they rippled in the increasing roar of the air rushing by me. Gradually I ceased to be myself and became instead a bird creature, an eagle man. I rose ever higher, the sun still huge in front of me, and I flew to it, streaking forward ever faster, until it had enveloped me entirely in its warmth, and I knew that I was home again, that I had come to rest while moving, that motion was rest, and that most of all it was good.